When No One Is Watching

Joseph Hayes

Donna —
All the best!

[signature: Joseph Hayes]

Synergy Books

When No One Is Watching
Published by Synergy Books
PO Box 30071
Austin, TX 78755

For more information about our books, please write to us, call
512.623.7270, or visit our website at www.synergybooks.net.

Publisher's Cataloging-in-Publication available upon request.

LCCN: 2010923529
ISBN-13: 978-0-9843879-4-6
ISBN-10: 0-9843879-4-3

10 9 8 7 6 5 4 3 2 1

To my father, Bill Hayes, a quiet hero who tirelessly provided sponsorship, support, compassion, and friendship to fellow alcoholics in search of lasting sobriety as he changed the world, one life at a time. And to all of the other quiet heroes of AA who do the same.

CHAPTER 1

I love this ride, Dano!" Blair Van Howe yelled exuberantly to his partner, who was passed out cold in the passenger seat. "I'd buy one myself, but the voters might not approve!" He laughed loudly as he leaned forward and accelerated.

Blair had never driven a Porsche before and was relishing every second of it. The power and responsiveness of the 911's massive engine, the tightness of the steering, and the way the tires gripped the road felt strangely seductive. He was driving fast, which was not his habit, but it was past midnight, and the neighborhood streets were empty. The events of the past two days had him riding a wave of exhilaration, and rocketing around the deserted streets of North Beverly in Danny's new Porsche 911 Turbo was a perfect way to conclude a thrilling week.

The north end of Beverly was a well-to-do enclave on Chicago's Far South Side. Danny Moran had grown up there, and Blair had been captivated by it from the moment of his first visit, when he and Danny were still in law school. The houses were large, stately old brick structures built during the early and middle part of the twentieth century, on spacious, tree-covered lots. The streets were winding and irregular, unlike the grid-like pattern so prevalent throughout the rest of the city. This was because the neighborhood abutted Dan Ryan Woods, the only forest preserve within the city limits. The woods served as a buffer between the affluent Beverly residents and the not-so-affluent areas to the north and east, and prevented any through traffic, giving the area a quiet and secluded ambience. Tonight, those wide, winding streets felt like Blair's private racetrack, an ideal place to be celebrating life with the assistance of a Porsche 911.

He was just a few blocks from Danny's house, where he would have to leave the Porsche and walk the short distance to his own home. He would also have to find a way to get Danny inside, which would undoubtedly be a challenge, given Danny's highly inebriated state. Before tackling that chore, he would treat himself to one more Porsche-delivered thrill to bring the evening to a fitting conclusion. The snakelike roads made it impossible to go for pure drag-racing speed, so he'd been delighting in the 911's maneuverability as he whipped around sharp turns with barely a tap on the brakes. Blair gunned the turbo-charged engine as he approached Hamilton Avenue, Danny's street, inspired by the sonorous whine emanating from beneath the hood. He felt as if he were one with the vehicle, as if it had nerves and reflexes and were an extension of himself. He jerked the steering wheel hard to the left, leaning into the turn as the Porsche careened around the corner.

Suddenly, he was jolted out of his euphoric state by the harsh glare of high-beam headlights flashing directly into his eyes, blinding him momentarily. Exhilaration turned to panic as he felt the back end of the Porsche swerving and realized that he had lost control. He slammed the brakes hard, and they responded with a deafening screech as the oncoming vehicle veered out of his path, missing the Porsche by inches. Two other sounds simultaneously assaulted his eardrums: the sound of shattering glass as the trophy that had been resting in Danny's lap was hurled into the dashboard, and the sickening sound of crumpling metal as the other vehicle slammed into some unknown object.

The terrifying cacophony lasted just a couple of seconds, and then everything was still. "Son of a bitch," Blair said under his breath. His entire body was shaking.

"Dano, wake up!" Blair shouted, staring at his partner, who was still tightly strapped into his seat. He hadn't even stirred. "Wake up, Dano!" Blair yelled louder, gripping Danny's shoulders and shaking him roughly. Still no response.

Blair reached down to unbuckle his seat belt and felt a sharp pain shoot through his right hand as it struck a shard of glass, the remnants of their shattered trophy. "Shit!" he cried as blood spurted from a deep gash in his right index finger.

He opened the door and climbed out, gingerly confirming that all of his body parts were intact and that he was unhurt. He surveyed the Porsche. There was not a scratch on it. With a feeling of dread, as if moving in slow motion, he turned around and gazed up the street in the direction from which he had just come. "Oh my God," he said in a trembling voice as he beheld the horrific scene ninety feet away. He felt dizzy and almost vomited. He glanced quickly back at Danny, desperately hoping he'd come to, but Danny remained peacefully oblivious.

The car was an old one. He couldn't tell what kind in the darkness, but it appeared to be 1960s vintage. That meant no airbags. From where he stood, Blair could see that the vehicle had run head-on into an enormous oak tree. The entire front end was grotesquely contorted and pancaked into the passenger area.

Blair approached the vehicle slowly. His stomach turned again as he stopped several feet from the driver's door. The windshield looked like it had exploded into thousands of tiny particles, glistening in the pale glow of the streetlight. The driver was slumped over the steering wheel, his face and head a bloody mess, the lower half of his body pinned beneath a mass of twisted wreckage. The man weakly opened his eyes. Blair stared at him, recognition setting in. He couldn't recall the man's name, but he remembered his face. He and his family were new to the neighborhood, and Blair had met them at a recent block party.

"Help me," the injured man said in a voice no stronger than a whisper. Then his eyes closed again.

Blair stared at him, feeling paralyzed, unable to think or act. He had always counted on Danny when things went wrong, and Danny always came through. Danny was right there, just ninety feet away, but he was dead drunk and utterly useless.

Blair moved closer to the car, and with a start, noticed a child in the backseat. She was weeping quietly, rocking back and forth, clutching a small stuffed animal.

"Are you okay back there?" he asked, trying to collect himself.

The child looked at him, then turned away without responding.

Blair looked closer and saw that the girl had the distinctive features of a Down syndrome child. She appeared to be seven or eight years old, but it was hard to tell in the darkness. "Are you okay?" he asked again. He couldn't help noticing the unmistakable sound of panic in his own voice.

"Help my daddy … help my daddy," the child repeated, staring straight ahead with unfocused eyes.

"Don't worry, kid. I'll call for help. They'll be here fast. Everything will be okay."

The child shot a glance in his direction, then looked away again. "Help my daddy," she whispered through her quiet sobs.

Blair yanked at the driver's door. It wouldn't budge. He peered through the open window and looked more closely at the tangled wreckage covering the driver's legs. He could see that the driver was pinned in tightly, and that there was no way he could extricate the injured man from the vehicle by himself. He had to get help. He raced back to the Porsche. Danny was still out cold. Blair opened the passenger door and shook Danny again, then slapped him firmly across the face. No response. "Goddamn it, Dano, wake up! I need you!" He shook Danny's shoulders violently. Danny stirred and mumbled, but did not open his eyes.

Blair pulled his cell phone from the holster on his belt and began dialing: nine, then one—and then he stopped before adding the other one. He stared at the phone for a long time. The events of the past few days flashed through his mind. He thought about all of the glorious publicity he'd received following the trial. He thought about the campaign. He was on the cusp of fulfilling a lifelong dream, and he had never wanted anything so badly. Then he envisioned the police giving him a breathalyzer test and taking him away in handcuffs. This would be an unmitigated disaster.

He closed the passenger door and paced back and forth in front of the Porsche, gripping his cell phone and struggling to control his scattered thoughts. He stopped, put his elbows on the Porsche's driver's side door, and peered through the open window. He closed his eyes and took a deep breath. Then he took a long look at his unconscious friend and partner. "I'm sorry, Dano," he whispered to himself. He put away his phone, and then he opened the door, leaned in, and unfastened Danny's seat belt. As Danny slumped forward, Blair grabbed him under the arms and began pulling him out of the passenger's seat. Danny was dead weight, so it required great exertion, but he finally succeeded in moving him into the driver's seat. Danny slumped forward, completely limp. Blair pulled the shoulder strap tightly around him and fastened it in place, leaving Danny sitting upright behind the wheel, his head hanging like a rag doll's.

Blair took a few deep breaths; then he removed Danny's cell phone from his jacket and dialed 911. "I've been in an accident. Eighty-ninth and Hamilton. I think the other driver is hurt pretty bad. We need an ambulance right away!"

"Of course, sir. We'll get right on it. May I have your name, please?"

Blair pushed the *end call* button and dropped the phone into Danny's lap. "Sorry, pal," he said softly, tears welling up in his eyes and blurring his vision. He looked around. There was not a soul in sight. He patted Danny on the shoulder, slammed the door, then briskly walked away.

CHAPTER 2

Earlier that evening

As CEO of Champions HealthCare, I know I speak for everyone in our company when I say congratulations and thank you to the most brilliant legal team I've ever laid eyes on—Blair Van Howe and Danny Moran!" Grant Peterson looked toward his two attorneys as the room erupted into raucous applause.

Peterson raised his arms in a gesture for silence, and the noise abated. "The future of our company was riding on this case," he continued, "and you delivered. Your preparation was tireless, your strategy brilliant, and the execution of that strategy in the courtroom absolutely flawless—a thing of beauty! Well done, gentlemen!"

The twenty-four board members and corporate officers seated in a private dining room of Chez Pierre, one of downtown Chicago's finest restaurants, rose to their feet, applauding again.

"Blair, Danny, would you mind joining me up here for a moment?" said Peterson.

Blair strode confidently to the podium with the smile and ease of a Hollywood movie star about to accept an Academy

Award. Danny Moran ambled along behind him, looking at the floor and forcing a slightly embarrassed smile.

"Gentlemen, it's a true pleasure watching real artists perform their craft," Peterson said. "You're the best. That was evident to everyone watching these court proceedings over the past few weeks. We are humbled and grateful to have you in our corner, and we're proud to count you among the true friends of Champions HealthCare. Please accept this as a token of our heartfelt appreciation."

From behind the podium, Peterson lifted a large glass trophy—a sculpture of the company's logo: a muscular athlete, laurel wreath around his head, arms raised skyward in victory. Beneath the glass figurine was an inscription that read, "In Recognition of the Outstanding Contributions and Friendship of Blair Van Howe and Danny Moran—Champions of Champions."

Blair beamed as he accepted the trophy. He raised it above his head with both arms as the assemblage of normally reserved corporate leaders cheered like rabid sports fans. He loved the limelight. He'd been in his element the past few weeks on center stage, handling the city's biggest trial in a decade, and he was basking in the accolades and adulation of the corporate leaders standing before him.

"Thank you," Blair shouted in a commanding voice, silencing the applause. "It's a real privilege to represent a world-class company like Champions HealthCare and the esteemed leadership team represented here in this room." He paused and looked intently at the eager faces staring back at him. "When we embarked on this mission, we all knew the stakes were incredibly high, and your courage and determination have paid off. We achieved a monumental victory this week, for the company, and just as importantly, for the thousands, maybe millions of people in desperate need of affordable health care. Think about what we've accomplished. From its inception, Champions HealthCare has had a mission of providing affordable health care options to people who don't have the luxury of health insurance provided by large employers. The concept is beautiful in its simplicity. Because we represent large groups of people, we should be able to negotiate favorable rates from health care providers, just like large employers do. But there were those who attempted to stand in our way. They refused to negotiate with us. They engaged in collusion and conspired against us. They were large, powerful institutions with a vested interest in keeping prices for the little people at unconscionable levels. They had a tremendous war chest and the best lawyers money could buy. But you had the courage of your convictions, and you took them on. And justice prevailed! You sent a real message, and no one will stand in our way now. We've pushed the door wide open, and countless people will now have real options for affordable health care. This is a great victory for them and for Champions Health-Care. And it is truly an honor to have been entrusted with your confidence and to have had the opportunity to fight this battle shoulder to shoulder with people like you."

Just as in the courtroom, Blair Van Howe was in complete command of his audience. His voice was rich and resonant, and his speech was unfailingly eloquent and effortless. He projected a natural charm that was at once folksy and comfortable, and yet also laden with power and demanding of respect. He was a man whose very presence commanded attention before he uttered a single word. He was trim and muscular, his athletic frame accentuated by his perfectly tailored Italian suits. Stunningly handsome, he could have been mistaken for a movie star or a fashion model, and he often was, although, at the age of thirty-nine, his once-sandy-brown hair was now silver-gray. He liked it that way. He thought it made him look distinguished, which was exactly what he wanted as he entered this new stage of his life.

"Gentlemen, I'd like to propose a toast," Blair continued. "Two toasts, actually. First, to Champions HealthCare. I have no doubt that you will have a glorious and successful future. May your stock soon hit a hundred dollars per share!"

The room again erupted into boisterous applause.

"Hear, hear!" a voice rang out above the crowd.

"To a hundred dollars a share!" shouted another.

"And second," Blair continued, "to my friend and partner, Danny Moran, the true mastermind behind our legal strategy. I was lucky enough to enjoy most of the spotlight, but Danny truly deserves most of the credit." He turned toward Danny and handed him the trophy as a waiter scurried forward with glasses of champagne for them both. Blair raised his glass and smiled warmly at his colleague.

"To Danny!" Grant Peterson echoed as the room burst into noisy applause once again.

"Way to go, Danny!"

"Here's to Danny!"

"We love you, Danny, you brilliant son of a bitch!"

Danny smiled modestly and nodded to the crowd. He raised his glass in salute, then lowered it to his lips and pretended to sip the champagne.

Grant Peterson raised his arms again. "Quiet, please. I have one more important announcement, and then you can get back to your celebration." The crowd settled down and looked at Peterson with anticipation.

"It involves our friend Blair Van Howe. As you know, Blair has provided us with outstanding legal representation for over eight years now, and I'm sorry to say that, as of tomorrow, he will no longer be acting as our attorney." Peterson paused for effect, staring at the puzzled faces before him. "That's because Blair will soon be providing another kind of representation for us and many others—as a United States Congressman for the great state of Illinois!" An excited buzz rippled through the crowd. "Just yesterday, Blair received the endorsement of the Democratic Party leadership to run against longtime incumbent Scott Carlson. He'll be announcing his candidacy at a press conference Monday morning, but he wanted his good friends here in this room to be among the first to know. Congratulations, Blair! See you in Washington!"

Once more, the room exploded with shouts and applause as well-wishers rushed forward to shake the candidate's hand. Danny slipped away from the podium unnoticed and quietly made his way back to his table, still carrying his untouched glass of champagne. It was Blair's moment now. The spotlight belonged on him, and Danny was happy to see his friend thoroughly enjoying the well-deserved attention. He was also genuinely pleased to see the Champions executives in such high spirits. They deserved to be. Yet Danny himself felt conflicted. Despite the celebratory atmosphere, he felt depressed, even a bit angry. Actually, he felt that way *because* of the festivities. The alcohol was flowing freely, and everyone in attendance seemed to be enjoying themselves immensely. Everyone seemed joyful and uninhibited—everyone except him.

Danny Moran was a man who loved to drink. He loved the taste of good beer and fine wine. He loved the way it made him feel. But it usually got the better of him, and he knew it. Once he started drinking, it was hard to stop, and with increasing frequency, he'd been drinking until he completely passed out. He often awoke the next day with absolutely no recollection of the previous evening beyond a certain point in time. That was scary. And staying out all night, then returning home in the morning with no explanation of his whereabouts had taken a serious toll on his marriage. That, coupled with his need to stay clear-headed and focused during trial preparation, had caused him to quit cold turkey over three months ago. But now the trial was over. He knew that he should abstain, but he desperately wanted a drink. He continued staring at his untouched glass of champagne as if engaged in a contest of wills with the pale golden liquid.

"Danny! Time for you to make good on your promise!" Danny looked up to see Brendan O'Malley, Champions' general counsel, standing before him, holding a mug of light beer. Danny stared at him blankly. "Don't pretend you've forgotten," Brendan said. "Remember? The day the lawsuit was filed? You assured me that someday you and I would celebrate our victory over a couple of pints of Guinness. Time for you to pay up! Let's go next door and grab a real beer. This stuff tastes like piss!" Brendan disdainfully set his beer mug on the table.

It was difficult to say no to Brendan O'Malley. Aside from his personal charm and the forcefulness of his personality, Brendan was Danny's primary contact at Champions Health-Care, and was responsible for sending a great deal of legal work to Danny and his firm. They had become good friends over the years and had spent countless hours together over the past few months, gearing up for the Champions trial. *What the hell*, Danny thought. He couldn't risk offending Brendan. *Just one beer*, he told himself, and with that decision, his spirits lifted immediately. He stood and smiled eagerly at the general counsel. "You're on, Brendan. A deal's a deal!"

Brendan put his arm around Danny's shoulders, and they made their way to the restaurant's bar, just around the corner from the private dining room.

Two hours later, Blair found Danny at the bar, drinking Guinness by himself and staring absently at a basketball game on the television behind the bar.

"Brendan told me I'd find you here," said Blair. "The party's breaking up. Ready to call it a night?"

"No, you go ahead, Blair. I may stay awhile," Danny replied, slurring badly. "I want to watch the rest of this game."

Blair eyed his partner with concern. "Who's winning?" he asked.

"I dunno."

"Who's playing?"

"Dunno."

"Well, you're my ride home, pal. I can't stay out all night. I've got to be fresh tomorrow so I can prepare for the press conference."

Danny reached into his pocket and handed Blair his valet parking stub. "Here you go, Blair. Take my car. I'll catch a cab later."

Blair was well aware of Danny's history of blackouts and all-nighters, and he had no desire to leave his friend in his present condition.

"That's okay, Dano," he said agreeably. "I'll wait. Just finish your beer, and I'll drive you home." Blair ordered a gin and tonic and joined his friend at the bar. He truly didn't mind waiting. He was still in high spirits, and a brief delay would permit him to savor this special evening just a while longer.

Twenty minutes later, Danny staggered out of the bar with Blair at his side, and they made their way to the valet stand. Blair felt a twinge of excitement as he saw Danny's new Porsche 911 glide around the corner. He handed the young valet a twenty-dollar tip, helped Danny into the passenger seat, then jumped behind the wheel.

"This ought to be fun!" Blair said, a broad smile on his face and a gleam in his eyes, as he glanced over at his passenger. Danny didn't respond. He had already closed his eyes.

***

Terry McGrath tiptoed up the stairs and quietly opened the bedroom door of his twelve-year-old son, Tommy.

"Is she asleep, Dad?" Tommy asked, springing out of bed, fully dressed.

"Yep," Terry whispered gleefully. "Fast asleep. Time to launch Operation Bulldog, buddy boy! Go wake Ashley."

"Yes, sir!" Tommy replied in a hushed but excited voice.

Tommy scurried into his younger sister's bedroom. "Ashley, get up! It's time!" Ashley was snoring hard and didn't stir. Tommy shook her vigorously. "Ashley! Operation Bulldog!"

Ashley opened her eyes and looked at him blankly for several seconds until comprehension set in. "Operation Bulldog! Yay!" She shouted and clapped her hands, an enormous smile brightening her face.

"Shhh! You'll wake Mommy. Be very quiet, Ashley, okay?"

"Okay, Tommy," she responded, in a loud stage whisper. She groped for her glasses on the nightstand and clumsily pulled on her jeans and a sweatshirt. They made their way down to the kitchen, where their father was writing a note on his wife's birthday card.

"Okay, kids," he said, "sign the card."

Tommy signed his name, then waited impatiently as Ashley slowly printed her name in large, crooked block letters.

"That's good enough, Ashley," he snapped as his sister began drawing awkwardly shaped hearts around her name. "Time to go."

"We're coming, Bully!" Ashley shouted exuberantly.

"Shhh!" hissed Terry and Tommy together.

"Come on, little girl," said Terry, taking his daughter's hand and walking toward the garage.

"Can we take Lucille?" Ashley asked.

Lucille was Terry's vintage 1957 Chevrolet, which his wife Nancy had bought him for his fortieth birthday a year earlier. Its body was a thing of beauty—cherry red, in mint condition—but its engine required constant maintenance, so he rarely drove it except on special occasions. "Absolutely," he responded. This was clearly a special occasion.

Terry opened the back door, and Ashley climbed in. "Wait, Daddy!" she yelled as he was about to close the door. "I forgot Mr. Growl. He wants to come, too."

Terry smiled patiently. "Okay, sweetheart, go get Mr. Growl. I'll wait."

Terry waited behind the wheel of the Chevy, basking in the moment. He loved being a husband and a father, and times like this made him realize how fortunate he was. God, this was fun! It felt like Christmas, but the roles were reversed. He and the kids had planned a special surprise for Nancy's fortieth birthday that required elaborate scheming and the utmost secrecy. They called it Operation Bulldog, which was fitting, since that was the surprise: a puppy—a bulldog, half English and half French.

Nancy had long wanted a dog in the family, but Terry had always resisted. He just wasn't a dog person. He thrived on cleanliness, neatness, and order, and he was convinced that having a dog around the house would be an impediment to all of those goals. He had begun to warm to the idea recently after seeing the joy on his daughter's face when she played with a neighbor's puppy. This had been a tough year for Ashley. She had been born with Down syndrome, but he and Nancy had mainstreamed her by sending her to the local public school with all the other kids her age. At eight years old, Ashley was just beginning to realize that she was different from the others, and it broke his heart. She deserved all the joy that life could bring her special little heart, and Terry was determined to do whatever he could to make her happy, even if it meant having a messy, smelly, drooling canine in his house.

So Terry embarked on Operation Bulldog, knowing that the addition of a puppy to the McGrath household would be a thrill for both Nancy and Ashley. The kids delighted in the grand conspiracy as they spent weeks secretly visiting breeders all over the city, looking for a purebred English bulldog, the breed Nancy had owned as a child. Their plans changed when Ashley fell in love with a funny-looking English-French mix at the pet shop in the local mall. They had purchased the puppy earlier in the day and were hiding it at the Martins' house, four blocks away on Hamilton Avenue.

As part of Operation Bulldog, Terry had enlisted the help of some of Nancy's friends from the neighborhood. They had taken her out for a Saturday night on the town in honor of her birthday and had promised Terry that they would be sure to get several glasses of wine into her, then get her home by midnight. Terry knew that the wine would have Nancy in a deep sleep shortly after returning home. Then he and the kids would spring into action. He and Ashley would drive over to the Martins' house to pick up the puppy, whom Ashley had already named Bully. While they were gone, Tommy would attach a red ribbon to the birthday card and place the card on the sink in Nancy's bathroom, where she would find it as soon as she woke up. The ribbon would lead out of the bathroom, across the bedroom floor, down the hall, through the kitchen, and into the laundry room, where it would be attached to the kennel holding their precious new family member. A large sign was attached to the kennel, reading, "Hi, Mom. I'm Bully, your new baby. Happy birthday!"

Terry's musings were interrupted by the sound of Ashley howling from the kitchen. "I can't find Mr. Growl!"

"Be quiet, Ashley!" Tommy said. "You can find Mr. Growl in the morning."

"No, I need him now! I told him he could come with me to get Bully. He wants to come!"

"Ashley, he's a stupid stuffed animal! He doesn't care. Go get Bully, and we'll find Mr. Growl tomorrow."

Ashley just shook her head and sobbed. Terry knelt beside her and gently put his hands on her shoulders. "Ashley? Look at me. Where did you last see Mr. Growl?"

"I don't know," she wailed.

"Shhh! Calm down, sweetheart. Is he in your bed?"

"No."

"Did you look all around your room?"

She nodded.

"Did you put him somewhere special, to wait for this trip?"

Her face brightened. "The car!" she yelled and raced back into the garage.

The scruffy white polar bear was in the backseat of Terry's Volvo, sitting upright and staring straight ahead, as if he'd been waiting for them. Ashley grabbed him unceremoniously with one hand and raced back to the old Chevy. Terry pulled out of the driveway, drove one block east, then headed north on Hamilton Avenue. Ted Martin lived just four blocks away and had promised to be up waiting for them, regardless of the hour. Terry smiled to himself as the Chevy chugged through the deserted neighborhood. He felt an overwhelming sense of contentment as he remembered the excitement in his children's faces. This was a special night, one he was determined to treasure and never forget.

Then he sensed that something was wrong. He sensed it for the briefest instant before he saw it. Just as he approached Eighty-ninth Street, a car rounded the corner at breakneck speed, clearly out of control. He heard the tires screeching as the vehicle came right at him. Instinct took over, and he did the only thing he could. He jerked the steering wheel hard to the right, his only thought being to avoid a collision. He saw the Porsche skid past him, missing the old Chevy by inches. In the next instant, he saw a giant oak tree, illuminated by his headlights, rushing right at them.

"Hold on, Ashley!" he screamed an instant before he felt an explosion of noise, impact, and pain as the Chevy smashed head-on into the tree.

CHAPTER 3

J esus Christ," muttered Detective Victor Slazak as his headlights illuminated the gruesome scene before him. The
front end of an old car was smashed up against an enormous
tree, the mass of crumpled metal and shattered glass leaving
no doubt as to the violence of the impact. He could see the
driver slumped over the steering wheel and two uniformed officers standing beside him, looking helpless as their attempts
to force open the passenger door proved futile. Their squad car
was parked on the other side of the street, its blue lights flashing silently. A black Porsche was in the middle of the road a
short distance away, perpendicular to the curb. Slazak climbed
out of his vehicle and strode briskly toward the wreck.

"Is he alive?" Slazak asked the uniformed officers.

"Yes, sir, but I think he's in bad shape," said the tall, thin
officer, who looked like he was fresh out of the police academy. His nameplate read "Wilson."

"Where the hell is the ambulance?" Slazak asked, looking
past the officers at the bloody face of the poor soul behind
the wheel.

"We called a few minutes ago. They said they'd get it here
as fast as they could," Wilson replied.

"Call 'em again, goddamn it!" said Slazak. "This guy can't wait!"

The uniformed officers looked at each other uncertainly. Wilson took a radio from his belt. "Dispatch, this is Officer Wilson again. We're still waiting for that ambulance at Eighty-ninth and Hamilton. Anything you can do to speed that along?"

Slazak grabbed the radio. "This is Detective Vic Slazak. Who's this?"

"This is Steve Burns, Central Dispatch."

"Listen, Steve, I need an ambulance here right away! Send the fire department boys, too, with their Jaws of Life and all that shit. We're going to have to cut this guy out of the driver's seat. We need them fast—I mean right goddamn now, Stevie boy!" He abruptly hung up and handed the radio back to Officer Wilson.

"What about the other guy?" Slazak asked, nodding toward the Porsche.

"I think he's okay. Just drunk," replied the other officer, a pudgy, fresh-faced kid whose nameplate read "Briggs."

"That son of a bitch," said Slazak as he turned back toward the wreckage. He reached through the broken driver's-side window and put his hand on the driver's neck, feeling for a pulse. It was there, but barely. He began examining the driver's wounds, when movement from the back of the car caught his eye. A small child was curled up in the fetal position on the floor, whimpering quietly.

"Hey, there's a kid back here!" Slazak called out to the two patrolmen.

"Yeah, we know," Wilson replied sheepishly. "I think she's okay, but we couldn't get her to talk."

Slazak glared at the officers, shaking his head, then leaned into the car through the driver's-side window. "You all right back there?" His voice sounded rough, and he knew it. The child continued weeping quietly and did not respond.

Slazak stared at the child in thoughtful silence for a moment. He considered himself to be a man of many talents, but playing nursemaid to a scared kid wasn't one of them. He reached behind the driver's seat, pulled up the button lock, opened the door, and leaned in. He did his best to assume a gentle, calming tone, but only partially succeeded. "We're here to help, kid. They're going to take care of your father, okay? Can you sit up for me?"

This time, the child responded and climbed slowly into a sitting position on the backseat, attempting to adjust her glasses as she did so, but they remained askew. Slazak surveyed her carefully. She was small, probably seven or eight years old. Short, straight brown hair in a bowl cut framed a tear-streaked face with the distinctive features of a Down syndrome child. A flash of pity jolted the hardened detective. He awkwardly put his hand on her shoulder and asked, "Are you hurt?"

The child hesitated, then shook her head.

"What's your name?" Slazak asked.

"Ashley. Ashley McGrath," she said in a voice that was barely audible.

"Ashley, my name is Vic. We're going to help your father now, okay? How about if we get out of the car?"

Without a word, Ashley reached over, took his hand, and climbed out of the backseat. Once outside the car, she stared at him for a long moment, a dazed look on her face. Then she threw her arms around his waist and held him tightly. Slazak stood there, patting her head, feeling awkward and helpless.

"About time!" Briggs called out as blaring sirens pierced the night, and the flashing red lights of the ambulance could be seen speeding toward the accident site. A fire truck followed closely behind. Several sleepy-eyed neighbors emerged from the surrounding homes and walked hesitantly toward the grim scene.

"Daddy!" Slazak looked up to see a young boy in his pajamas sprinting toward the smashed Chevy in an obvious state of panic.

"Tommy!" Ashley yelled, pulling away from Slazak and running toward her brother. "Daddy's hurt, Tommy! We crashed into the tree!"

Tommy stopped momentarily and stared at his sister, then bolted toward the wreck, reaching it just steps ahead of the ambulance crew. "Daddy!" the young boy shrieked, as he took in the sight of his father's battered body, his bloody head hanging limply over the steering wheel and his lower half looking grossly contorted. "Daddy, wake up! Wake up!" he wailed as he grabbed his father's shoulder and began tugging it.

The two emergency medical technicians reached Tommy simultaneously. The tall, muscular African American who had been driving the ambulance put his hands on Tommy's shoulders firmly yet gently, and said in a reassuring voice, "We're going to get your father out of the car now and take him to the hospital. I need you to step back and let us do our job, okay, son?"

Tommy stepped back from the car without taking his eyes off his father, grief and horror etched on his face as his body was racked with deep, convulsing sobs. Ashley stood by his side, holding Mr. Growl in one hand and staring at her shoes.

As two firemen hurried past carrying their Jaws of Life and other rescue implements, the other EMT, a stocky young woman with short red hair, put an arm around each child and guided them away from the wreck. "Come on, kids," she said in a comforting voice. "You can wait here in the ambulance while we take care of your dad, okay?"

She helped the distraught children into the rear of the ambulance, then pulled a gurney from the vehicle and raced back toward the old Chevy. Passing Detective Slazak, she nodded toward the Porsche and asked, "What about him?"

"Not hurt—just drunk and passed out," Slazak said, doing his best to conceal his contempt in front of the children. "I'll deal with him right now." He walked purposefully toward the Porsche. "You better hope this guy makes it, you drunk son of a bitch," he said under his breath as he strained to see through the car's tinted windows.

Slazak yanked open the driver's-side door and peered in. The man behind the wheel didn't look like the typical drunk driver he encountered late at night, if there was any such thing as typical. He appeared to be about forty, with neatly trimmed black hair that was starting to gray around the temples. He was wearing a dark suit and had not even loosened his tie or unbuttoned his collar. His head rolled from side to side as he struggled to open his eyes and squirmed against a seat belt that seemed too tight.

Slazak leaned toward the driver and detected the unmistakable smell of alcohol. "You prick," he said under his breath. Then he shouted into the driver's face, "Wake up, mister!"

The driver managed to open his eyes and stared uncomprehendingly back at Slazak before his eyelids fluttered and closed again.

"Need any help, detective?" Officer Wilson had ambled up behind him, doing his best to avoid appearing useless.

"Get me a glass of cold water," Slazak said without looking up. He surveyed the inside of the vehicle. Although there were no broken windows, shattered glass was scattered across the floor, the dashboard, and the area between the front seats. He walked slowly around the outside of the car, examining it carefully. He stopped when he reached the passenger side. In the glare of the streetlight, Slazak could see that the door was not flush with the body of the vehicle. He ran his fingers across the uneven surface. It was obvious that whoever had attempted to close the door had not shut it completely. Officer Wilson arrived with a large Styrofoam cup filled with cold water.

"Get pictures of this car, Wilson, inside and out. Be sure you get this door," Slazak ordered, pointing at the passenger door. "Don't touch anything, just get pictures." Although the crime scene technicians would surely take photographs when they arrived, Slazak believed in being abundantly thorough and leaving nothing to chance. The crime scene unit might miss something.

Slazak grabbed the Styrofoam cup, walked back around to the driver's side, and without hesitating, threw the ice-cold water directly into the driver's face. The man gasped, and his eyes opened wide.

"Wake up, pal! Step out of the car," Slazak ordered.

The driver stared at him, trying hard to focus.

"What happened?" the driver stammered.

Slazak glared at him. "I was hoping you could tell me. The way I see it, you got drunk, went for a ride in your fancy car, and passed out behind the wheel. Step out of the car, sir."

With trembling hands, the driver unfastened his seat belt, then climbed unsteadily out of the vehicle, gripping the open door to maintain his balance.

"May I see your driver's license?" Slazak asked curtly.

The driver fumbled with his wallet, and with some difficulty, extracted his driver's license and handed it to the detective. Slazak studied it hard. The name sounded familiar: Daniel J. Moran. He had heard it somewhere recently, but couldn't place it. He handed the license to Wilson and stared hard at the driver. "Been drinking tonight, Mr. Moran?" he asked. His tone was harsh and confrontational.

The driver stared back, a bewildered look on his face, and said nothing.

"Hey, I know this guy," Wilson remarked, handing the driver's license back to Slazak as he scrutinized Danny Moran's face. "He's a lawyer. Been in the news a lot lately. He handled that Champions HealthCare trial."

Recognition set in with Slazak as well. He stared hard at Danny, then glanced in the direction of the mangled Chevy, fury rising within him. "Look at that, hotshot!" he shouted. "Take a good, hard look, you drunk son of a bitch!" He pointed at the paramedics, who were moving a limp body from the wreckage. "Because of you, two little kids may lose their father!" Slazak's face was red with rage and was within inches of Danny's. Danny had been unable to focus on anything beyond the policemen in front of him, but he was now staring past them at the horrific sight ninety feet away.

"Oh my God!" he gasped.

"Get him out of here," Slazak growled at Wilson, his voice filled with contempt. "Give him the breathalyzer and the sobriety tests."

"Come with me, sir," Wilson instructed, grabbing Danny by the elbow and guiding him toward the squad car.

Slazak shook his head and cursed to himself as he watched Danny Moran stagger to the squad alongside the lanky patrolman. He took a deep breath and turned back toward the Porsche, trying hard to control his emotions so that he could focus on doing his job. He pulled a small flashlight from his pocket and leaned back into the car. Drops of water glistened on the headrest and the driver's seat. The crime scene investigators would scold him for contaminating the scene, but he didn't care. It was a crude but effective way of awakening a drunk driver to question him before he had time to concoct a story or call a lawyer.

In the midst of the shards of glass scattered across the floor, a shiny metallic object reflected the flashlight's beam—a cell phone. Slazak carefully picked it up with a handkerchief and checked the call log. One call had been placed to 911 thirty minutes earlier; other than that, no calls had been made or received all evening. He placed the phone into a plastic bag. He would turn it over to the evidence boys if they ever showed up. He continued scanning the interior of the vehicle with his flashlight. As the narrow beam passed over the passenger seat, he brought it to an abrupt halt, training the flashlight on a dark substance spattered across the fine leather, glistening in the beam of light. He couldn't discern the color against the dark leather, so he delicately dabbed the area with the corner of a handkerchief, then held the white cloth in front of the flashlight. The bright crimson stain was unmistakable—it was blood. Wet blood.

CHAPTER 4

Kimberly Van Howe awoke to the sound of running water in her bathroom. Her bedside reading lamp was on, and her paperback novel was still in her hands. The clock on her nightstand read 1:25.

She walked unsteadily into the bathroom, wearing nothing but one of Blair's oversized T-shirts. Her eyes were still half-closed as she snuggled up to her husband from behind, wrapping her arms around him while he washed his hands at the sink.

"Hello, Congressman," she purred softly.

Blair recoiled at her touch and said nothing, but continued running water over his hands. Kimberly stood back to look at him in the mirror. She gasped as she saw the blood spattered across the sink and swirling down the drain.

"My God, Blair! What happened?"

Blair pulled his hand from the running water and held it up. Blood oozed from a large gash in his right index finger. "I was in an accident," he responded in a shaky voice.

Kimberly grabbed a hand towel and wrapped it around the bloody finger. "Are you hurt? Anywhere else, I mean?" She stepped back and surveyed her husband from head to foot. He was pale and obviously shaken.

"No, I'm not hurt, but the accident—it's bad. I think the other guy is really hurt ... I took off ... I called 911 and then I ran home ... I left Danny there."

"Slow down, Blair, you're not making sense," Kimberly said, her face turning as pale as her husband's. She guided him toward their bed, and he sat down. "Now tell me exactly what happened," she instructed him. Her voice was firm and steady, but alarm and dread were evident in her eyes.

Blair stared at the floor, gripping his towel-wrapped finger tightly. "I was driving Danny's Porsche. When we left the restaurant, Danny was loaded, so I drove. When we got near Danny's house, I took a turn too fast. It was late, the streets were empty, and I didn't expect to see any other cars. But when I made the turn onto Hamilton, there was another car coming right at me. He swerved and missed me, but he smashed head-on into a tree. I got out of the car and went to check on him, and he was hurt—bad, I think."

"Then what happened?" Kimberly asked.

Blair stood up and began pacing, unable to look at his wife. "I couldn't get him out. He was wedged in. And then ..." He looked up at his wife for just an instant, then looked down again. "I just panicked. I thought about the campaign, what this means to you, what it means to your father, and I just panicked."

"Blair, what did you do?" Kimberly demanded, her tone becoming sharp.

Blair stopped his pacing and hung his head. "I moved Danny into the driver's seat. He was passed out. Then I called 911 on his cell phone. And then I left."

Kimberly stared at her husband in stunned silence for a long moment. Then she exploded. "Jesus Christ, Blair, what were you thinking? This could ruin everything! This election is our big chance. We've both wanted this for so long. Now it could all blow up in a big, messy scandal! Shit! I can't believe this!"

Blair avoided his wife's glare. He walked back into the bathroom and found some gauze in the medicine cabinet and wrapped it tightly around his finger with white medical tape. He looked at himself in the mirror, then stared down at the sink. "I need to go back there. I need to straighten this out," he said quietly, more to himself than to his wife.

"Like hell you do!" Kimberly shouted. "What's done is done! That would only make it worse. We better call my father."

Blair continued staring at the sink for a long moment. "I guess we should," he said reluctantly. He hated the idea of having to break this news to Kimberly's father, Sam McIntire, but he could think of no one better equipped to deal with a situation like this.

Sam McIntire was a legend on the Chicago political scene. He had held a variety of public offices over the past thirty years, including State's Attorney, Comptroller for the State of Illinois, Cook County Assessor, and Chairman of the Democratic Party at both the city and state levels. The title on his business card at any particular point in time was almost irrelevant, however. Simply put, he was the consummate power-broker, one of the most influential Chicago politicians of his generation. He had all the right connections and knew how to work the system. He had launched and guided the careers of mayors, senators and governors. Those who were unwise enough to cross him invariably watched their careers and political fortunes abruptly falter or slowly slide into oblivion.

As a young politician, McIntire had set his sights on the big prize: the governor's mansion. Unfortunately, the talents that served him so well—backroom deals, arm-twisting, coercion, and his reputation as a "fixer"—were considered baggage by the party leaders, too much dirty laundry for a candidate seeking such a high-profile public office. So he had to satisfy himself with his role as a master behind-the-scenes powerbroker, someone who could make things happen and fix what needed fixing when the guys in higher offices were afraid to get their hands dirty.

Within twenty minutes of his daughter's phone call, McIntire burst through the back door of the Van Howe house without knocking, ready to take charge. At sixty years old, he was still an imposing figure, standing nearly six feet six inches tall and pushing 300 pounds. Despite his girth, he moved quickly and had an aura of energy and intensity around him. He instinctively pulled down the shades in the kitchen. "Let's talk in here," he ordered in a voice that left no room for argument. They gathered around the kitchen table. McIntire inserted a fat cigar between his lips, but didn't light it.

"Okay, Blair, Kimberly gave me the short version on the phone: you got into an accident, the other guy might be hurt pretty bad, and you left the scene. Now give me the whole story. Every detail."

Sam listened intently as Blair recounted the evening's events in considerably more detail than he had shared with Kimberly. When he mentioned the little girl in the backseat, Kimberly exploded again. "Jesus, Blair, you didn't tell me someone saw you there! What a disaster!"

Sam remained unfazed. "Tell me about the girl," he asked, his eyes narrowing.

"She was young, probably seven or eight years old," Blair replied. "I think she might be mentally disabled. She didn't look normal."

"Did you say anything to her?" Sam asked.

"Not much. I asked if she was hurt. She didn't really answer, but she looked okay. She just said, 'Help my daddy,' or something like that, and then I told her I was going for help." Blair paused and drew a deep breath. "But she wasn't the only person who saw me. When I approached the car, the driver opened his eyes, just for a few seconds, and asked me to help him."

"The driver saw you?" Kimberly looked horrified.

Blair looked down and nodded. "Yeah, and I recognized him. He's new in the neighborhood. We met him and his wife at that block party over on Leavitt Street a few weeks ago. They live next door to the Olsons, I think. I can't remember their name."

"McGrath?" Kimberly asked.

"Yeah, I think that's it. Anyway, he looked right at me when he asked for help."

"Then what happened?" Sam asked.

"Then I ran back to Danny's car and tried to wake him up, but he was still passed out. I thought about what a disaster this would be for the campaign ... and I just panicked. I moved Danny into the driver's seat, then I called 911 on his cell phone and took off." Blair looked from his father-in-law to his wife through watery eyes, then hung his head. "I'm so sorry," he said softly, his voice thick with emotion.

"You should be!" Kimberly screamed through tears of rage. "Everything we've dreamed about and worked for—we're so close—and now you may have ruined it all! How could you, Blair?"

Her father shot her a stern glance and held up a beefy hand in a gesture for silence. This was a time for cool calculation, not recrimination. He leaned back in his chair and folded his arms across his massive chest. "Well, here's how I see it," he said. "We can't change what happened. Those are the cards we've been dealt, and we need to play them as best we can. The fact is, you may not be implicated at all, Blair. The police will find Danny in the driver's seat, seriously drunk, and they'll draw the obvious conclusion: Danny passed out at the wheel and caused the accident. There's no reason for them to think anything else, so they probably won't even investigate. That was actually some pretty quick thinking on your part, and it may just save your ass."

"But I can't do that to Danny," Blair protested. "After everything he's done for me, I can't lay this off on him."

"You already have, Blair," Sam said coldly. "You made that decision at the accident site, and now you have to live with it. Hell, look at it this way. If he hadn't gotten drunk, this never would have happened. Don't risk destroying your career over this. Think of all the good you can do for so many people if you win this election."

"But what about Danny? This could ruin him!"

Sam stared thoughtfully at his son-in-law, tapping his unlit cigar on the kitchen table. "Leave that to me. I may be able to pull a few strings to keep the damage to a minimum." Sam stood up and began pacing. "So, here's the play, Blair. If anyone asks, you took a cab home. You were never at the accident scene, and you know nothing about it."

"What if the little girl remembers seeing me there?"

Sam winced and tried hard to conceal his frustration. "Chances are, it won't even occur to her to mention it," Sam replied coolly. "If she does, people will think she's just confused. She's seven years old, probably in shock, and maybe retarded. Who will believe her? You were never there—got it?"

"Damn! I just thought of something else," Blair said, closing his eyes and looking as if the thought were causing him physical pain. "The valet at the hotel— he saw me get into Danny's car. He handed me the keys."

"Does he know you?" Sam asked, growing irritation evident in his voice.

"No, I've never seen him before," Blair replied.

"What did he look like?" Sam asked.

"Short and slight, Hispanic, young. Twenty, maybe."

"Probably nothing to worry about," Sam said confidently. "The police aren't likely to talk to him. Why would they? Anyway, he probably deals with dozens of people every night and wouldn't have any reason to remember you."

Blair looked defeated and utterly dejected. He knew he'd made horrible decisions earlier that night and was overcome with remorse and self-loathing. Yet Sam's words had some validity. He couldn't undo what had been done or dwell on those poor decisions; he needed to move on. He honestly believed that he could do tremendous good as a United States congressman, and there was something to be said for considering the greater good. And he had his family to think about. Both Kimberly and Sam wanted this as much as he did, maybe more, if that were possible. He would trust in Sam's judgment and heed his advice. No one knew more about these kinds of things than Sam McIntire.

"Okay, Sam, I'll do it your way," Blair said with quiet resignation, staring at the blood-soaked bandage on his finger.

Sam nodded slowly. "It's your only choice, Blair. No matter what happens next, you just need to act as if you know nothing about all this. You took a cab home by yourself. It's as simple as that."

Blair looked down at the kitchen table for a long moment. "Sam?"

"Yeah?"

"What if the driver survives? He could put me at the scene."

Sam eyed him coldly. "Well then, let's just hope he doesn't."

CHAPTER 5

Early Sunday morning

The temperature was mild, but Blair Van Howe shivered at the thought of facing his best friend. *Act like you were never there.* That's what Sam had advised. And Blair knew he was nothing if not a great actor. It's what he did best. Yes, he was smart, and certainly a capable lawyer, but he was not possessed of a brilliant legal mind, and he knew it. He wasn't a deep thinker or a masterful strategist, like Danny. But he was a gifted communicator. The ability to speak—articulately, eloquently, and persuasively—came naturally to him. So did acting, and those two talents coalesced perfectly in the courtroom. It was his stage, and he had pulled off many a masterful performance there. With a jury as his audience, he was absolutely convincing playing whatever role the situation demanded. Sometimes it required anger or righteous indignation, sometimes humility and sincerity. Some situations called for him to be the brash showman; other circumstances called for humble, folksy charm. Blair delighted in the challenge of immersing himself in a role and leading his audience exactly where he wanted them to go. But not this role, and not with Danny Moran as the audience.

Danny had been his closest friend since they attended law school together at Northwestern. Fate had brought them together as dormitory roommates their first year, and they quickly became fast friends. Law school had been a struggle for Blair at first, but Danny had made it his personal mission to see Blair succeed. Danny had helped him develop the organizational skills necessary to handle the massive amount of work and inspired Blair to push himself to do the best he possibly could. Danny had spent countless hours explaining the intricacies and nuances of contracts, torts, constitutional law, and all of the various other subjects they studied in law school. Largely due to Danny's coaching and support, Blair had finished in the top third of their class and graduated from law school with a sense of accomplishment and confidence he was certain he would not have attained if left to his own devices.

Danny had graduated first in their class and was heavily recruited by all the premier law firms in Chicago. He joined Preston & Harrington, known to be the most selective law firm in the city. The firm was also known for its highly sophisticated and successful trial practice, and was unquestionably the most politically connected of all the city's elite law firms. Its client list read like a *Who's Who* of Corporate America. Danny was a natural in that environment. Although not flamboyant or one to seek the limelight, his legal talents were quickly recognized, and he rapidly rose through the ranks, becoming head of the firm's powerhouse litigation department at the age of thirty-five. Danny also proved himself to be extremely adept at cultivating relationships within both the corporate universe and political circles. His manner was unfailingly low-key and unassuming, but his legal and political savvy, insights, and creativity quickly made him one of the most sought-after advisers in the city.

It was Danny who had paved the way for Blair to join Preston & Harrington eight years ago. It was Danny who was the mastermind behind the high-profile trials Blair had handled, even though Blair enjoyed most of the visibility and the credit. And it was Danny who had made the right introductions and paved the way for the launching of Blair's political career. Danny had been there to help every step of the way. Now the tables were turned: Danny needed his help.

At six thirty Sunday morning, Blair pulled his black Lexus out of the driveway and drove through the quiet streets of North Beverly toward an unfamiliar destination, the lockup at the local precinct house. Danny had called twenty minutes earlier asking for help. Blair had not even been to bed yet, partly because he was too upset to sleep, but also because he was expecting Danny's call. They were partners and best friends. Who else would Danny call? If the roles had been reversed, he certainly would have called Danny.

Danny had sounded uncharacteristically distressed when he called, and said nothing other than that he was in jail and in trouble, and needed help. Blair asked no questions and promised to be there as fast as he could. Having had absolutely no experience with arrests or lockups, Blair was clueless about the process for procuring Danny's release; however, Sam had assured him that he'd make a call and that Blair would encounter no trouble.

Ten minutes later, Blair pulled up in front of a drab, old concrete building that resembled a fortress. The world seemed eerily quiet as he pulled the handle of the heavy wooden door and stepped inside. A balding, overweight police sergeant looked up from his Sunday newspaper as Blair approached.

"I'd like to see Danny Moran," Blair said uncertainly. "I understand he's in custody here."

"And who are you?"

"My name is Van Howe. Blair Van Howe."

"Okay, I was told you'd be coming. You can have a seat over there, and we'll bring him out." The sergeant motioned toward some time-worn wooden benches across the room.

Within minutes, Danny was escorted to the reception area by another paunchy, middle-aged police officer. Blair started at the sight of his partner. Danny was always impeccably dressed and groomed, with an air of self-confidence and positive energy about him. At the moment, he was none of those things. He was unshaven, his clothes were rumpled, and his eyes were bloodshot. He looked haggard. Even worse, he looked humiliated—and scared.

Danny smiled weakly at Blair as he was led past him to the duty sergeant behind the counter. He signed some documents relating to his discharge and personal effects.

"You're free to go, Mr. Moran," said the sergeant. "The State's Attorney's Office will be contacting you." He glanced up from his paperwork and gave Danny a hard look. "You better hope that guy survives. If he doesn't, you'll be looking at homicide charges on top of the DUI and reckless driving."

Danny said nothing. He collected his belongings and turned toward Blair, who was now standing behind him.

"Hello, Dano," Blair said softly. "I don't know what happened, but whatever it is, I'm here for you. You'll get through this." He did his best to sound reassuring.

Danny was unable to meet his gaze. He stared at the grimy tile floor, a tear trickling down his cheek.

"Come on, pal, we can talk outside," Blair said, putting his arm around Danny's shoulder and leading him outside.

They walked in silence to Blair's Lexus and climbed in. As Blair started the ignition, Danny turned and faced him. "I'm in serious trouble, Blair. I almost killed someone last night. This is such a nightmare." He sounded despondent.

Blair turned off the ignition and gave his friend his full attention. "Take it slow, Dano. Why don't you tell me exactly what happened?"

"That's just it—that's the worst part. I don't even know what happened. I don't remember anything! All I remember is waking up in my car a block from my house with a policeman staring me in the face, telling me that I had run somebody off the road. He said the guy was really hurt and that he might not make it."

"You don't remember anything about the accident at all?"

"Nothing. It's a total blank!"

"Well, don't be too quick to jump to conclusions. Maybe it wasn't your fault. Maybe the other guy was driving recklessly."

Danny looked doubtful. "But that won't matter in court. I was drunk. There'd be a presumption that I was at fault. And I probably was. Hell, I blacked out. I'd have to be really drunk for that to happen. But it just doesn't make any sense. I know sometimes I drink too much, but I never drive when I'm drunk. I just don't. That's been programmed into my brain forever. How could I have done that?"

"We'll find the best DUI lawyer in town, Dano. You may not be able to get off completely, but—"

"I'm not worried about getting off! I'm worried about what I've done! This guy might die because of me. And the cop told me he's got two little kids. How can I live with that?"

"Well, don't assume the worst. Maybe he'll pull through."

Danny turned toward the window and wiped tears from his eyes. "It's so scary, Blair, not having the faintest recollection of what happened." There was pain etched across his face and anguish in his voice.

"What's the last thing you remember, Dano?"

Danny closed his eyes and thought for a moment. "I remember having a couple of pints of Guinness with Brendan. After that, it's just a total blank. I've been trying all night to force my memory to come back, but it's no use. It's just not there." Danny hung his head and took a deep breath as if bracing himself for the cold truth. "I guess it doesn't matter," he said with quiet resignation. "Whether I remember it or not, it's pretty clear what happened. I got loaded, I tried to drive home, then I either passed out at the wheel and ran that poor guy off the road, or I ran him off the road and then passed out. Any way you cut it, I'm responsible. It's my fault, and now I've got to deal with the consequences."

"Let's get you home, pal," Blair said sympathetically, starting the ignition. "You need some rest. Are Karen and Allie home yet?" he asked, referring to Danny's wife and teenage daughter, who had been visiting relatives in California during the trial.

"Not yet," Danny replied. "They get home this afternoon."

Throughout their conversation, Blair had been struggling with his own anguish. He was trying to play the role, trying to act as if he knew nothing. That's what he had promised Sam and Kimberly he would do. However, his resolve was wavering as he witnessed the damage that course of action was inflicting upon his friend. And that damage and pain would only get worse over time. Danny could go to jail. He would almost certainly be sued. He would be publicly disgraced, and perhaps worst of all, he'd have to live with guilt he didn't deserve. And this was Danny Moran, his best friend, who had done so much for him. But just when Blair thought it was a role he couldn't play, when he was within seconds of revealing the truth, Danny had made it easy. "I'm responsible," Danny had said. "It's my fault." And Danny truly believed that. It was just too easy to let him continue believing it.

CHAPTER 6

Detective Victor Slazak sat in the leather recliner in his living room, intently watching the baseball game on his new big-screen TV. The room was hot and stuffy, but he didn't mind. It felt like the old days, before central air-conditioning had become commonplace, and that's how baseball should be watched on a Sunday afternoon during June in Chicago.

The house was a 1950s-era bungalow in Mount Greenwood, a working-class neighborhood on the southwestern outskirts of the city. Like many of his neighbors, Slazak had grown up in Mount Greenwood and had never found any reason to leave. Most of the residents were policemen, firemen, or other city workers, drawn there by the availability of affordable housing within the city limits.

The yellow brick bungalow was small, but that didn't bother Slazak; he lived alone and liked it that way. He had tried marriage twice, and each marriage had lasted less than a year. Now forty-four years old, he was content with his station in life and felt no need for companionship, either at home or on the job. He wasn't good at relationships, he told himself. They were messy and complicated. They required tact and diplomacy, which meant holding your tongue and dancing around the truth. They required flexibility and compromise. He wasn't good at any of those things and had no desire to be.

On the job, he was brutally honest and direct with his colleagues. He said what was on his mind, without apologies and without making any effort to be politically correct or considerate of the feelings of others. Not surprisingly, he had alienated more partners than he could count, but the department tolerated him and allowed him to work alone, for one simple reason: he was unquestionably the best detective on the force. What he lacked in diplomacy, he made up for with uncanny intuition, street smarts, a tireless work ethic, and a relentless drive to find the truth. He was a perfectionist who got results. And his job was his passion.

His other passion was baseball. It was his only real interest outside of the job. His father had raised him to be a White Sox fan from the time he could talk, and he had started traveling to Comiskey Park on his own at the age of eight. A true "South-Sider," he despised the cross-town rival Cubs. He would tell anyone who asked that he had two favorite baseball teams, the White Sox being one, and whoever happened to be playing the Cubs, the other. He took great pride in the fact that he had never set foot in Wrigley Field, home of the Cubs on the city's north side, and never would.

Today was Slazak's idea of the perfect day for baseball. The White Sox were playing the Cubs as part of their annual interleague series, and he was relishing the prospect of watching every pitch on his new high-definition TV, one of the few luxuries he permitted himself.

By the third inning, Slazak realized that one of his passions was interfering with the other. He was watching every pitch, but he was distracted. He couldn't stop thinking about the car wreck he'd been called to the previous night. He couldn't shake the rage he felt at that hotshot lawyer who had almost killed Terry McGrath and left two young children without a father. Yet something else was distracting him, too—a nagging sense of duty that was telling him he should be investigating the incident right now. Witnesses needed to be interviewed while events were still fresh, before their memories became fuzzy and before they had a chance to concoct some other version of what had happened.

Slazak picked up the old Titleist golf ball on the table beside him and began tossing it softly from one hand to the other as he stared at the TV. It was an old habit. When the wheels began turning in his mind, he tossed the golf ball back and forth. The more intense the deliberations, the quicker the tosses became.

There seemed to be little mystery to the previous evening's events. A guy got drunk and ran somebody off the road. How much simpler could it get? Still, some part of him required certainty, and the only way to attain that was through diligence, hard work, and attention to detail. Experience had taught him that, every once in a while, things were not as they seemed. He had seen other detectives embarrassed when they got it wrong. He had seen them ridiculed by their colleagues and criticized by their bosses. He refused to subject himself to those risks, so he forced himself to be thorough and meticulous in his handling of even the simplest cases.

"You shithead! Can't you get anybody out?" Slazak yelled at the White Sox pitcher. It was just the top of the third inning and the Cubs had already scored five runs, putting him in a foul mood. His cursing was interrupted by the ringing of his cell phone.

"What?" Slazak shouted impatiently into the phone.

"Detective? This is Officer Wilson. We met last night at that car wreck. You asked me to call you today."

"Yeah, fill me in, Wilson. Did you take him to the ER?" Slazak had instructed Wilson to take the suspect to the hospital for two reasons: first, to protect the police department against liability claims in case the suspect had been seriously injured, and second, because the emergency room routinely took blood tests, and it was a great way to get irrefutable evidence of intoxication. Most people signed the consent form along with all of the other hospital paperwork and didn't think to object to a hospital-administered blood test.

"Yeah, I took him there. Had to wait almost two hours before they examined him. He was fine. He wouldn't take the blood test, though."

"Shit," Slazak muttered. Another Cub base runner had scored as Wilson delivered this news. "So he wasn't hurt at all?"

"Nope."

"Not even any minor scrapes or cuts?"

"I wasn't in the room when the doctor examined him, but I didn't see any. The doc said he was fine and sent us on our way. We got to the station around four o'clock, and they put him in lockup. I heard he was bailed out by one of his law partners this morning."

"Did you get any information out of him?"

"He said he was at some French restaurant downtown last night. The big shots at Champions HealthCare threw some sort of party in his honor. Other than that, he didn't say much."

"Okay, thanks, Wilson. Hey, one more thing. Find out where his partner lives." He hung up.

Slazak turned his attention to the ball game once again. The golf ball flew from hand to hand with increasing speed as two more innings went by. As the fifth inning ended, Slazak grabbed the remote control and turned off the game in disgust. The Cubs were pounding his beloved White Sox 10–1; he couldn't bear to watch. He stood up, tossed the golf ball straight up in the air, caught it with his right hand, and shoved it into his pocket.

Slazak retrieved a small spiral notebook from his bedside table and studied it for a few minutes. He had jotted down the addresses of both Danny Moran and Terry McGrath from their driver's licenses. They both lived in Beverly, just a few blocks apart from each other, about four miles northeast of Mount Greenwood. It was Sunday, his day off, but he needed to get away from baseball for awhile. There was work to be done.

CHAPTER 7

"Daddy, we're home!"

Danny awoke with a start at the sound of the cheerful teenage voice. He blinked hard and looked at his watch. It was three thirty in the afternoon, and he was lying in bed in gym shorts and a T-shirt. He rolled out of bed and moved slowly out of the second-story bedroom toward the stairs, trying to ignore the pounding in his head.

His wife, Karen, and their seventeen-year-old daughter, Allie, had been visiting Karen's parents in San Francisco for the past ten days. They knew that Danny worked nearly around the clock when he was in trial and needed to be free from distractions, so they used those opportunities to travel whenever they could. Despite being consumed by the trial, Danny had found himself greatly missing them by the time it was over and had been eagerly awaiting their return—until now. A wave of dread passed over him as he made his way down the stairs.

Allie met him at the bottom of the stairs. "Hi, Pops! Congratulations on your trial! I missed you!"

She flung her arms around him enthusiastically, oblivious to his haggard appearance. He was bleary-eyed and unshaven, and obviously had been sleeping in the middle of a Sunday afternoon. She was equally oblivious to the look of shame and embarrassment clouding his face.

Danny could see that none of that was lost on Karen. She dropped her suitcases and stared silently at her husband for several long moments.

"Danny? Are you okay?" she asked apprehensively, glued to her spot just inside the door.

"I'm afraid I've got some bad news," Danny began, hesitation in his voice.

"What? What happened?" Allie asked, immediately becoming alarmed.

"I was in an accident last night."

Allie gasped. "Are you okay?"

Danny nodded, and they walked slowly into the living room, where he sat down on the sofa. Allie sat next to her father, eyeing him with concern. Karen stared at them from across the room, one hand over her mouth.

"What happened?" Allie asked again, her eyes widening.

"I'm not exactly sure," Danny said slowly. "I went to the victory celebration downtown last night. I was driving home sometime after midnight, and I think … I think I almost collided with another car. He drove off the road into a tree. I hear he's hurt pretty badly."

"What do you mean 'you think' you almost collided?" Karen asked, her voice shaking. "You don't know for sure?"

Danny shook his head, staring at the floor.

"You were drinking again, Danny, weren't you?" Karen asked, her tone harsh and accusatory.

"I'm afraid so," he replied softly. "I honestly don't remember what happened. I woke up at the accident scene, and I just have no recollection of what happened."

"What's going to happen, Daddy?" Allie asked. "Are you going to be arrested? Will we get sued?"

"I don't know, sweetheart," he replied, unable to look his daughter in the eye.

Allie leaned toward her father and gently grasped his forearm. "Don't worry, Daddy, we'll get through this," she said, obviously trying hard to sound confident and reassuring, but not quite succeeding. "Everything will be okay, I just know it."

"Allie, would you give your father and me a few minutes alone?" Karen asked, her voice trembling.

"Sure, Mom," Allie said quietly, keeping her eyes fixed on her father. She embraced him tightly and left the room.

Karen waited until she heard the sound of Allie's bedroom door closing. "I can't do this, Danny," she said, her voice breaking as she began pacing across the room. "I just can't take it anymore. You were sober for three solid months, and I was finally starting to feel hopeful … and then I come home to this!"

"Karen, I'm so sorry," Danny said, standing and walking toward his wife. She put her hands up, gesturing for him to stop, and turned away from him.

She was sobbing now, and Danny reached out and put a hand on her shoulder. She recoiled. "You *should* be sorry, Danny! But that's not enough. We've talked about this before—the late nights, the nights you don't come home at all, drinking until you can't even talk, drinking until you pass out and can't even remember where you were or what you were doing. I can't live like this anymore, I just can't! And now someone's gotten hurt because of it, and there'll be legal implications, not to mention the shame and humiliation!"

"You have every right to feel that way, Karen, and I'm truly sorry for what I've put you through. I don't know what I can possibly do to make it right, but I'll find a way."

Karen turned and looked directly at him. "There's nothing you *can* do, Danny," she said with quiet resignation, her voice steady now. "It's too late."

CHAPTER 8

Vic Slazak drove toward North Beverly at a leisurely pace, giving himself time to formulate a plan for each of the interviews he hoped to conduct that afternoon. As he cruised past the luxurious homes, some part of him felt a twinge of regret that he hadn't taken his father's advice and gone to law school. Had he done so, he might be enjoying life in an affluent neighborhood like this one.

His father had spent forty years as a Chicago cop, and had made it abundantly clear that he was disappointed in his son's career choice. He had insisted that his son was far too smart to settle for the meager pay and lifestyle offered by the Chicago PD, but Slazak hated school and hated the thought of spending his working days cooped up in an office. So he joined the police force, believing that working as a homicide detective would provide plenty of opportunity for him to use his wits. He had proven that to himself throughout his career; however, his hypercritical father would never believe that. As with most of the people in his past, Slazak's relationship with his father had become permanently strained, and they seldom spoke anymore. When they did, the conversation was typically limited to brief exchanges about sports.

Slazak's ruminations were interrupted by the ringing of his cell phone. It was Officer Wilson, calling to pass along Blair Van Howe's address. As luck would have it, Van Howe lived less than two blocks from Danny Moran, so he might be able to catch both of them on this trip. But first, he would drop in on the one person who might be in a position to actually remember something about the previous night's accident: Ashley McGrath.

A frizzy-haired teenager with thick glasses and braces opened the door hesitantly in response to his loud knock. She looked nervously at the lean and wiry stranger with the intense dark eyes and greasy brown hair.

"Is Mrs. McGrath home?" Slazak inquired.

"No, she's at the hospital," the girl replied in a timid voice.

"Who are you?" asked Slazak.

"I'm Tammy, the babysitter."

Slazak pulled his badge and identification card from his pocket and showed it to the girl. "I'm a police officer, Tammy, and the person I really need to talk to is Ashley. Is she here?"

Tammy studied Slazak's ID carefully. "Yeah, she's in the backyard," she said, after satisfying herself that his face matched the photograph on the ID. "You can come through this way."

She guided Slazak through the house to a sliding glass door that led to a cedar deck and a large backyard that clearly belonged to a family with young children. The yard was dominated by a monstrous, brightly colored fort, complete with swings and slide, and bicycles, balls and toys of all types were scattered everywhere. Ashley McGrath was seated at a miniature picnic table, holding a small, sleeping puppy in her lap. Her face was expressionless as she gently stroked the puppy, staring absently into the distance.

"Ashley? Remember me?" Slazak asked in as gentle a voice as he could muster.

She turned and looked at him calmly for a second or two, then looked away. She nodded.

"I'd like to ask you a few questions about last night, okay?"

Ashley continued staring straight ahead and said nothing.

"It's okay, Ashley. He's a policeman," said Tammy, trying to be encouraging. "He's here to help. You can talk to him."

Ashley bowed her head and looked at the sleeping puppy.

Slazak pulled a lawn chair alongside the little girl and leaned toward her. "Ashley, do you remember what happened last night? Do you think you can tell me about it?"

The girl nodded slowly.

"Did you see what made your daddy crash?"

She nodded again.

"Tell him, Ashley," Tammy urged.

"We were going to get Bully. Another car came right at us, really fast," the young girl replied in a soft monotone voice.

"Then what happened?"

"Daddy tried to get out of the way, but we crashed into the tree. My tummy hurt from the seat belt. My glasses fell off."

"What happened next?"

"Daddy was hurt. His head was all bloody, and he didn't answer when I talked to him," she said in a faraway voice. "Then the man came and looked in the window."

"The policeman?" Slazak asked.

"No," Ashley replied. "Another man came before the policeman. He looked at Daddy, and he talked to me."

"Are you sure it wasn't one of the policemen, Ashley?"

Ashley nodded, still staring straight ahead as if in a trance, while stroking the little bulldog.

"Do you remember what he said?" Slazak asked.

"He said he would get help for Daddy."

"Do you remember what he looked like?"

Ashley looked down at the puppy and did not respond.

Slazak leaned in closer to the little girl. "Ashley, this is really important, okay? Do you remember what the man looked like?"

Her lower lip began to quiver as tears welled up in her eyes. Slazak didn't know whether she felt bad because she was unable to answer his question or whether his questioning had caused the child to relive the terrible event. He touched her gently on the knee. "That's all right, Ashley. You've been very helpful. Just one more question, okay?"

She nodded.

"Is there anything else you think I should know about last night?"

She turned and looked at him through tear-filled eyes, then looked down again. "It's my fault," she said in a voice that was barely audible.

"What?" Slazak asked, startled by the comment.

"It's my fault," she said again, her voice quavering. "I couldn't find Mr. Growl, and I made us late. If I hadn't made us late, we wouldn't have been there when the other car was." She began sniffling. A tear fell on the little puppy's back, and she quickly wiped it off.

Tammy stepped between them, knelt in front of the child, and wrapped her in a tight embrace. "Oh, Ashley," she said through her own tears. "Don't ever think that way! It wasn't your fault at all. It was just an accident."

She looked reproachfully at Slazak, who took that as a sign that it was time to leave.

"That's right, kid," Slazak said softly, struggling to keep his own emotions in check. "It's not your fault." He stood up, unsure what to say or do next. "I'll be leaving now," he said, directing his comment to the babysitter. "I can find my way out," he said awkwardly when the babysitter failed to respond. "Bye, Ashley."

CHAPTER 9

Danny Moran sat alone in his study. The room had always felt warm and comfortable to him, with its dark wood paneling, antique mahogany desk, and the old black-and-white photos of his parents and grandparents adorning the walls. It was his sanctuary, a place where he could stay up late preparing for trial or just relishing the silence and solitude that he often craved after a busy day.

He sat there now, trying to collect his scattered thoughts and decide exactly what he needed to do to address his current predicament. At the moment, the silence pervading his house was decidedly not comfortable; it was tense—painful, even. His wife and daughter had been home for over an hour now, but Karen hadn't spoken with him since he told her about the previous evening's events and she had glared at him with those angry, incriminating pale blue eyes. He could hear her shuffling around the house, sniffling quietly, while slamming drawers and doors not-so-quietly as she tended to her unpacking. That was her way when they had a disagreement, and he hated it. He would have much preferred that she explode and say whatever was on her mind, but she would never do that; she forced him to endure the silent treatment.

"Danny?" He was surprised to hear her calling his name. She stood in the study doorway, looking aloof. "There's someone here to see you," she said coolly. He followed her to the living room, where his heart sank at the sight of his visitor.

Victor Slazak stood before him. "Mr. Moran, I'm Detective Slazak. We met last night. I was hoping we could visit for a few minutes."

Danny composed himself quickly. "Sure, Detective. Have a seat," he said, motioning to the living room sofa. Danny sat at the other end of the sofa and faced the detective. Karen stood behind an armchair across the room, obviously intent on listening.

"Sorry to stop by unannounced," Slazak said, "but I was in the neighborhood and thought I'd drop in. This shouldn't take long. I just have a couple of things I'd like to ask you about."

Danny stared at the detective, saying nothing. Slazak continued. "First, I'm following up on last night's events—you know, just trying to piece together exactly what happened. I was hoping I could ask you a few questions."

Danny looked unsure of himself. "Detective, I've never been in this situation before, and I don't really know how it works. I don't want to seem uncooperative, but I feel like I should consult with an attorney before I agree to any further questioning."

That was the response Slazak had been expecting. He was disappointed, but did his best to appear nonchalant. "I understand," Slazak said. "That's certainly your right, Mr. Moran. I just thought that since there's not much in dispute here, and since you're a lawyer yourself, you might be willing to answer just a few simple questions."

"Sorry, Detective. I know you have a job to do, and I respect that. But let's defer any questioning until after I've had

JOSEPH HAYES

a chance to confer with my attorney. What's the second item on your agenda?"

"I just wanted to make sure that you weren't hurt in the accident. Are you okay?"

"I'm fine, Detective. Not a scratch on me. Thanks for asking."

"By the way, do you happen to know your blood type?"

"Type O, I believe."

Danny watched as Slazak scribbled something in his notebook and wondered whether he'd been tricked and had made a mistake by answering those innocent-sounding questions. He decided to bring the meeting to a close. "Do you have a card, Detective? Once I've retained counsel, I'll ask my attorney to call you."

Slazak stood up, put away his notebook, and handed Danny his card.

"How's Mr. McGrath?" Danny asked with some trepidation as he walked Slazak toward the door.

"Not good," Slazak replied curtly. "He's in a coma. His doctors don't know whether he'll pull through or not."

Danny watched the detective hurry down the front walkway and climb into his car. "You better hire that lawyer fast!" he heard Karen say from behind him. He turned around to see her walking briskly away.

Danny trudged back into his study and sat down wearily, as if the brief encounter with the detective had worn him out. He turned his chair around and stared out the window into the backyard. A small hummingbird was darting around the bird feeder hanging just outside his window, tentatively nipping at the cherry-colored liquid inside the plastic cylinder.

"What was that about, Daddy?" Allie stepped into the study, trying her best to appear calm.

"That was a detective, asking questions about last night," Danny replied in a tired voice, without turning around.

"Are they going to arrest you?"

"I don't know, sweetheart." He wished he could say something reassuring to his daughter, but he couldn't find the words.

"What happens next? What should we do?" Allie asked.

Danny started at the question. He had heard it from hundreds of clients under all kinds of circumstances, usually when they were in a tough spot. His mind snapped into focus as he turned and faced his seventeen-year-old daughter. "Well, for starters, I think I need to follow the advice I always give to my clients when they're in a jam. If you've done something wrong, whether you're a politician, a corporation, or just a regular guy, the best place to start is to take responsibility for your actions. That means apologizing and doing what you can to make things right." He paused as he considered what that meant in his current situation. "I better go to the hospital to check on Mr. McGrath."

Allie looked skeptical. "Are you sure that's a good idea?"

"It's the right thing to do." Danny's voice was quiet and sad, but his mind was clearly made up.

"Then I'll go with you, Daddy."

"Thanks, Allie, but I better go alone. This is likely to be difficult for everyone. There's no telling how his family will react."

Allie wrapped her arms around her father and hugged him tightly. "I love you, Daddy," she whispered hoarsely as tears rolled down her cheeks.

***

Danny was intimately familiar with Oak Lawn Community Hospital, having visited his mother there almost daily during the final weeks of her battle with lung cancer the year before. He made his way to the intensive care unit and approached the reception desk.

"Can you tell me what room Mr. McGrath is in?" he asked the frail-looking gray-haired receptionist behind the desk.

She checked her chart. "Room 214. That's just around the corner, third door on the left." She motioned to the corridor directly behind her.

Danny took several steps in that direction, then hesitated and turned back toward the elderly receptionist. "How's he doing?" Danny asked.

She shook her head sadly. "Still in a coma … such a shame. Those two little kids … His wife and her brother are in there now."

Danny walked slowly toward the room, burdened with a crushing sense of guilt and dread. The prospect of facing Nancy McGrath was almost more than he could bear. He walked past room 210, then room 212, and all of his instincts told him to turn around and leave, but he willed himself forward. As he reached room 214, a petite, middle-aged woman walked out of the door, nearly bumping into him. She looked haggard, dark circles under bleary eyes, as they stared at each other. It seemed to Danny that Nancy McGrath recognized his face, but couldn't place it.

"Mrs. McGrath, we met once before, at the block party a few weeks ago. I'm Danny Moran."

For an instant, she looked confused. Then it clicked. Danny could see that she recognized his name. He assumed the police must have told her.

"Were you the driver? Last night?" she asked, her voice trembling, a look of disbelief on her face.

Danny nodded silently, looking down, desperately groping for the right words. "Mrs. McGrath, I can't begin to tell you how sorry I am. How's Ter—"

"How dare you come here!" she shrieked through tears of rage, slapping him hard across his face.

A short, well-built man in a dark polo shirt rushed out of the room. "What's going on?" he demanded as two young nurses also hurried to the scene.

"It's *him*!" Nancy McGrath yelled, pointing an accusing finger at Danny. "He's the bastard who ran Terry off the road." She glared at him with hatred in her eyes. "How could you?" she screamed between sobs.

One of the nurses put an arm around Nancy as her brother roughly grabbed Danny by the upper arm and began escorting him from the scene. "Get your ass out of here, pal, and don't come back! Because of you, she might lose her husband, and two little kids might lose their father, you low-life piece of shit!"

"I just wanted to tell her how sorry—"

"She doesn't care! Beat it!" He shoved Danny in the direction of the reception desk.

Danny walked quickly past the startled receptionist and toward the elevator, head down, his face still stinging.

"I hope you rot in jail!" he heard Nancy McGrath scream from behind him. "You go to hell, you lousy drunk!"

CHAPTER 10

Blair Van Howe hurriedly flipped through the pages of the Monday morning *Chicago Tribune*. Nothing. Then he scanned the pages of the *Sun-Times*. Nothing there, either. He was alone in a small conference room at the Marriott Hotel. In less than an hour, he would be giving the most important speech of his life, his campaign kickoff speech, yet he was distracted and unfocused.

"Don't worry, there's nothing in the papers this morning, Blair." Van Howe looked up as Sam McIntire bustled into the room, his giant frame barely fitting through the door. Blair looked at him, doubt evident in his eyes.

"I made some calls," Sam continued, matter-of-factly. "The story will probably break later today, but I bought us a little time, anyway."

"The timing couldn't be worse," Blair muttered, shaking his head, his eyes still skimming over the newsprint. He pushed the papers away, shook his head rapidly as if to clear the cobwebs, and let out a deep breath. "How is this going to affect the campaign, Sam?"

Sam poured a cup of coffee and handed it to his son-in-law. "It shouldn't have any effect at all," he answered confidently.

"The other side may try to make something out of it. They could suggest some sort of guilt-by-association theory. And there'll probably be some questions from the press. They'll point out that you were with Danny that night and ask if you knew he was drunk, whether you could have intervened and gotten him home safely, that kind of thing. But if you handle it right, it won't go anywhere. People will accept that you weren't there and that you can't be responsible for your partner's actions. It'll all blow over in a day or two."

Blair paced back and forth across the small conference room, arms folded, trying to evaluate Sam's assessment.

"You know, Blair, there's a way you might even turn this to your advantage," Sam added thoughtfully, rubbing his large chin.

"How's that?" Blair asked doubtfully.

"Look, a big part of your campaign involves getting tough on crime, as well as ethics and personal responsibility, right?"

Blair nodded. "Yeah. So?"

"So this gives you the perfect opportunity to bring those issues to life. Instead of being defensive about this issue and trying to avoid it, you tackle it head-on. You bring it up yourself and use it to further your agenda. You use it as an opportunity to condemn drunk driving, demand tougher laws and better enforcement in that area, and you tie all that into your overriding themes about ethics and personal responsibility."

"You want me to turn on Danny? I can't do that, Sam!"

"I'm not saying turn on him. You're not condemning Danny, you're condemning what he did. He made a mistake, and people who make mistakes need to be held accountable, right? Especially people who hold positions of responsibility and trust. You can bring that message to life with this story. But Blair ..." Sam paused. Blair stopped pacing and looked at him. "Whether you choose to talk openly about this incident or not, one thing is absolutely clear. You have to distance yourself from Danny. There's no way around that."

Sam McIntire had more political savvy than anyone Blair had ever met, and Blair had always listened intently to Sam's views and advice. He knew from experience that Sam's instincts were invariably right on the mark. Everything Sam had been saying made perfect sense until he suggested abandoning Danny, even condemning him, or at least his actions, which meant the same thing for all practical purposes. Blair sat down and stared at the shiny wooden conference table. "I don't know if I can do this to Danny," he said quietly. "It's just so ... wrong ... even if we could pull it off. And what if, somehow, the truth comes out? Then what?"

"Goddamn it, Blair, what's done is done!" Sam exploded, putting his beefy hands on the table and leaning across toward his son-in-law. "If Danny hadn't gotten drunk, none of this would have happened. Get over it! You have an opportunity that most people could never even dream of, and you'll never have it again if you don't grab it right here and now. Don't piss this away!"

Sam sat down opposite his son-in-law. "Look, Blair," he said in the most sincere tone his gruff persona was capable of generating. "You're like the son I never had. You are, without a doubt, the most naturally gifted politician I've ever laid eyes on. I've never seen a better communicator or anyone who could charm people and earn their trust like you can—not even Ronald Reagan or JFK. You've got a gift. A long time ago, I wanted to be governor more than anything else in the world, but I didn't have what it takes to get there. I realize that now. But you do! This is just a stepping stone. United States congressman will be a shoo-in. You could be governor.

You could be a senator. Hell, you could wind up in the White House! I really believe that. And I want that for you and for Kimberly. Think about how much good you could do for so many people."

"Do you really mean that, Sam?"

"Hell, yes, I mean it!"

They both looked up as Kimberly walked in, looking stunning, her blonde hair shimmering against an elegant, yet conservative, navy blue dress. "Ten minutes until showtime!" she announced cheerfully. "Are we ready?"

"Hi, honey," Blair replied, his spirits beginning to lift after Sam's pep talk and the sight of his gorgeous wife brimming with enthusiasm. The press would love her. "Your dad and I were putting the finishing touches on my speech. I just need a few minutes alone to get my game face on."

"You got it, sweetheart," she answered brightly. "Come on, Dad." Kimberly leaned over, kissed her husband on the cheek, and bounced out of the room.

Her father walked around the table, slapped Blair on the shoulder, and said, "Knock 'em dead!"

***

As he had done countless times before, Blair Van Howe effortlessly slid into role-playing mode. He was playing the part of the rising political star, captivating the heart and soul of the populace with a combination of energy and flair, sincerity and passion, and most of all, unparalleled charisma. From the podium, he looked at the throng of reporters, politicians, labor leaders, corporate titans, and old friends. He felt that familiar rush that came from being on center stage, mesmerizing his audience. All hesitation and doubt were left behind in that small conference room. As he launched into his speech, he visualized himself as the reincarnation of JFK and knew beyond any doubt that he could play that role perfectly.

The purpose of the speech was simple: to announce his candidacy for United States Congress. Yet there was so much more at stake. This would be his first opportunity to educate the electorate about Blair Van Howe—who he was and what he stood for. The themes certainly were not new: bringing a fresh outlook to Washington, insisting on fiscal responsibility, holding political leaders accountable by demanding change and action, making ethics and personal responsibility a priority for our elected leaders and everyone else. Yet Blair Van Howe made these ideas sound compelling and urgent. He instilled in his listeners a sense of hope and excitement like no other politician had generated in them before. This was a man who could inspire, a man people would trust and respect, a man they would root for—and, most important, a man they would vote for.

The room exploded into applause as he finished his remarks—not the polite, tepid applause typically heard following a politician's press conference. This was raucous, excited cheering, the kind that results from a truly inspired, and inspiring, performance. Blair looked out over the crowd and saw Sam McIntire standing against the back wall. Their eyes met. Sam nodded and smiled, a satisfied smile indicating that all of his instincts had just been resoundingly confirmed.

Following the speech, Blair and Kimberly lingered in the auditorium, shaking hands, chatting, and basking in the glow of the enthusiastic feedback. When the crowd had dispersed, they went in search of Sam and found him in the conference room, talking on his cell phone in a low voice, his back toward them. He terminated the call, then turned to face them, a broad smile crossing his fleshy face. "You're on your way, Blair!"

"Thanks, Sam. And thanks for the pep talk. It really helped."

"No problem. You just convinced everyone in that room that they just had their first glimpse of one of our rising political stars. I hope you convinced yourself, too."

"I'm ready, Sam," Blair responded, shaking Sam's hand enthusiastically, still riding high from his speech.

"Then let me put your mind to rest on one other thing," said Sam, with a look of satisfaction. "Terry McGrath is dead."

CHAPTER 11

Vic Slazak had not come to the press conference to listen to another politician engage in flowery self-promotion. He was there on official police business, although no one knew that but him. He was determined to wrap up the investigation of Saturday night's car wreck, and that meant talking to the key players promptly. A few pieces of the puzzle weren't fitting into place, and that was nagging at him. From spending half a lifetime in police work, he knew that criminal investigation was a messy business and that there were often unanswered questions. He could accept that, but only after he'd made a real effort to solve the puzzle. In this case, that meant speaking to the short list of people who were either at the accident scene or with Danny Moran earlier Saturday evening. He was determined to have those conversations on his own timetable, and not be put off by the personal agendas of anyone involved, including the new Democratic candidate for Congress.

Slazak had stopped by the Van Howe home the previous afternoon, following his visit with Danny Moran. Mrs. Van Howe had greeted him at the door and informed him that her husband was not at home. She seemed flustered when he asked if one of the two cars in the driveway was her husband's. She acknowledged that it was and stated that he was meeting with members of his campaign team and must have gotten a ride from one of them. She claimed to have just recently gotten home and that she didn't know where her husband's meeting was or when he would be home.

Slazak had called Van Howe's law office that morning when the switchboard opened at eight o'clock. He was told that Mr. Van Howe would not be available that day because he was holding a press conference that morning and had meetings scheduled throughout the entire day.

Slazak had slipped quietly into the press conference just as Blair Van Howe was taking the podium. Slazak loathed most politicians and typically found himself silently ridiculing them whenever he listened to their speeches. One of the essential job skills in his line of work was to have a good bullshit detector, and he generally found it easy to dismiss both the substance and the sincerity of most political speeches as superficial, disingenuous bullshit. This guy was different, however. Slazak had to admit that Blair Van Howe was in a class far above most other politicians. He was a captivating speaker, and his audience was clearly enthralled. And he looked the part: tall, fit, and good-looking; silver-haired, yet youthful. This was a guy who could go places.

When the speech concluded, Slazak stood in the back of the media room, cell phone to his ear, acting as if he were preoccupied with a call as the crowd slowly dispersed. He followed Van Howe with his eyes as the candidate waved good-bye to some of his well-wishers, then walked briskly through a door just behind the stage. Slazak waited a few moments, then followed.

***

Blair staggered backward and flopped into a chair in the small conference room, as if the impact of the words had knocked him off his feet. The wave of euphoria he had been riding disintegrated instantaneously as Sam's words sank in: Terry McGrath was dead.

For the past thirty minutes, Blair had been blissfully oblivious as Terry McGrath and the accident had been pushed completely out of his conscious mind. That harsh reality came rushing back with Sam's announcement. Sam had shared the news as if it should be a relief to him. It had quite the opposite effect, as a suffocating sense of guilt bore down on him—guilt because his actions had resulted in the death of another human being, and, just as devastating, guilt that he had allowed his best friend to take the blame.

Blair was jarred from his dazed state by a loud knock on the door. "Mr. Van Howe? Got a minute?"

Blair, Sam, and Kimberly all turned and stared at the lean figure with the deep, gravelly voice standing before them.

"Who are you?" Sam asked gruffly.

"My name is Vic Slazak." He pulled out his badge, looking directly at Blair and ignoring the others. Slazak noticed that Van Howe looked nothing like the charming, confident politician he'd witnessed just a few minutes earlier. He looked worried and unfocused. "I'm investigating an accident that happened Saturday night involving one of your partners, Daniel Moran," Slazak continued. "I understand that you were with him earlier in the evening. I just want to ask you a few questions."

Sam glared at Slazak with undisguised hostility. "Listen, Detective, Mr. Van Howe is a candidate for United States Congress. He just finished his speech five minutes ago, and we're about to pay a visit to the mayor. Can we do this another time?"

"That's okay, Sam," Blair interjected, assuming his most charming and accommodating demeanor. "We've got a little time. Have a seat, Detective. What would you like to know?"

Slazak remained standing in the doorway, eyeing Sam McIntire steadily. "I'd like to meet with Mr. Van Howe alone, if you don't mind."

Sam started to protest, but Blair cut him off. "Sure, no problem, Detective." Then turning to Sam and Kimberly, he asked, "Can you two give us a few minutes?"

Sam shot Blair a hard look and walked out of the room with his daughter, without saying a word. Slazak closed the door behind them.

"This shouldn't take long, Mr. Van Howe."

"Take as much time as you need, Detective."

They sat down opposite each other, and Slazak pulled out a small, rumpled notebook.

"I'll get right to the point, Mr. Van Howe. Since you bailed Mr. Moran out of jail, I'm sure you know the basic story. He got in a wreck sometime after midnight on Saturday night, and it's likely he was intoxicated. The other guy—McGrath is his name—he's hurt pretty bad. I don't know whether he'll pull through or not. Anyway, it's probably all pretty straightforward, but I want to be sure we've investigated this as thoroughly as possible. That's why I'm talking to you."

Slazak stopped speaking and looked at Blair, inviting a response. Blair calmly returned the detective's look and said nothing. Through his years of trial work, he knew better than to volunteer information. There was no need to share the news he had just heard about Terry McGrath, or to say anything else, since no question had yet been posed.

Slazak continued. "Were you with Mr. Moran anytime Saturday evening?"

"Yes, I was. One of our clients was hosting a dinner downtown at Chez Pierre. Danny and I were both there."

"Which client?"

"Champions HealthCare."

"You and Mr. Moran just handled that trial for them, right?"

"That's right."

Slazak nodded slowly, looking at his notepad. "How did you get to the restaurant?"

"Danny picked me up, and we drove together."

"In his Porsche?"

"Yes."

"Where did Mr. Moran park his car?"

"With the valet, in front of the restaurant."

"Did you notice whether Mr. Moran was drinking during the evening?"

"I saw him with a glass of champagne in his hand when some toasts were being made. Other than that, I didn't notice."

"Did you drive home with Mr. Moran?"

"No."

Blair Van Howe had been rattled when the detective had appeared in the doorway, but his confidence was growing with each response. He was sliding into the role, playing the part of a cooperative witness who wanted to be helpful, but simply had no useful information—the role of a man who wasn't there and just didn't know anything about the accident.

"So you drove in together, and you live within two blocks of each other, but you didn't drive home together?"

"I had a busy day planned for Sunday, so I wanted to go home early. Danny was having a good time and wasn't ready to leave when I was, so I just took a cab." Blair drummed his fingers slowly on the table as he spoke.

"When you last saw Mr. Moran, did he appear to be intoxicated?"

"I honestly didn't notice, Detective," Blair responded, a trace of aggravation entering his voice. "Most people there were drinking. We were celebrating. But I really wasn't paying attention to whether Danny, or anybody else, had too much to drink." Blair lowered his head. "In retrospect, I wish I'd been more observant," he said softly. "I know Danny's had some drinking issues in the past. Perhaps I should have been thinking about that when he said he wanted to stay later. I could've stuck around awhile and driven him home if I'd noticed that he was drunk. I was just fixated on my own schedule and not paying attention to him. I should have been a better friend." He sighed deeply and looked up at Slazak. "Anything else, Detective?"

Slazak stared at him steadily for a long moment, then looked at Blair's hands silently tapping the conference table. "What happened to your finger?" Slazak asked casually, nodding toward the bulky white bandage covering the index finger on Van Howe's right hand. He had noticed it earlier, during the speech.

Blair's eyes darted to the right for a fleeting moment, and then he looked back at the detective, assuming a sheepish grin and shrugging his shoulders. "I'm a klutz. I was drinking a glass of water the other day, and the glass slipped out of my hand. I tried to catch it before it hit the sink, but I was too slow and grabbed it just as it shattered. Bled like crazy!" He held the bandage in front of his face and stared at it. After a moment, he folded his hands and leaned across the table toward Slazak. "Detective, there's one more thing I want you to know," he said earnestly, as if making a closing argument to a jury. "Danny Moran is a good man. He's a good father and husband. He's been a great friend to me and to a lot of other people. He's kind and compassionate, one of those rare men who's always thinking more about others than about himself." Blair stopped, looking for a reaction. Slazak stared back impassively, saying nothing.

"Where is this heading, Detective? For Danny, I mean?" Blair asked, concern in his voice.

"That depends," Slazak replied. "As of now, he's charged with DUI. If Mr. McGrath dies, he'll probably be charged with manslaughter. If that happens, he'll need plenty of character witnesses to say the kind of thing you just said." A flash of anger crossed the detective's face as he closed his notebook, stuffed it into his pocket, and stood up to leave. "Anyway, that's not up to me," he continued, assuming a more nonchalant tone. "I just gather the facts, prepare my report, and the State's Attorney's Office takes it from there. I just have to clear up a few little mysteries, then my part will be done."

"Mysteries? I thought you said this looked routine and that the facts speak for themselves."

Slazak shrugged. "They probably do, but there are still a few details I can't figure out—like the fact the accident was called in to 911 on Mr. Moran's cell phone, but he was still passed out behind the wheel when I got there. I don't get it. But that will be easy enough to clear up. Those calls are recorded and I can get copies of the recordings." He looked carefully at Van Howe for a reaction, but the seasoned trial lawyer didn't flinch.

"Oh, yeah, it seems there was a witness, too," Slazak continued in a matter-of-fact tone. "She may be able to shed some light on that." The candidate's eyes darted to the right again for the briefest instant, and then he looked steadily back at the detective.

"If there was a witness, that should solve all your mysteries, right?" Blair suggested calmly.

"Yep, I think so. Thank you for your time, Mr. Van Howe."

"You're welcome, Detective."

Slazak walked briskly out the door and returned a moment later to find Blair Van Howe slumped in his chair, looking drained and troubled, tapping his fingers rapidly on the table. He quickly sat upright at the sight of the detective.

"Sorry, Mr. Van Howe, there's one other little mystery I forgot to mention. There was blood in Mr. Moran's car Saturday evening that wasn't his, and you know how the press is. There are bound to be stories about Mr. Moran's troubles. Now that you're running for office, some overzealous reporter might think it's fair game to suggest that you might have been involved. I think you and I would both like to be in a position to dispel any crap like that, so I was wondering if you'd be willing to provide a blood sample?"

"Look, Detective, as far as I'm concerned, you can have blood samples, hair samples, saliva samples, whatever you want," Blair responded testily, looking at his watch. "But I'd like to check with my campaign team first. I'm new at this and I want to get their counsel. They may tell me that's a bad idea. Maybe the very fact that I'm giving a blood sample would be a suggestion of guilt or complicity. Let me check with them and get back to you. Now, if you'll excuse me, I have an appointment with the mayor."

He rose abruptly and strode past the detective and out of the small conference room, reaching for his cell phone as he did. He dialed Sam McIntire's cell phone number as soon as he was beyond earshot. "Sam, we need to talk—now!"

CHAPTER 12

Danny Moran sat in the posh reception area of the law firm of Leo J. Lewis and Associates. It seemed strange. He had visited countless law offices over the years, but never as a client. He felt confused and vulnerable, utterly reliant upon the lawyer he was about to meet to steer him in the right direction.

The reception area was quiet, like a library, but it had the look and feel of a modern art museum, with sculptures and paintings from the proprietor's private collection prominently on display throughout the area. The man-made artwork was complemented perfectly by nature's own masterpiece: a glorious view of Lake Michigan glistening in the summer sunshine, sailboats gliding leisurely in every direction. Under other circumstances, Danny might have found the tranquil setting to be soothing and relaxing. At the moment, however, the serenity of the surroundings brought neither pleasure nor peace to his troubled heart.

Several hours earlier, Danny had heard the grim news about Terry McGrath's death. In addition to the guilt and sadness generated by that news, he felt an even more disturbing emotion: stark fear. He knew that the clock had just started ticking with Terry McGrath's death, and that very soon he would be facing manslaughter charges. It was that concern that brought him to the office of the most famous white-collar criminal defense lawyer in town, Leo J. Lewis.

"Danny! Nice to see you again." Leo emerged from around the corner and warmly shook his visitor's hand.

"Hi, Leo," Danny replied in a subdued voice. "Thanks for seeing me on such short notice."

"Don't mention it, pal. I was only too happy to make time for one of the city's preeminent lawyers. Let's step into my office, shall we?"

Danny Moran and Leo Lewis knew each other by reputation and had met and exchanged pleasantries at various bar association functions and charitable events. Although they belonged to the same profession and both were well known and highly regarded in legal circles, they operated in entirely different universes. Danny represented big business and was immersed in the local political scene. Leo was a criminal defense attorney. He represented the rich and powerful when they got crosswise with the law. Although Danny had referred several wayward clients to Leo over the years, there had never been any other form of professional interaction between them.

Leo led Danny into an enormous corner office that seemed extravagant even to someone like Danny, who was accustomed to dealing with a prominent, well-heeled clientele. Two sides of the office consisted of floor-to-ceiling windows overlooking the vast expanse of Lake Michigan to the east and the urban sprawl stretching northward along the lakefront as far as the eye could see. The other walls appeared to be a shrine to the great Leo J. Lewis. Danny walked slowly across the office, hands in his pockets, taking in the countless photographs of Leo smiling broadly with celebrities and politicians, and the framed newspaper articles touting Leo's many notable courtroom victories.

"You got some pretty good press yourself last week, Danny," said Leo, as Danny's eyes scanned the headlines shouting from the walls. "I was following the Champions trial pretty closely. You and Blair did a masterful job on that one."

"Thanks, Leo. Unfortunately, I think I'm about to get some pretty bad press. Criminal charges, too. That's why I'm here. I was hoping you might be able to help."

"It would be an honor, Danny. Please, have a seat. Now, tell me what's going on."

Leo sat down behind his ornate mahogany desk, and Danny sat opposite him. Leo reminded Danny of a massive bullfrog, with his sagging jowls, thick lips, and enormous, bulging eyes, magnified by thick glasses. He was short and considerably overweight, but looked stylish and meticulously well groomed, from his shiny black shoes to his manicured fingernails to his neatly trimmed black hair, which was slicked straight back. Although three-piece suits were not in vogue, Leo never wore anything else, and the blue pinstripes looked fashionable on him, adorned with gold cuff links and matching tie clip.

Danny took a deep breath and began recounting the events of Saturday evening and early Sunday morning in as much detail as he could recall. He described the visit from Detective Slazak the previous afternoon and shared the news that Terry McGrath had passed away earlier in the day. Leo sat upright in his chair, hands folded, staring intently at Danny as Danny spoke. He took no notes and did not interrupt.

"Anything else?" Leo asked when Danny had finished.

"No, that's about it. That's all I remember, anyway."

Leo rose from his chair and began pacing in front of the window, his eyes focused on his well-polished shoes. "Here's how I see this, Danny," he began. "They'll probably want to arrest you—soon. They'll throw the book at you. For starters, DUI, reckless driving, and manslaughter. And you're right about the press. They'll jump on this fast. I'm surprised they haven't already." Leo stopped pacing and stared at Danny. "You better prepare yourself for that, Danny. You can imagine how they'll spin this: Hero last week, despicable scoundrel this week. It won't be pretty." Leo looked down and began pacing again, more quickly now. "So, here's what we do," he said decisively. "I'll put a call in to the State's Attorney's Office. We'll make an appointment for you to turn yourself in quietly. That way, they won't be able to come to your home or office and make a spectacle out of this. Then they'll file charges, and there will be an arraignment. A man of your stature will almost certainly be released without bail on your own recognizance."

"Then what?" asked Danny, looking dejected.

"Then we talk. We see if they want to cut a deal."

"Is there any reason to think they'd consider a deal?"

"Hell, yes! For starters, they're scared shitless of me! I kick their ass on a regular basis. They won't want to look bad."

That part rang true with Danny. Leo Lewis was brash and bombastic. He was a showman and had a reputation for turning a courtroom into a three-ring circus, but he was the ringmaster of that circus and always in control. He had a keen intellect and was lightning-quick on his feet. His ability to read and manipulate a jury was legendary. He had made many a prosecutor look utterly foolish as they helplessly watched their "sure thing" convictions melt away.

"But what have we got to work with here, Leo?" Danny asked, doubt evident in his voice. "What defense do I possibly have?"

"Look, Danny, we may not have much, but I don't need a lot. Just give me a tiny crack in a prosecutor's case and I can turn it into a gaping hole. That's called reasonable doubt, and that's all we need."

"I understand that, Leo, but where's the crack in their case? Where's the reasonable doubt?"

Leo stopped his pacing, turned his back toward Danny, and gazed out over the glassy blue waters of Lake Michigan. "First, they can't prove you were drunk," Leo said with an air of confidence. "You didn't take the breathalyzer and you were smart enough to avoid giving them a blood sample at the hospital. So all they have on that point is the subjective impressions of a couple of police officers. Those guys are stooges," he said disdainfully. "I'll rip them apart on the stand!"

"But how do we explain the fact that I was passed out behind the wheel when the cops arrived?"

"Easy. You just finished a two-week trial and you were exhausted. You just fell asleep at the wheel."

"But how does that help, Leo?" Danny protested. "If I fell asleep at the wheel, I still caused the accident, right?"

"Maybe, maybe not. How do you know? Maybe the other guy was the one driving recklessly. How do we know he wasn't?" Leo's voice took on a tone of excitement as he began doing what he did best, conjuring up reasonable doubt. "Think about it, Danny. There could be plenty of explanations other than you got smashed and passed out at the wheel. Like I said, maybe you were exhausted and fell asleep at the wheel. Maybe someone slipped something into your drink. That happens all the time now with that date rape drug. Hell, Danny, for all you know, someone else could have driven you home, caused the wreck, and framed you. It's possible. You honestly don't know what happened! There are a whole lot of maybes here, and all those maybes add up to reasonable doubt. That's my specialty," he announced boastfully. "Here, have one of these." Leo took a pencil from a canister on his desk and handed it to Danny. It bore an inscription that read "Leo J. Lewis: Reasonable doubt for a reasonable fee."

Danny shook his head and smiled weakly. "You know, Leo, that last scenario you mentioned—that someone else was driving—that's actually what it feels like. I don't remember the accident. I don't remember getting into my car, and I find it really hard to believe I would have gotten behind the wheel if I were drunk. I just don't do that. But I've got to face reality. The facts seem pretty clear. I *was* behind the wheel. I *was* drunk. No jury will buy these far-fetched scenarios. I don't practice criminal law, but I know where the jury's sympathies will lie. A man is dead. His wife is now a widow, and two little kids are without a father. And all the legal presumptions will go against me. How do we possibly overcome all that? Should I even try? Maybe I just need to accept responsibility for what I've done, cut the best deal I can, and hope the prosecutor shows at least a little mercy."

"Don't be too quick to fall on your sword, Danny," said Leo, sounding offended at the suggestion that he might lose. "Yes, we should talk to the prosecutor's office, but let's not be too quick to surrender. Unless they offer us a fabulous deal, we should be prepared to fight."

"I don't know if I have the stomach for a fight, Leo. I'm responsible for what happened. It's that simple."

"Goddamn it, Danny, listen to yourself!" Leo snapped. "You sound like you're giving up already." Leo bit his lip and struggled to maintain control. He walked slowly toward Danny and leaned against his desk, facing him. "Look at it this way," Leo began. His voice was calm and earnest now. "You can't change what happened. You have no control over that now. But you can shape your own future. You can do a lot of good for your family, your friends, and your clients—*if* you stay out of jail and avoid a conviction. If you're convicted, you'll probably be disbarred, for Chrissakes, so you really need to avoid a conviction. I assume that's why you came here, Danny. Am I right?"

Danny nodded hesitantly as he stared at the intricate pattern of the Persian rug beneath his feet.

"Look, Danny, I'm the best at what I do. I'm your best shot. But you've got to trust me. You've got to let me help you, okay? Don't forget, you honestly don't know what happened, so don't be too quick to presume you do. We'll have plenty of time to think about this and work on your story."

"My story? I won't lie, Leo," Danny said in a voice that was soft, yet resolute. He glanced up and saw Leo grimace with exasperation. "I won't commit perjury."

CHAPTER 13

Sam McIntire and Kimberly Van Howe stood in the hotel lobby visiting with a couple of aldermen who had attended Blair's speech. Sam abruptly cut the conversation short when he noticed his son-in-law hurrying toward them, looking distressed.

"Wipe that look off your face," Sam growled under his breath as soon as Blair was within earshot. "You're a candidate now. You need to be smiling and looking happy whenever you're in public. Shaking hands, kissing babies, all that shit."

"Sam, that cop ..."

Sam shot him an angry look. "We'll talk in my car."

They took the elevator to the underground parking garage and made their way to Sam's shiny black Cadillac. Sam and Blair climbed into the front seat, and Kimberly sat in back. Sam started the ignition, then surveyed the surroundings. The parking garage was deserted. He shifted in his seat, turning his large frame toward Blair.

"Now, you were saying? The cop?"

"What did you tell him, Blair?" Kimberly demanded, her voice sharp. Her father glared at her with a look she knew well—the one that meant *keep quiet and let me handle this.*

"I told him I drove to the banquet with Danny Saturday night, but I took a cab home because I had a lot to do the next day, and Danny wasn't ready to leave when I was."

"Shit, Blair, why did you tell him you drove together?" Kimberly scolded. "That gives you some real explaining to do. That—"

"Kimberly!" Sam snapped. "Let him talk!"

Blair turned toward the backseat and faced his wife. "Plenty of people saw us drive up together. He'd have no trouble confirming that."

"So, do you think he bought it?" Sam asked.

"I don't know," Blair replied, worry in his voice. "He didn't act suspicious, but he was hard to read. But he knows a lot, Sam. And he won't let it go, I'm sure of that."

"What does he know?" asked Sam.

"He knows that Danny left the car with the valet, and he kept asking if I noticed whether Danny was drunk at the banquet. I've got to believe he'll track down the valet and ask him the same thing. What if the valet remembers me getting into the car?"

"There were probably a lot of people there Saturday night," Kimberly pointed out. "Is there any reason he'd remember you?"

"Well, a new Porsche might be something he'd remember. And I gave him a twenty-dollar tip."

Kimberly hung her head and cursed silently to herself in the backseat. Sam said nothing, but rubbed a beefy hand over his face, as if washing himself with an invisible washcloth.

"What else does he know?" Sam asked, his tone becoming more brusque and irritable.

"He said there was a witness."

"Did he say who it was?"

"No. It must be the little girl I saw."

"Well, we've talked about that before. She was in shock, she was confused, she's retarded… What else?"

"He knows that Danny's phone was used to call 911. He said he'd be checking the recording."

"Shit!" Sam muttered, shaking his head and staring harshly at his son-in-law. "What else, Blair?"

Blair lifted his right hand in front of his face, spreading the fingers and staring at the bulky white bandage. "He said there was blood in Danny's car. He wants me to give a blood sample."

"How can this be happening?" Kimberly asked, whimpering and wiping her eyes. "This is a nightmare! It's an absolute disaster!"

Sam took a deep breath and rubbed his face again. "Okay, so now we know what we're up against," he announced, his brain obviously shifting into high gear. "We need this to go away and go away fast."

"And how do we make that happen?" Blair asked doubtfully.

"Here's the plan, Blair," Sam replied in a decisive tone. "Part of this is on me and part of it is on you. I'll see what I can do through my contacts with the Chicago PD and the prosecutor's office. Your job is to make sure Danny confesses. If he does, the investigation is over. You need to convince Danny that it's in his best interest to put this behind him, fast! I can probably get the state's attorney to agree to a plea bargain on pretty favorable terms. Then you need to sell it to Danny. That would tie up this entire sordid mess very nicely. I'll get on this right away." Sam paused, looking for a reaction. "Are you on board, Blair?"

"Of course he is, Daddy!" Kimberly shouted from the backseat. "We have no choice!"

Blair looked away from the imposing figure beside him and stared out the window at the deserted parking garage. Sam looked steadily at his son-in-law. "Blair?"

Blair sighed deeply. "Okay, Sam," he said in a voice that was barely audible. "I'll give it a try."

"Maybe I'm not being clear," Sam said, his voice low and ominous. "Trying isn't good enough. You *need* to make this happen. There's no room for failure here, understand?"

Blair looked down, staring at his bandaged finger for a long moment. "I understand," he said at last.

CHAPTER 14

Shortly before one o'clock on Monday afternoon, Vic Slazak pulled up in front of the elegant downtown restaurant.

"Good afternoon, sir. Welcome to Chez Pierre." A smiling young man in a black-and-tan valet uniform approached the dirty Crown Victoria as Vic Slazak stepped out. "Will you be having lunch with us today?"

Slazak flashed his badge. "Nah, not today. I just wanted to ask you a couple of questions, if that's okay."

"Certainly, sir. Fire away," the youth said agreeably.

"Were you working here Saturday night?" Slazak asked.

"Yes, sir. We were pretty busy Saturday."

"Do you recall seeing this gentleman?" Slazak pulled out Danny Moran's mug shot and handed it to the valet.

"Hmmm ... looks familiar."

"He was driving a new Porsche, a black 911 Carrera."

The valet's face brightened. "Yep, now I remember! I'm better with cars than I am with faces. I was the one who parked it for him. Sweet ride!"

"Were you the one who brought the car back out for him when he left here?"

"No, that must have been Carlos. I left here around eleven thirty. The place was mostly cleared out by that time. There were just a few stragglers with that corporate function in the private dining room. This guy must've been one of them." The young man looked again at Danny's picture as he returned it to the detective. "I would have remembered driving that baby again!"

"Where's Carlos?"

"Not here yet. He doesn't do the lunch shift. I think he works another job during the day. But he'll be here tonight, probably a little before five o'clock."

"Got an address or a phone number for him?"

The kid shook his head. "Sorry. All I know is he moved here from Mexico about a year ago and he lives with some relatives near Humboldt Park."

"Okay, thanks, kid. I'll catch up with him later."

"You're welcome, officer. Hope you can stay for lunch next time," the youth called out cheerfully.

Slazak reached for his cell phone and punched in a number as he pulled away from the valet stand. "That you, Nolan? I need a favor."

Mike Nolan was one of the nerdy technicians who had worked in the evidence lab for years. Although he and Slazak could not have been more different, there was a mutual respect between them. Nolan was the best there was at analyzing complex evidence and finding precious nuggets of information that escaped the eyes of mere mortals. He also had a knack for piecing together complicated puzzles and arriving at logical and insightful explanations. His manner was persnickety and effeminate, characteristics that normally would have made him a target for merciless teasing by the rougher elements on the force. However, through some combination of his quick wit, his arrogance, and his reputation for being the best at what he did, he was accepted and respected, and any teasing was entirely good-natured. While Nolan was known to be a stickler for policies and procedures, he had a long history of secretly complying with Slazak's unorthodox requests and playing a significant role in helping the rogue detective solve the cases that no one else could.

"What is it this time, Slazak?" Nolan asked in a voice that suggested he was being put out.

"Just a couple of little things, Nolan, but I need them fast and I need them on the QT."

"As usual," Nolan replied curtly. "What do you need?"

"A blood sample was taken yesterday from an auto accident scene at Eighty-ninth and Hamilton. The driver's name is Moran. I need that report ASAP."

"Those reports usually take three to five days, Slazak."

"I know, but I need it fast. See what you can do."

"Okay. What else?"

"There was a 911 call from the accident scene. Probably came in a little after midnight. Make me a copy of that recording, will you?"

"Why don't you just call the 911 control center yourself? That's routine stuff. They'll play it for you right over the phone."

"I tried. I called them a little while ago, and they said they were having some technical problems. I'm pretty sure that's bullshit, which is why I'm calling you. I want to be sure nothing happens to that tape. It may be important."

"Anything else?"

"That's it for now. Thanks, Nolan. I owe you."

"Yes, you do, Slazak. And I won't forget it."

***

At five o'clock sharp, Slazak again pulled his beat-up black Ford to the valet stand at Chez Pierre, where they were accustomed to a different class of vehicle.

"Nice to see you again, sir," said the annoyingly chipper young man he had met earlier that afternoon. "That's Carlos right over there." The valet pointed to a young man wearing an identical black-and-tan uniform, hanging a set of keys on the rack behind the valet stand. "Hey, Carlos, this gentleman is here to see you."

Carlos dutifully approached them. "Good afternoon," he said in a heavy Mexican accent, smiling nervously. He was short and slightly built, and looked considerably younger than his nineteen years.

Slazak sensed his nervousness. "Hi, Carlos," he said in a friendly voice. He offered his hand, and Carlos shook it weakly, looking down. "Relax, pal, there's nothing to get uptight about," Slazak assured him. "I just want to ask you a few questions, okay?" He handed Carlos the mug shot of Danny Moran. "Do you remember seeing this man here on Saturday night?"

"Sí, señor, he was here." Carlos relaxed visibly upon hearing the nature of the question.

"How do you remember him? There must've been a lot of people here Saturday night."

"I remember this one." Carlos said it insistently. "He was one of the last to go home. He had too much to drink. He walked like this ..." Carlos swayed from side to side, doing his best to imitate a staggering drunk.

"Do you remember his car?"

Carlos nodded vigorously, obviously pleased to be able to answer the detective's questions. "It was a Porsche, black. It looked new. I drove it." He smiled proudly.

"So you saw him get into the car and drive off?"

Carlos looked confused. "Oh no, señor. He got into the Porsche, but he didn't drive it. The other man did."

Slazak stared hard at the young valet. "Another man drove the Porsche?"

"Sí, señor."

"What did he look like?"

Carlos stared back blankly. "I … I don't remember. I was excited to be driving a Porsche, and when I got out, the gentleman handed me a big tip, twenty dollars. I must have been looking at the money and not at his face."

"This is important, Carlos," Slazak said, urgency in his voice. "I really need your help. Try to remember what the man looked like."

Carlos looked down, shaking his head, appearing crestfallen. "I don't remember," he said sadly, obviously disappointed in himself.

Slazak silently cursed himself for not having the foresight to bring another picture—a picture of Blair Van Howe. "Do you think you might remember if I showed you his picture?"

"Sí … maybe … I don't know," Carlos replied in a dejected voice.

"I'll be back tomorrow with a picture. Thanks, amigo, you've been a big help." He patted the young man on the shoulder, climbed into his car, and drove off.

After driving several blocks, Slazak pulled to the side of the road and turned off the ignition. It was rush hour in downtown Chicago, and hordes of people scurried past him on their way to train stations, subways, and bus stops. He paid no attention to them. He sat in his car with the engine off, staring straight ahead, tossing the old golf ball from one hand to the other.

CHAPTER 15

Tuesday

It was lunchtime, so the office was quiet. Danny Moran sat at his desk, wondering what to do next. News of his accident and Terry McGrath's subsequent death had made the front page of both the *Tribune* and the *Sun-Times* that morning. The firm's executive committee had convened an emergency closed-door meeting to discuss the subject, and Danny had just been advised of the outcome. He was being placed on an indefinite leave of absence, pending resolution of the criminal charges against him.

Danny felt paralyzed as he stared at the empty boxes on his desk. He didn't know whether to take just the active files he was working on, so that he could arrange an orderly transition to a colleague for temporary assistance, or whether he should pack up all of his personal belongings, assuming he would never be coming back.

He looked down at the two newspapers in front of him. The harsh headlines had left him feeling physically stunned when they leapt off the pages at him earlier that morning. Now they lingered as a loud and painful reminder of his predicament, echoing the accusations of his own conscience.

"Prominent Attorney Involved in Fatal Crash" was the headline splashed across the front page of the *Tribune*. "Drunken Lawyer Causes Fatal Accident—Kills Neighbor," blared the *Sun-Times*.

Page 3 of the *Sun-Times* contained another article entitled "Rise and Fall: Careers of Well-Known Attorneys Move in Opposite Directions." The article explained how, just a week earlier, Danny Moran and Blair Van Howe were considered two of the city's most prominent attorneys, who were basking in the glory and acclaim resulting from the Champions HealthCare trial. Blair Van Howe seemed to be following a meteoric trajectory toward even greater renown and accomplishment, as his political career was off to an auspicious start. In stark contrast, Danny Moran's distinguished career and promising future had been all but destroyed in the blink of an eye. The story made Danny out to be a despicable scoundrel, a wealthy, self-indulgent drunk whose reckless disregard for the law left two small children to face life without their father.

Danny's eyes skimmed over the words again. Even his longtime partner appeared to have turned on him. "Drunk driving is a heinous offense," the congressional candidate had said to the reporter. "This accident is a tragic and compelling illustration of the cost of such behavior. It causes countless deaths and injuries throughout this state, leaving ruined lives and broken families in its wake. I will do everything in my power to shine a bright spotlight on this problem. We need to make this a priority for law enforcement authorities and see that violators are dealt with severely and held accountable for their actions."

Blair peered around the corner into Danny's office. "Stop reading that shit, Dano. You know how the press is."

Danny looked up as Blair walked in, closing the door behind him. "The thing is, I can't argue with any of it, Blair. It's harsh, and it hurts to read it, but I can't argue with the truth. They're not saying anything I'm not saying to myself."

Blair sat down opposite Danny and pointed a finger at the newspaper article open in front of him. "Well, I want you to know that they quoted me out of context. Most of what I said to the reporter was about you—what a good and decent man you are, a great father, and a great friend to countless people, including me. That prick of a reporter left all the good stuff out."

"There's no need to explain, Blair. We both know how the media works. Besides, your comments were perfectly appropriate. That's exactly what you should have said."

"I heard about the executive committee's decision. I'm really sorry."

Danny shrugged and smiled weakly. "Again, they did exactly what they should have done. They don't have much of a choice, do they?"

Blair leaned forward, folded his arms on Danny's desk, and looked intently at his friend. "Listen, Dano, I know it must seem like everyone is abandoning you, but I want you to know that you've got friends who care, and they're working behind the scenes to help you through this. I'm doing what I can, and Sam is working his angles. We want to help."

Danny looked puzzled. "Help? How? What exactly are you doing?"

"There have been discussions, Dano, with the right people. I think we're close to arranging a deal on very favorable terms."

"What kind of deal?"

"A plea bargain. Here's what it would look like: You would have to plead guilty to negligent homicide, as well as

DUI. You'd lose your driver's license for a year, maybe two. You'd have to do some community service, and you'd receive a seven-year prison sentence, almost all of it suspended."

"*Almost* all?"

The State's Attorney's Office is insisting that you serve at least some jail time. Sixty days. Like I said, the rest of the sentence is suspended, so as long as you stay out of trouble, sixty days is all you'd serve."

"So, I'd have to go to jail, and I'd have to plead guilty to a felony? That means the State Bar will probably revoke my law license. Think about the humiliation that would cause my family."

"But think about the alternative, Dano. If you go to trial, there'd be a ton of publicity. It'll be brutal. Think about what that would do to your family. Besides that, you could lose. In fact, you probably will lose, in which case you could be in prison for *ten years*, maybe longer. What does Leo Lewis recommend?"

"You know Leo. He'd love to try the case, partly because he's a publicity hound, but also because he loves a challenge. He thinks there's a chance that if I tell a good story, I'd be acquitted. But Leo is also practical, and he said the same thing you just did: If I'm convicted by a jury, I could be looking at a long time in jail, so if I don't want to take that risk, I should consider a plea bargain."

"Talk to Leo about this, Dano. Sam will be filling him in so this can go through the right channels, but I wanted to talk to you first. It's a good deal. I'm sure Leo will tell you the same thing."

Danny picked up the picture of his daughter from his desk and stared at it with unfocused eyes. "This is all happening so fast. I can't even think straight. I'm going to need some time to sort everything out."

"They won't give you much time, Dano. The state's attorney may take a lot of heat if he cuts a deal. The only reason he's open to this is that, if you cut the deal now, he can put the right spin on it and make himself look good. He can take credit for acting quickly and decisively and procuring a confession and a plea bargain in a matter of days. They'll play up the seven-year sentence and won't focus on the fact that most of it is probated. But if you don't give him that victory, he's got no incentive to bargain. As you get closer to trial, he's got more taxpayer money invested in the case, and the media coverage will pick up again, so a plea bargain will look like a copout for him at that point. You've got to take the deal now, or it'll be gone."

Danny continued staring at Allie's picture as he put it down on his desk. "I can't put my family through a trial, Blair."

"And you can't risk ten years in jail, not when you could be in and out before the summer's over."

Danny pushed his chair back from the desk and stared at the floor for a long moment. "You know, even if I went to trial and got off, that just wouldn't be right. Think about the McGraths. How would they feel if I were acquitted? I'd have a hard time living with that." He looked up at Blair. "I need to accept responsibility for what happened. This is the right thing to do, isn't it?"

"It's the right thing to do, Dano."

"I'll call Leo and tell him to take the deal."

CHAPTER 16

Wednesday

"You wanted to see me, Lieutenant?" Lieutenant Thomas Rollins looked up from a file to see Vic Slazak standing in his doorway.

"Come on in, Slazak. Shut the door."

Slazak shut the door, but remained standing in the hope that the meeting would be quick. The two men had gone through the police academy together and had known each other for over twenty years, but had never been friends. Their opinions of each other were formed many years ago and hadn't changed. Slazak considered Rollins to be a lazy, unimaginative bureaucrat who was much more comfortable behind a desk than on the streets. He was a political animal, intent on rising through the ranks, and Slazak knew from personal experience that he wasn't above being sneaky and deceitful to get ahead. Rollins's opinion of Slazak was equally unflattering. He made no secret of the fact that he considered Slazak an undisciplined cowboy and a prima donna in a job that required teamwork. However, like everyone else, Rollins tolerated the maverick detective because he recognized that Slazak got results and made him look good.

Slazak was neither pleased nor disappointed when Rollins moved to his precinct two years ago and became his boss. He'd had worse. For the most part, the two interacted as little as possible. Their meetings were something neither of them enjoyed and were therefore infrequent. They typically involved situations where Rollins was forced to confront Slazak about some conflict Slazak had created with a colleague, or had to ask Slazak to do something he almost certainly wouldn't want to do.

"The Moran case is over," Rollins said brusquely. "You can close your file."

"Over? What do you mean? I've still got some leads I'm chasing down." Slazak made no effort to conceal his irritation with the overpaid desk jockey in front of him.

"I don't know what leads you think you have," Rollins scoffed, "but you can stop wasting your time. Moran confessed. He's copping a plea. Close it out, Slazak."

"He confessed?" Slazak looked incredulous. "Are you sure?"

"Positive."

"Well, I think there's more to this story, and if you don't mind, I'm going to run down those leads before I close the file."

"I *do* mind, Slazak," Rollins snapped. "Jesus Christ, it doesn't get any easier than this! You found the guy drunk behind the wheel of his own car, and now he's confessed. I don't want you burning any more of the department's time on this."

Slazak stepped closer to the desk and glared down at the bald head of the overweight lieutenant. "Look, Tom, I'm telling you, something's not right about this. The valet told me that Moran drove home with someone else that night, and the other guy was driving! There was blood in Moran's car, and he doesn't have a scratch on him. And guess what? His best friend, Blair Van Howe, who lives two blocks away and was at the same party, shows up with a big bandage on his finger the next day. On top of that—"

"Forget it, Slazak! The goddamn guy confessed! If we start pursuing some crazy theory that a candidate for the United States Congress was somehow involved, the press will jump all over this. We'd be tarnishing a good man's name and interfering with a congressional election in a case where we already have a confession. Close the file—that's an order! This meeting is over."

Slazak glared at his boss, summoning every ounce of self-restraint he could muster to keep himself from saying something he might regret. He turned and flung open the door.

"Close the door, if you don't mind," Rollins asked curtly.

Slazak ignored him, leaving the door wide open as he stormed away.

***

"Nolan? Slazak here. Got that blood analysis yet?" Slazak spoke into the wireless speakerphone in his car, golf ball passing quickly from hand to hand.

"For the Moran case? I was just told that case was closed." Nolan sounded confused.

"I'm still looking into a few loose ends. It may be re-opened. I need that report, Nolan!" The urgency in Slazak's voice was unmistakable.

"Well … I don't have it yet. It's on its way, but I was asked to give it to someone else."

"Who?"

There was a long pause. "I … I really can't say. Look, you're putting me in a bad spot, Slazak."

"Okay. Sorry, Nolan. Go ahead and give the report to whoever asked for it. Just make me a copy, will you?"

"What's going on here, Slazak?" Nolan's voice sounded worried, which was unusual. He had performed dozens of questionable favors for Slazak over the years and had never shown a trace of nervousness. To the contrary, he seemed to relish those covert assignments.

"You don't want to know, trust me. Can you do me this favor?"

"I'll see what I can do," Nolan responded unconvincingly.

"What about the 911 recording? Did you make me a copy?"

"Can't you call them yourself and have them play it for you?"

"I've been trying. They're stonewalling me. They keep saying that they're still having some technical problems, but I'm sure that's bullshit. Did you get a copy?" Slazak asked insistently.

"Yeah, I've got it. But Slazak …" There was a long pause. "I've got a problem."

"What?"

"I've been told that the Moran case is closed, and I was given strict instructions not to provide any evidence regarding that case to anyone, particularly you."

"Shit!" Slazak muttered.

"Hey, I've got orders. I'm in a tough spot here."

"Sorry, Nolan, I'm not swearing at you. This is just really screwed up." He thought for a moment. "Listen, Nolan, if you're not comfortable giving me that information, no sweat. I'll try to get my hands on it another way. But whatever happens, don't destroy it, and don't let anyone else destroy it, either. I'm counting on you to preserve that evidence, got it?"

"What if I'm ordered to destroy it?"

"Don't do it! Destroying material evidence is a crime. Following orders may keep your bosses happy, but it won't save your job if the shit hits the fan. It won't keep you out of jail, either. I'm telling you, Nolan, this is very important evidence, and if it gets lost or destroyed, it's your ass!"

"I should've known better than to get mixed up in your shady deals, Slazak," Nolan grumbled ruefully. "Next time you need a favor, call somebody else!" He hung up.

***

At five o'clock sharp, Slazak's dirty Crown Victoria lurched to a stop in front of the valet stand at Chez Pierre. He grabbed the rumpled manila folder holding the recent newspaper photographs of Blair Van Howe.

"Hi, kid," he called out to the smiling valet he had met earlier that week. "Is Carlos around?"

"Sorry, Detective, he doesn't work here anymore."

Slazak stared at the young man in open-mouthed surprise. "Since when?"

"He came by about an hour ago and dropped off his uniform. Said he was leaving town. Some kind of family emergency, I think. Seemed to be in a real hurry."

"Any idea how I can reach him?"

The valet shook his head. "Sorry, sir. No idea."

Slazak climbed back into his car. "Son of a bitch!" he yelled, pounding the steering wheel as he pulled into rush-hour traffic and headed toward the South Side. He grew even more agitated as he contemplated his drive home. He hated driving between downtown and Mount Greenwood at this time of day. The trip was barely fifteen miles and took less

than thirty minutes on the weekends, but it could take ninety minutes during weekday rush hour. Slazak made his way
slowly through the downtown traffic toward the Dan Ryan
Expressway, the main route to the South Side, bracing himself
for the grueling bumper-to-bumper drive ahead of him.

He passed Thirty-fifth Street and gazed at U.S. Cellular
Field, just off the expressway to his right. "The Cell," as the
locals called it, was the home of his beloved Chicago White
Sox. He found himself in a better frame of mind as he drove
past and was reminded that the White Sox were presently in
first place, two games ahead of the pesky Minnesota Twins.
He relaxed considerably, realizing that he needed some unin-
terrupted quiet time to process the day's events and that navi-
gating the slow-moving expressway actually gave him time to
think.

Slazak wondered whether he was wasting his time pursuing the leads relating to the Moran case. Rollins had made it
abundantly clear that the case was officially closed. And perhaps it should be; after all, the guy had confessed. Was there
really any point in looking for some other explanation when
the primary suspect had already admitted his guilt? On the
surface, the facts seemed to speak for themselves. Why try to
make it more complicated than it probably was?

On the other hand, he wasn't one to let go of an unsolved
puzzle. He held himself to a higher standard and took great
pride in his ability to find answers to questions most people wouldn't even think to ask. Moran could have confessed
whether he was guilty or not, because his alternative was a
messy trial and almost certainly a conviction and a harsh sentence. Perhaps he truly didn't remember what happened but
was surmising that he was guilty, because it certainly looked
that way. But the valet had seemed confident that someone

else was in the driver's seat when the Porsche left the restaurant Saturday evening.

His musings were interrupted by the shrill ringing of his cell phone. He recognized Rollins's phone number on the caller ID, and his mood immediately soured. Despite his strong desire to ignore the call, he picked up.

"Hello?" It sounded more like an expression of annoyance than a greeting.

"Slazak? This is Rollins. Got a minute?"

"Sure, what's up, Lieutenant?" Slazak asked, struggling to conceal his irritation.

"I need you on a special assignment, starting tomorrow."

"What kind of assignment?" Slazak asked suspiciously.

"Can you come by the station? I'd rather fill you in face-to-face. It's a sensitive project."

"I'm stuck on the Dan Ryan, moving along at about two miles an hour. I won't be able to get there for at least an hour. Can we just talk now?"

Rollins hesitated, then said, "Okay, Slazak, here's the scoop. I need you on a stakeout up in Lincoln Park. It may last a few days or it could be weeks. It just depends on what happens."

"A stakeout? In Lincoln Park? That's not my thing and it's not our jurisdiction! Why me?"

"Like I said, it's a touchy matter, and we need our best. The chief of police himself asked for you by name."

"What am I supposed to be looking for?"

"We think there's a high-dollar prostitution ring being run out of a three-flat on Fullerton Avenue. The reason it's a big deal is because we think some prominent citizens are patronizing this little enterprise. When we're able to confirm who's involved, you'll understand why this is such a big deal."

"Come on, Tom! This is bullshit!" Slazak exploded. "You can send a rookie with a camera over there. There's nothing special I can add to an operation like that."

"Maybe, maybe not, but like I said, the chief wants you there, so that's that. You're on the four-to-midnight shift, starting tomorrow and continuing until further notice."

Slazak made an obscene gesture in the direction of the speakerphone, but held his tongue.

"You still there, Slazak?"

"Yeah."

"Good. One more thing. I've received reports that you're still poking around on the Moran case in direct violation of my orders. I won't say this again, Slazak—that case is closed. I won't have you wasting the department's time on that or causing us any embarrassment. It's over and you're done with it! If you violate my orders on this, there'll be hell to pay! Got it?"

"Why do I feel like the more I'm told to stay away from this, the more I shouldn't?"

"Goddamn it, Slazak, just do your job!" Rollins shouted as he hung up.

"You're damn right I'll do my job, you stupid piece of shit," Slazak muttered to himself. "And you can't stop me!"

CHAPTER 17

Thursday

A large crowd was gathered in Daley Plaza in the heart of downtown Chicago for the weekly lunchtime concert. A rhythm-and-blues band was playing loudly, and the crowd was responding enthusiastically to the infectious energy of the lead vocalist, a hefty, middle-aged black woman with a stunning voice and an ability to engage the audience. The normally reserved array of business people were boisterous, many of them gyrating to the pulsating beat.

Sam McIntire stood on the fringe of the plaza as far from the deafening music as he could get. He had not come there to enjoy the concert.

At two minutes past noon, a uniformed police officer sidled up next to him. The officer was nearly as tall as Sam, with a dark complexion and mirrored sunglasses, the bulging physique of a serious bodybuilder giving shape to his dark blue uniform. His nameplate read "Capetta."

"You're late, Frankie," Sam growled without looking at the officer.

"Nice to see you, too, Sam," the officer replied nonchalantly. "Big crowd," he remarked, observing the obvious.

"Talk to me," Sam ordered.

"Everything went as planned. The valet is long gone. I told him his three sisters would be deported unless he left town immediately. I gave him the two grand and told him never to come back and never to mention our meeting. He won't be back."

"Good. I may have another job for you. This one will be trickier."

The officer folded his muscular arms across his chest. "I can handle it," he said coolly. "What do you need?"

Sam stared straight ahead, applauding politely as the band finished another crowd-pleasing tune.

"There's this cop, a guy named Slazak. He's becoming a problem."

CHAPTER 18

Slazak had been in a foul mood all day, thinking about his new assignment. While there was at least a remote chance that Rollins was shooting straight with him about the stakeout, his gut told him that was bullshit. A more likely scenario was that Rollins was pissed at him for ignoring orders or for his display of "attitude," and this was his way of letting Slazak know who was boss. The other possibility was that his pursuit of the Moran case was making somebody nervous—somebody who had some stroke. Both of those possibilities made Slazak even more determined to do exactly what Rollins had ordered him not to do.

Rollins had insisted that no more of the department's valuable time be spent on the Moran case. Slazak told himself that he would honor that request. However, no one would tell him how to spend his free time. He wasn't on duty until 4:00 p.m., when his shift at the North Side stakeout began. Until then, he was off the clock and would do whatever he pleased.

He placed a call to Chez Pierre and asked to speak to the person in charge of personnel. He was connected to Arnie Schultz, a nervous-sounding man with a high-pitched voice.

When Slazak informed Mr. Schultz that he was calling on police business and was trying to locate Carlos, the valet, Schultz launched into a rambling and disjointed discourse, the gist of which was that Carlos Ramirez had produced all of the necessary documentation to confirm that he was eligible to work in this country legally. Slazak assured the skittish personnel director that he wasn't interested in immigration issues and that no one was questioning Chez Pierre's hiring practices; he simply needed to locate Carlos. Schultz calmed down a bit and indicated that he would be happy to provide the last known phone number and address he had on file for the young valet, but because of privacy laws and confidentiality concerns, he would need proof that the caller was truly a representative of the police department. Slazak informed Schultz that he would drop by later that afternoon to obtain the information and would bring his badge and police ID with him.

Slazak's next challenge was trickier—getting a copy of the 911 recording and the blood analysis, when those with access to that information were apparently under strict orders not to share it with him. He sat in the leather recliner in his living room, staring at the blank TV screen, tossing the old golf ball from hand to hand, pondering the possibilities. This was an occasion when having lots of friends on the force would have come in handy, and his lone wolf approach to detective work definitely put him at a disadvantage. Despite twenty years on the force, he couldn't think of a single colleague he could count on to help him out with a delicate task for the sake of friendship. So he considered his quandary from another angle: Who owed him? Again, because he usually worked alone, he was rarely in a position to do meaningful favors for fellow officers. But there was that one time, about ten years ago, with Robbie Walsh. Walsh definitely owed him big-time.

Robbie Walsh was in his late thirties and had been on the force approximately fifteen years. Slazak had lost track of him, but knew that he was working in some sort of administrative capacity, which was precisely where he belonged. It was difficult to envision anybody less suited than Walsh to be a street cop. Walsh was a moon-faced carrot-top with a serious weight problem. He could not have been more than five feet six, but must have weighed at least 230 pounds. He was unfailingly friendly and cheerful, a genuinely nice person who didn't have a mean bone in his body. Unfortunately, those traits didn't serve him well when he was patrolling the rougher neighborhoods on Chicago's South Side. He was utterly out of his element and completely ill-equipped to deal with the hardened street thugs he encountered on a daily basis.

Slazak remembered the incident vividly. He had heard the call on his police radio. "Backup needed at 4900 South Ashland. Officer down, another officer under fire. All units in the vicinity respond immediately."

Slazak had been less than a mile away and rushed to the scene. It was a drug bust gone bad. He saw one officer lying on the pavement, next to the blue-and-white squad car. Walsh was taking cover on the other side of the car as three gangbangers approached from across the street with guns drawn, all three firing in Walsh's direction. Slazak sprang out of his car, drew his weapon, planted his feet, and without so much as flinching, proceeded to empty his firearm. Two of the three thugs dropped instantly, dead before they hit the ground. The third fled the scene and was apprehended several hours later when he showed up at a local hospital seeking treatment for multiple gunshot wounds. Slazak helped the terrified Walsh to his feet just as a small army of blue-and-whites arrived on the scene, sirens blaring. "I owe you, Slazak," Walsh had stammered in a trembling voice. "I'll never forget this." Shortly after that, Walsh had transferred to the safety of a desk job downtown.

"Okay, Robbie boy, it's payback time," Slazak said quietly to himself as he dialed headquarters. The switchboard patched him through, and Robbie Walsh answered on the first ring. He greeted Slazak with his customary cheerful enthusiasm, and the two chatted like old friends for several minutes, each bringing the other up to date on their current assignments. Robbie explained that his career path had taken a perfect turn, and that he was now working for the department's public relations division. Essentially, that meant that he was a goodwill ambassador whose job entailed giving speeches at schools and representing the department at various community functions, with the goal of maintaining a positive public image for the Chicago Police Department and developing closer ties with the community. It suited him perfectly.

Slazak explained that his job hadn't changed one iota, but that he still enjoyed the work, despite the bureaucracy and the bureaucrats. He then cut to the chase and informed Robbie that he was calling because he needed help working around that bureaucracy. He mentioned that he was working on a very sensitive case that could involve members of the department, and therefore he needed to obtain some evidence through unorthodox channels. Robbie's cheerful and accommodating demeanor turned serious and nervous as he listened to the details of Slazak's request and absorbed what was being asked of him. He promised to give the matter some thought and call Slazak first thing Monday morning. He said he wanted to give himself the weekend to consider the various ways of accomplishing Slazak's request. The response was about what Slazak had expected, and he hoped that, given a little time, Robbie's conscience and sense of obligation would bring him around.

On his drive toward the Lincoln Park stakeout, Slazak stopped at Chez Pierre and obtained the address and phone number the restaurant had on file for Carlos. He called the number from his cell phone and struggled through a conversation with a young-sounding female who spoke little English. Two words told him all he needed to know: "Carlos gone."

The stakeout was tedious and unproductive. Slazak parked across the street, several doors down from the swanky Lincoln Park three-flat, from 4:00 p.m. until midnight, when his replacement arrived. He had seen two attractive young women leave the building at around nine o'clock. No one had returned, and there were no other comings or goings for the duration of his shift.

Slazak pulled into his driveway shortly before 1:00 a.m., feeling utterly exhausted. Stakeouts always made him feel that way. When he was conducting an investigation, he could spend sixteen hours a day running all over town, working furiously, and still feel alert and fresh. Normally, his work energized him. But not stakeouts. They were dreadful, and they were draining.

He opened a can of beer and flipped on the large flatscreen TV. The house was stuffy and hot, so he opened the windows and turned on the rotary standup fan next to the television. Then he sat back in his recliner and channel-surfed with the remote control, looking for the sports channels, but finding nothing of interest.

He guzzled the beer, pulled the golf ball from his pocket, and slowly passed it from hand to hand. He struggled to keep his eyes open, but within minutes, he was dozing. His right arm dropped over the side of the chair, still clutching the golf ball.

His sleep was uneasy. He dreamed that he heard noises in his house, heavy footsteps and hushed whispers. The golf ball dropped from his hand and hit the wooden floor with a loud thud. He opened his eyes with a start and tried to sit up straight. He grunted with surprise and pain as he was yanked violently backward by some type of strap across his neck.

Slazak was instantly wide awake, a burst of adrenaline rushing through his veins. The eerie glow from the blank television screen provided more than enough light for him to assess the situation. Someone was standing behind his chair, powerful arms holding a strap tightly around his neck. There was an intruder on either side of him, each holding a gun to his head. In front of him stood a giant of a man, also brandishing a shiny silver handgun. The man had a nylon stocking pulled over his head, giving him a demonic appearance in the flickering gray light of the television. He wore distinctive dark clothing that Slazak knew all too well—the uniform of the Chicago Police Department. Through his peripheral vision, he could see that the intruders on either side of him were dressed the same way.

"Don't say a word, Slazak," said the big man in front of him in a deep, menacing voice. "I'll do the talking." The intruder turned around and pushed the power button on top of the television, plunging the room into darkness.

"Here's the deal, Slazak. You do exactly as I say, and you may live a while longer. You don't, you're a dead man. We can get to you at any time."

Slazak tried to lunge forward, but the strap around his neck was pulled even tighter, biting into his skin. "Who are you, you prick? Who sent you?" Slazak demanded, barely able to force the words out of his constricted windpipe.

He felt searing pain and saw a flash of light as the pistol to his left crashed into his skull. He felt blood oozing down his face.

"He said he'll do the talking, asshole!" snarled the man to his left. "Now shut your goddamn mouth!"

Slazak turned and glared at his assailant, trying in vain to see through the nylon mask just inches from his face. He spat into the nylon and immediately felt a sharp blow to the other side of his head, leaving him dizzy and enraged. He struggled in vain against the restraint that was crushing his windpipe.

"Knock it off!" bellowed the big man in front of him, who obviously was the leader. "Are you trying to be stupid, Slazak, or does it just come naturally? Now, listen to me." He leaned in so that he was within inches of Slazak's face. "Not another word, not another move, or we'll kill you right here and now. That would make our job real simple. Got it?"

Slazak glared at the masked man, saying nothing.

"Here's how it's going to work, Slazak," the man continued. "You're going to leave town—tomorrow. If you're still here tomorrow night, you're a dead man. If you ever come back, you're a dead man. *Capisce,* amigo?"

The big man pulled a thick white envelope from the pocket of his trousers. He threw it on Slazak's lap. "The Chicago Police Department appreciates your many years of service and wishes you a happy retirement, Mr. Slazak. There's fifty grand in there to help ease you into your new life. And you'll get your full pension, starting immediately, direct deposit into your new bank account—in Las Vegas. If I were you, I'd try to stay alive so I can enjoy it. Think of it this way—the longer you live, the more the Chicago PD has to pay you. But if you screw up, if you come back here, or if you mention a word of this little meeting to anyone, then I get to do what I do best. In that case, all you'll get from the police department is the flag they put on your casket. Don't be stupid, Slazak!"

CHAPTER 19

Danny Moran awoke early on the final day of his incarceration. He knew he should feel excited to be going home, but he didn't. In fact, he felt completely incapable of experiencing anything resembling excitement. If anything, he felt an even greater sense of remorse. He had spent all of July and August in prison, but those sixty days had passed quickly. It was too easy. He felt like he deserved more punishment.

The state correctional facility in Kankakee was a minimum-security prison about sixty miles south of Chicago. It was no country club, but it wasn't exactly Alcatraz, either. The facility had a well-equipped, state-of-the-art exercise room and an outdoor running track. It had a decent-sized library, as well as limited access to computers and the Internet. Most of the guards were surly and the food was bad, but with a few exceptions, the inmates seemed like a group of fairly normal individuals who were determined to keep their noses clean while they did their time. The truly dangerous element of the prison population resided elsewhere, so Danny never felt afraid or threatened, nor did he ever feel abused or oppressed. And something about that bothered him. His conscience told him he deserved worse than he was getting.

Danny had always been one to use his time productively and efficiently, because time was one commodity that seemed far too scarce in his busy life. Now, for the first time in his adult life, he had an abundance of time on his hands. He could have used it to plan for his future, since he'd been forced to leave the law firm and needed to develop plans for a new career. He could have used the time to focus on his physical and mental well-being by embarking on a physical fitness program and spending time in the library. He did none of those things. He was consumed with self-loathing, which numbed his mind and rendered him completely unable to focus on anything.

During his first several weeks in prison, Danny had tried on a daily basis to compose a suitable letter of apology to the McGrath family, but he just couldn't get it right. The feelings were heartfelt, but no matter what words he used, the family might think he was writing to ask their forgiveness. He wasn't. He knew he didn't deserve their forgiveness. Hell, he couldn't even forgive himself; why should they forgive him? So he gave up trying.

Had he been able to, Danny would have responded to his guilt and pain by drinking himself into oblivion. He desperately wanted to be lulled into that sweet forgetfulness that only alcohol could bring. However, drinking was not an option, so Danny did his best to pass the time by immersing himself in work assignments that didn't require much in the way of thought or human interaction. The prison was undergoing a complete repainting that summer, so from breakfast until dinner, he slapped fresh paint on the walls of the offices, corridors, and sleeping quarters in the old prison building. Although painting was a task that he had always despised because he found it tedious and mind-numbing, that was precisely what made it attractive now. In the evenings, he worked in the library, entering data from the ancient card catalog into the library's new computer database. Again, it was a way to avoid human contact and the torture inflicted by his conscience whenever he allowed himself to think.

Danny had three visitors during his stay in prison. Karen had come a single time, within a week of his incarceration, to inform him that she was leaving him and leaving Chicago. She told him she could no longer handle his drinking and that she couldn't stay in a place where shame and humiliation would always be with her. She said that she would stay with Allie until he was released from prison, and then she would move back to California to be near her family, leaving Allie behind to finish her senior year of high school with her friends. Danny made no attempt to change her mind. He couldn't blame her.

Blair Van Howe also paid him a visit, and Danny had been delighted that at least one of his old friends seemed to care enough not to ostracize him; however, his happiness over the visit faded when he saw Blair on television that evening, speaking to a throng of reporters in front of the prison.

"Why are you spending time with a convicted killer?" one of the reporters had asked.

"Danny Moran made a mistake, and it resulted in a terrible tragedy," Blair responded. "People should hear about these tragedies, and I intend to do my part to call attention to them. Those who drink and drive must be held accountable. Mr. Moran is paying for his mistake, and I hope others will learn from it. However, I also believe in compassion—for the poor, the unemployed, the sick, and, yes, even those who have made serious mistakes and run afoul of the law. Our society is well known for both its sense of justice and its sense of compassion, and we must strive to keep it that way."

Danny understood politics and tried not to take offense at the fact that Blair's visit had almost certainly been orchestrated by his campaign team to further his political agenda, yet some part of him hoped that friendship had brought him there as well.

The only other visitor was his daughter. Allie came every weekend, often on both Saturday and Sunday. Those visits were the only source of happiness in an otherwise bleak and depressing existence. Her fresh face, her bright smile, and her cheerful demeanor were a striking contrast to everything and everyone else around him. Just a few months ago, he had thought of her as a child, innocent, naïve, and dependent. Now, as she was about to begin her senior year in high school, she suddenly seemed mature, confident, and dependable. Perhaps it was his own crisis that had caused her to grow up fast, or perhaps she already had and he had simply been too busy to notice. Either way, he needed her now, and she was there for him. He didn't know how he would have coped without her.

Danny walked toward the visiting area, his spirits lifting with the realization that he was surveying the grim prison surroundings for the last time. The guard swiped his ID through an electronic card reader. He heard a loud metallic click, and the heavy metal door swung open. His eyes fixed on the beautiful young woman standing across the room. She was almost as tall as he was now and had the same pale blue eyes and perfect rosy complexion as her mother, although her face was framed by a thick mane of unruly raven hair, unlike Karen's bone-straight blonde tresses.

They stood and stared at each other for a moment; then Allie rushed toward her father and held him in a tight embrace.

"Hi, Pops," she said in a voice thick with emotion.

"Hello, little girl."

"Let's go home," Allie said. She grabbed her father's hand, and they walked through the large wooden doors into the bright September sunshine.

CHAPTER 20

Sam McIntire lumbered into the cramped office and flung the morning *Tribune* across the desk toward his son-in-law. "Feast your eyes, buddy boy!" he said with a broad grin.

Blair read the front-page headline: "Van Howe Opens Wide Lead in Polls." According to the article, he was leading his opponent, Scott Carlson, by ten percentage points, and the gap was widening.

"Hot damn, Sam! We're on cruise control now!"

"Bullshit!" Sam responded in his booming voice. "You can't coast during a campaign. We've got some real momentum now, and we need to keep pouring it on."

"And we will," Blair replied with conviction. "Hell, I'm not going to stop until the polls close on November fifth. I've never had this much fun in my life!"

He meant it. Blair was playing the most exciting role he'd ever played, and he was loving every minute of it. The media attention, the enthusiastic crowds, the opportunity to rub shoulders with the city's business and political leaders—it was a thrill beyond anything he'd ever known or even imagined. And for Blair, it was absolutely effortless. He felt as if he were doing what he was born to do.

Kimberly Van Howe and Sam McIntire were relishing their roles, as well. Kimberly maintained an active campaign schedule, visiting schools, hospitals, soup kitchens, and other charitable enterprises. Her mission was only partly to win the votes of those she was visiting. Mostly, her public appearances were intended to help shape the Van Howe campaign image as one characterized by compassion and a desire to help the underprivileged. Kimberly accomplished that goal with flying colors. The press loved her. She looked great on camera and came across as witty and engaging whenever reporters were anywhere near. In the eyes of the media, she was unfailingly cheerful and accommodating, although behind the scenes she was short-tempered and demanding with everyone, including her husband and father.

Sam McIntire was living the fulfillment of a dream. Although Blair had hired a professional campaign manager, Sam was the primary architect of the Van Howe campaign strategy. Having spent a lifetime immersed in the Chicago political scene, Sam knew it as well as anyone alive, and he navigated those waters with a level of adroitness that left the entire campaign team in awe. His unparalleled network of relationships and contacts secured a level of clout and high-profile support that no political opponent could hope to match.

"Let's take a look at the calendar," Sam suggested. "I want to get these fundraisers locked in."

They walked out of the small office and into a large room filled with portable cubicles and telephones, which were fully manned by eager volunteers in the afternoons and evenings, but empty at the moment, as it was not yet 8:00 a.m. Piles of posters, bumper stickers, and lawn signs were everywhere. The office itself was stark, but functional. The location was ideal. It was on Western Avenue, the primary commercial street running north and south through the Beverly neighborhood, in the heart of the third congressional district. A large red, white, and blue sign in the front window proclaiming "Van Howe for Congress" provided great visibility, and the location was easily accessible to the legions of young volunteers from the area who were clamoring to be part of the Van Howe campaign team.

Hanging in the center of the painted cinderblock wall, surrounded by a collage of campaign posters, was an enormous whiteboard calendar covering the remaining sixty days until the election. It showed all of the speeches, fundraisers, and meetings that had been scheduled, as well as target dates for advertisements and various other communications.

"The mayor wants to host a fundraiser for you at his beach house a week from Saturday," Sam said, tapping that date on the calendar with a massive index finger. "I'm trying to line up the governor for the following week."

"Will we get a decent-sized crowd?" Blair asked. "That's pretty short notice, isn't it?"

"Not at all. When people are invited to a reception hosted by the mayor or the governor, they'll show up, don't worry about that," Sam replied confidently.

"Are we planning them too close together?"

"Nope. Like I said, people will show, and we can't wait. The clock is ticking, and we need the dough now. We should absolutely blitz the airwaves during October—television, radio, newspapers, and the Internet. That'll cost us some serious money."

"Stuart has been working on the new ads," said Blair, referring to his media consultant. "He's come up with some great stuff. I think you'll like it."

"Excellent! I may have some good stuff, too. I just heard from a source who tells me he's got some dirt on Scott Carlson," said Sam in a conspiratorial tone.

"What kind of dirt?" Blair asked, a troubled look crossing his face.

"Apparently, our friend Scotty has a long history of extracurricular activity with his female staffers, including some who were underage."

"We're not going there, Sam!" Blair said emphatically. "I don't plan on saying a word about that during the campaign, and I don't want it leaked to the media or anyone else, either. I mean it! I don't want anyone to think we won by slinging mud. This campaign is all about taking the high road. Besides, we're up ten points in the polls. There's just no need to go there."

"All right, Blair, don't get so worked up about it," Sam said, sounding disappointed. "Just remember, it's there if we need it. By the way, speaking of dirty laundry, Danny Moran was released from prison a few days ago. He can get on with his life now, so you can stop beating yourself up over that."

Blair looked down, his mood immediately darkening at the reminder. "We should find a way to help him get his life on track," he mused. "Maybe we can help him find a job."

"Don't tempt fate!" Sam said sharply. "You dodged that bullet once, and you were damn lucky. Any link between you and Danny Moran from this point forward is a potential land mine. You can't be doing him favors or associating with him in any way. As far as you're concerned, he's a criminal. He committed homicide. You can't be consorting with someone like him."

"Come on, Sam, we both know that's not true. Danny's no criminal. For Chrissakes, he's probably the most ethical person I've ever known. In fact—"

"Drop it, Blair! He's out of your life now. Got it?"

Blair looked at his father-in-law uncertainly, saying nothing.

"Look, Blair," Sam continued. "You're entering public life now. Politicians make sacrifices. They make hard decisions. Sometimes you'll need to do things you find distasteful, but you do it for the greater good. You can do great things as a congressman, so you need to put your career first, and Danny Moran is poison to your career. You understand that, don't you?"

Blair avoided Sam's gaze and looked absently at the large whiteboard calendar. He sighed deeply and slowly nodded. "I understand, Sam," he said with quiet resignation.

CHAPTER 21

"Last call, Danny. One more?" The bartender nodded at Danny's half-empty beer mug.

According to the clock behind the bar, it was one forty-five. "No thanks, Pete," Danny replied, draining his beer in one long swallow and leaving a five-dollar bill on the bar. "I better shove off."

"Need a cab?"

"No, I can walk. See you tomorrow, Pete."

Danny stood up from his bar stool and walked unsteadily out the door. The night air felt cool as he stepped outside, but he knew he'd be sweating by the time he completed the two-mile trek. He really didn't mind the walk; it had become his sole form of exercise, and it provided an opportunity to sober up at least a bit before getting home. Besides, he didn't have much choice. His driver's license had been revoked. It would be two years before he could drive again.

Danny's routine had evolved over the four weeks since he'd been released from prison. At first, his desire to be there for his daughter was enough to keep him sober all day. He was there when she returned home from school at three o'clock in the afternoon and made a point of staying around the house whenever she was home. He was determined to be a good parent, but the role reversal that had started earlier that summer continued. Allie seemed to be watching over him more than the other way around. She was keenly attentive to him, making a point to hurry straight home from school every afternoon to be with him. They would eat dinner together, and then Allie would busy herself doing homework, chatting on the phone, and engaging in all of the other activities that kept a seventeen-year-old girl busy. When she was occupied with such things, Danny would sneak a couple of drinks, but he made a point of never getting loaded around his daughter. When she retired for the evening, he would hustle to one of the Western Avenue bars as fast as his feet would carry him, where he would drink heavily until closing time at 2:00 a.m. After that, he'd stumble home and pass out. He would sleep the morning away and have the early afternoon to get over his hangover before Allie got home from school.

About two weeks after he returned home, the pattern changed. Afternoon tennis practice had begun, so Allie rarely got home before six o'clock. She had also started dating Jason Merrick, the star linebacker on the high school football team. The local football pundits were predicting that Jason would be a consensus All-American, and he was being heavily recruited by Notre Dame, Stanford, Michigan, and countless other big-time college football programs. He seemed to be the all-American kid in every other respect as well, and Danny was pleased to see his daughter so happy. However, between tennis practice, Jason, and her busy social life, Allie's presence at home seemed to be getting increasingly scarce.

As Allie's schedule changed, Danny found little reason to stay sober all day. He started drinking in the early afternoon, mostly at home. He'd try to avoid becoming too blitzed during the day, in case Allie showed up for dinner. If she didn't, he would make his way to the bar early in the evening. When she did make it home for dinner, she didn't stay long, so neither did he. Once she was gone, he would scurry up to one of the local watering holes with a sense of urgency and pass the evening sitting on a bar stool with the other lost souls who were seeking the comforting numbness of inebriation.

Danny had settled into that pattern, and this night was just like almost every other night over the past two weeks. His walk home down Western Avenue took him right past the Van Howe campaign headquarters. He stopped and stared at the smiling visage of his former partner on the massive campaign poster in the front window. Blair certainly looked the part: handsome and confident, his charisma coming through, even in photographs. Danny felt the same mixture of emotions he always felt now when he thought about Blair. He was genuinely happy for his old friend, knowing that he was on the threshold of what was certain to be a successful and illustrious political career. At the same time, he was deeply hurt by the fact that his best friend had completely abandoned him. Other than the one visit while he was in prison, which almost certainly was a PR ploy, he hadn't had a single conversation with Blair since his incarceration. Danny understood. He knew politics, and he knew the media. Blair didn't have much choice. But it still hurt.

The cool autumn mist turned into a gentle drizzle, and Danny picked up his pace. He was wet and shivering by the time he walked through his front door. The house felt quiet and lonely, as it had since he returned from prison. The empty closets and drawers were a constant reminder that Karen was gone. He hadn't been able to put away the pictures of her that were still scattered around the house. Doing so would have seemed like an admission that she was never coming back—something he knew, but still did not want to accept. Although Karen had always been cool and aloof to everyone, including him, he still adored her and missed her terribly.

As he stared at a picture of the two of them on the beach in San Diego, he reached into his pocket and pulled out the long white envelope with a feeling of dread. The messenger had delivered it to him just as he was leaving the house late that afternoon. He knew what it was. The messenger was obviously a process server. He had purposely avoided opening it when it was thrust into his hands because it would have spoiled his evening at the bar, which was the highlight of his dreary day. But now he had to face it. He had been fearing that it was only a matter of time before Karen filed for divorce.

Danny braced himself as he opened the envelope with shaking hands. He felt a jolt like an electric shock as he read the caption on the complaint: *In the Matter of Nancy McGrath v. Daniel J. Moran.* He was being sued in state court for the wrongful death of Terry McGrath.

He stared at the harsh words, feeling as if the air had been sucked from his lungs. He began to feel light-headed and dizzy. His stomach turned. He raced into the bathroom and vomited.

CHAPTER 22

Blair and Kimberly Van Howe mingled with the crowd of supporters packed into the tiny campaign headquarters. Champagne was on ice, reporters milled about, and television cameras were at the ready. The large-screen television at the front of the room provided updates on the election results, local and national. Although the polls had closed only an hour ago, the projections had Van Howe leading by a seemingly insurmountable margin.

"Blair, phone call!" Sam McIntire's voice boomed over the crowd. A buzz of anticipation rippled through the crowd as Blair elbowed his way toward the small office in the back. He picked up the phone, a wave of excitement washing over him.

"Hello?"

"Blair, this is Scott Carlson. I'd like to be the first to congratulate you. You've run a fine campaign, and I wish you the very best. I concede."

Blair gave Sam the thumbs-up sign as he listened. Sam disappeared momentarily, then returned with Kimberly, who looked like a kid on Christmas morning. Blair motioned to Sam to shut the door and stared at his wife and father-in-law for a long moment. Then he broke into a broad grin. "It's over," he announced, trying his best to remain poised and calm, but his voice quavered with excitement. "That was Scott Carlson. He just conceded."

Kimberly shrieked, threw both arms up in the air, then rushed to embrace her husband. "Washington, here we come!" she shouted.

Sam wrapped his gigantic arms around both of them at once. "You two are on your way! I couldn't be happier for you." The tough old veteran of many a political war wiped his eyes with the back of his hand. "Now go tell the troops," he instructed, opening the door for them and lingering behind to compose himself.

Blair and Kimberly walked hand-in-hand toward the front of the room. Their beaming smiles left no doubt as to what had just occurred. There was a feeling of electricity in the air as they made their way through the crowd, shaking hands, giving high fives, and receiving slaps on the back. The buzz escalated as word of the phone call spread faster than the Van Howes could make their way across the room.

Blair took the podium and raised his hands in a gesture for silence. The exuberant crowd was slow to comply, and he waited patiently, bathed in the bright lights of the television cameras. Presently, the room reached some semblance of quiet, and Blair leaned forward toward the microphone. "Let's pop the champagne!" he shouted. The room burst into wild and delirious applause. Blair raised his hands again and waited for the noise to die down enough to be heard. "Scott Carlson was kind enough to call me and offer his congratulations—and his concession."

The room erupted again. The shouts and whistles, hugging, and high-fiving went on for quite a while, and Blair made no effort to cut it short. Champagne corks began popping. The crowd took up a chant: "Van Howe, Van Howe, Van Howe!" came the loud, rhythmic shouts.

Someone handed Blair and Kimberly champagne glasses. "I'd like to propose a toast," Blair shouted over the crowd, raising his glass. "To all of you, without whom this would not be happening. We're making history here. We're looking at the greatest margin of victory over a sitting congressman in the past hundred years!" The crowd exploded into raucous applause once again. "But this isn't my victory. It's *our* victory! It's *your* victory! *You* made it happen, and *you* deserve the credit. When I go to Washington, I'll be representing *you* and the things this team believes in. You can be sure I will never forget that. Aside from the day I married my beautiful bride, this is without a doubt the happiest and most exciting day of my life. Thank you from the bottom of my heart!"

Blair and Kimberly clinked glasses, took a sip of the cheap champagne, and raised their clasped hands into the air. Once again, the room exploded into joyous pandemonium.

***

Less than two miles away, Danny Moran sat in his living room watching the election results on television, a bottle of Crown Royal at his side.

"Way to go, Blair!" he yelled at the television screen, slurring badly as he watched his former partner giving his victory speech. There were plenty of other races in the State of Illinois being decided that day, including governor and one of the United States Senate seats, as well as the races for the other nineteen national congressional seats. However, none of those races had attracted nearly the media attention of the Van Howe campaign. One reason for that was that a once-popular six-term congressman was being unseated. Another reason was the stunning margin of victory, with the newcomer racking up nearly 75 percent of the votes. The primary reason for all the attention, however, was the undeniable fact that this candidate had captivated the media and the electorate with a mixture of charm, charisma, and excitement, the likes of which few voters had experienced in their lifetime. He was dynamic and inspiring, eloquent and sincere. He was someone people wanted to believe in and get behind. The fact that his photogenic wife had become a media darling in her own right was an added bonus. She was lively, quick-witted, and funny most of the time, yet tender and compassionate when the situation called for it.

Danny Moran wasn't taken in by that part of the story. He knew Kimberly Van Howe and suspected, quite accurately, that when she was behind the scenes, she was ruthless, demanding, and impatient with everyone on the campaign team.

As he settled down in front of the TV again, Danny heard the back door slam loudly, followed by the sound of determined footsteps heading in his direction. He glanced sideways in his daughter's direction as she entered the room. "Look, Allie, Blair won in a landslide! You just missed his speech."

Danny stumbled into the study and picked up the telephone, intending to place a congratulatory phone call to the new congressman, but his memory was foggy, and he couldn't remember Blair's cell phone number. He recalled that Blair's number was programmed into his own cell phone, so he staggered back through the living room, the kitchen, and dining room, searching in vain for his cell phone. There was no telling where he'd left it, and the chances of finding it in his present state were not good.

He'd been on a bender for some time now. He couldn't remember exactly when he started, but it was Tuesday evening now, and he remembered being smashed at the high school football game Saturday night. He had caused something of a commotion when he had stumbled badly into a crowd of teenagers while climbing the bleachers. No one had gotten hurt; they just had a good laugh at his expense. Allie had been mortified when she saw him there and insisted that she drive him home at halftime. He remembered her ranting in the car on the way home about how he had humiliated her, but he didn't remember much else about that conversation or the rest of the evening. He couldn't remember whether he'd even spoken with his daughter since that time, and was actually hoping that he hadn't, since he'd been drunk ever since.

Allie had been increasingly hostile toward him over the past few weeks. Danny could see the disappointment in her face whenever she looked at him. The look had been one of concern at first, but it had evolved into something different. It had become a look of contempt, and that was precisely the look on her face at the present moment, although Danny was too oblivious to notice.

"He looks great, doesn't he?" Danny asked, flopping into the sofa and returning his attention to the TV.

Allie stormed across the room and slammed the power switch on the television. She turned and faced her father, hands on her hips, feet spread wide, tears of rage streaming down her face. "I don't give a shit about Blair Van Howe!" she yelled, her voice breaking. "Look at you! You've been drunk for days! You're drunk all the time! How can you live like this?"

Even in his inebriated state, Danny was stunned by the viciousness of the assault. Allie had never screamed at him like that before, and he had never witnessed the hostility he was now seeing in his daughter. "I'm sorry, Allie," he said, shamefully hanging his head and avoiding her glare. "You don't deserve this."

"No one deserves this, Daddy!" she screamed. "How many lives can you destroy? You drove Mom away, you're driving me away, Mr. McGrath is dead, and now Jason!"

Danny looked bewildered. "Jason?"

"Yes, Jason! He's been suspended from school and thrown off the football team—because of you!"

"Because of me?"

"Yes, because of you!" she shrieked. She was sobbing now and having difficulty speaking. "That creep Eddie Janek, the biggest derelict in our school, he wouldn't stop harassing me since he saw you at the football game. He kept calling you a low-life drunk. Jason told him to shut up, and Eddie just got even louder, so Jason punched him. Now Eddie's in the hospital with a broken jaw and Jason's off the team. All those scholarship offers—gone!

"Allie, I had no idea. I didn't mean to—"

"Stop! I don't want to hear it! There's nothing you can say. You're killing yourself, and you're dragging down everyone around you!" She stopped ranting and put a hand over her eyes, her shoulders shaking as a fit of quiet sobbing overtook her. After a few moments, she looked up at him, the fury now gone, replaced by a look of utter dismay. "I can't take this anymore," she said despondently. She turned away and ran out of the house, the sound of her quiet sobs echoing in Danny's ears.

Danny stood and walked to the window. He saw his daughter climb into Jason's car and drive away. He stumbled into his bathroom and splashed cold water on his face. He stared into the mirror and recoiled at the hollow-eyed drunk staring back at him. He turned away, unable to look at himself. He sat down on his bed, tears flowing down his cheeks. His quiet weeping quickly gave way to a fit of loud, uncontrollable sobs.

He reached into a dresser drawer, pulled out an unopened pint of Jack Daniels, and staggered into the backyard. He unscrewed the cap, but didn't pull it off, staring hatefully at the bottle for a long time. He began shaking his head. "No more," he said quietly to himself. "No more," he said louder, resolve creeping into his voice. "No goddamn more!" he shouted as he hurled the bottle against the brick wall of his house.

CHAPTER 23

Blair and Kimberly Van Howe sat hand in hand, enjoying the comfort of the luxurious stretch limousine whisking them off to O'Hare Airport. They savored the quiet and the solitude. The days following the election had been just as hectic as the days leading up to it. Their schedules were jammed with celebratory dinners, cocktail parties, non-stop phone calls, e-mails, visits from well-wishers, and interviews with the seemingly endless stream of media types, eager to get some face time with the newly elected congressman.

They should have been exhausted, but they weren't. They were riding a wave of exhilaration like nothing they had ever experienced before—exhilaration over the election results, over the prospect of moving to Washington, and over the realization that they were embarking on a new adventure, with a future that looked dazzlingly bright.

Kimberly squeezed her husband's hand and gave him a warm, wet kiss on the lips. He pulled her close to him and, for an instant, thought about making love right there in the backseat of the limo. He realized that probably would not be considered "conduct becoming a United States congressman," so he pulled back and stared deeply into his wife's eyes. She gazed back at him with a longing and affection that had been lacking for years. Their relationship had cooled over time. It wasn't that it was strained; they had just drifted apart. But now she seemed warm again. Somehow the campaign had rekindled the romance in their lives. They saw the best in each other on the campaign trail, and were proud of one another, each acutely aware of how much the other was bringing to their new partnership.

They were on their way to Washington for a long weekend getaway. They had thought briefly about heading to a remote tropical island for some well-deserved rest and relaxation, but they both felt their new home beckoning and decided they couldn't wait to visit. The new congressional session was still two months away, but Kimberly was eager to start house hunting, and Blair wanted to begin learning the city and making acquaintances. Kevin Larmon, a long-term congressman from a nearby district, had offered to show him around, and Blair was more than happy to take him up on that offer.

"How do you feel, Congressman?" Kimberly purred.

"I feel like we're a couple of high school kids going to our first big dance," Blair gushed. "I'm not sure what to expect or how to behave, but it's a thrill just to be going!"

"Me, too, babe," she replied warmly. "We've got a great new life ahead of us. It doesn't get much better than this!"

"It's just about perfect, sweetheart." He sat back and sighed wistfully. "The only thing missing is Danny. I wish we were able to share this with him."

Kimberly's gaze turned hard. "You really know how to ruin a nice moment," she snapped at him. "Danny Moran is out of your life. He's part of your past and has no place in your future. Get over it!"

The mood in the car became subdued, and they rode the rest of the way to the airport in silence. Their spirits lifted once they boarded their plane, as they were recognized and treated as celebrities by the flight crew and countless passengers, who offered excited greetings and congratulations. Just as on the campaign trail, it energized them and imbued them with a feeling of excitement and self-satisfaction.

"You're like a rock star, honey!" Kimberly remarked, feeling giddy again. "Better get used to it!"

Blair's spirits soared even further as the plane approached Dulles Airport and he beheld the nation's capital in all of its splendor from the air.

Kevin Larmon met them at the airport and acted as their personal escort for the next three days while the Van Howes looked at homes in Georgetown and received an insider's tour of the nation's capital. To their surprise and great pleasure, the rock star treatment continued. Everywhere they went, people seemed to already know the newly elected congressman from the third district of the State of Illinois.

"How do these people know me already?" Blair wondered aloud.

"You'll be amazed at life in Washington, Blair," Larmon replied. "It's a pretty close-knit scene in the political circles around here. Everybody knows everybody else, and there aren't many secrets. Your campaign and election got a lot of attention around here. You're a big wheel already, I promise you. People can't wait to meet you!"

***

As the Van Howes strolled across Washington Mall the evening before their return to Chicago, Blair stopped and put his hands on his wife's shoulders. "I'll make you proud, Kim. This is the role I was born to play. Just watch me!"

Kimberly stared back, a determined look on her face. "And this is only the beginning," she said.

CHAPTER 24

Danny's hands shook as he picked up the telephone. Partly, that was because his body wasn't quite through the detoxification process, but mostly it was because of his apprehension about the phone call he was about to make. He hadn't seen or spoken with Allie since she stormed out of his house on election night. She had left a message on his answering machine the following day, informing him that she would be staying with her friend Megan for awhile. She had left explicit instructions telling him not to call her. She said she needed time alone to think things through and would call him when she was ready to talk. That was eight days ago, and she hadn't returned home or called.

It was a few minutes before three o'clock, and Danny realized he had a short window to catch her before tennis practice began. He took a deep breath and dialed her cell phone.

"Allie, it's Dad." His voice sounded shaky and he knew it. "Can you talk for a few minutes?"

She hesitated. "Okay," she said, sounding distant.

"I'm calling to apologize," he began, his voice thick with emotion. "For last week, for my drinking, for everything I've put you through." He took another deep breath to keep his voice from breaking. "You mean more to me than anything in the world, and I'm so sorry for all the pain I've caused you." He could hear her quietly sniffling on the other end of the line. He continued, his voice breaking as the sound of his daughter's weeping unleashed his own tears. "I've been so consumed with guilt and shame over everything that's happened that I couldn't look outside of myself and see how it was affecting you—how I was affecting you. I don't blame you for leaving, and I don't blame you if you don't want to come home, but I wanted to let you know that I've stopped drinking. I haven't had a drop since I saw you last. I'm going to try as hard as I possibly can to stop for good this time. I really mean that."

"I'm sorry, too, Daddy," Allie said, choking back her sobs. "I just couldn't stand to see you that way. I couldn't bear to stand by and watch you slowly kill yourself, but I shouldn't have run off. It was selfish. I should've been there for you. I'm … so … sorry." She began crying harder and was unable to speak.

"Allie, stop, please! You have nothing to apologize for! This is all on me," he said with a sense of urgency. "Look, sweetheart, I know my life is in shambles, but I'm going to fix it. I'm ready to move on. I can't live like this anymore, either, and I can't do this to you—I won't! I really hope you'll come home, Allie-Baba," he said, calling her by her childhood nickname. "I don't blame you if you won't, but you'll be off to college next fall, and I'd love to spend as much time with you as I can between now and then."

Megan glanced over at Allie from the tennis court and hurried to her side when she saw Allie crying. Allie looked at her friend through tear-filled eyes and waved her off, turning her back and walking in the opposite direction. "Daddy, I'd love to come home—I really would—but I'll only do it on one condition."

"Name it, sweetheart."

"I know you really mean it when you say you'll quit drinking, but remember, you've tried before, countless times, and you always slipped back into it. This problem is bigger than you. It's bigger than both of us. You need help. You've got to realize that. I can't go through this anymore unless you agree to get some help. Will you do that? For me? For both of us?"

Danny had always dreaded that subject. He'd been able to quit on his own before, usually during trials or after Karen had really lit into him following an all-nighter. And he'd gone without a drink for a full week now. But Allie was right, and he knew it. He'd always slipped back into the habit. "I'll get help, Allie," he said with quiet resolve. "I'm not sure where to turn, but I'll figure it out, I promise."

"Let me help you, Daddy," Allie said, her voice taking on a tone of enthusiasm. "I've been talking to some people about this. I hope that doesn't embarrass you, but I've been amazed at how many people have family members with the same problem." She was talking fast and excitedly now. "I've heard some real success stories about AA. Jason's uncle has been involved with the AA program for years. He says it's absolutely changed his life, and he'd be happy to take you to a meeting. Can I have him call you?"

It didn't bother Danny that his daughter had been talking to others about his drinking. He was way beyond embarrassment. To the contrary, he felt encouraged that Allie was truly concerned about him and hadn't written him off. Still, he instinctively avoided her question. "How's Jason?" he asked. "I've been thinking a lot about him, and I feel terrible about the position I put him in."

"He's okay, Dad. He doesn't blame you. He's upset with himself for losing his cool. He knows that someone as big and strong as he is can't go around hitting people. At least he wasn't thrown out of school. He may have to go to a small college next year and then try to transfer to a Division I program, but he'll figure it out, and he'll be okay. He's a special guy, Daddy, and he won't let this keep him from his dreams. But back to you—what about AA? Like I said, his uncle will take you. He's a great guy. You'll like him. Can I have him call you?"

Danny thought for a long moment. For a seasoned trial lawyer and accomplished public speaker, he was terrified at the thought of standing up in front of a roomful of strangers and saying, "Hello, my name is Danny, and I'm an alcoholic." But he was even more afraid of losing his daughter. "Okay, I'll go," he heard himself say, as if the words were coming from somewhere else. "Tell him to call me."

"I will! Thanks, Daddy!" Allie gushed. "I've been praying that this is the answer for you."

"I hope so, too, Allie."

"I'll be home for dinner, Pops."

"I can't wait to see you, little girl," Danny replied, wiping the tears of relief from his eyes, his spirits soaring at the thought.

"Me, too. By the way, Jason's uncle's name is Andy. Oh, and Pops?"

"Yes, sweetheart?"

"We'll get through this together. I'll always be there for you, I promise. I love you so much!" She hung up.

CHAPTER 25

Danny walked into the South Side Diner and looked around. It was empty, which was not surprising, since it was four thirty in the afternoon. Danny had eaten at the diner countless times, but it was invariably well past midnight, and he had never been there sober. It was situated at 104th and Western Avenue, centrally located among the neighborhood's many drinking establishments; therefore, it served as a popular destination for the late-night crowd who came by in droves, either hoping that a hearty meal might soak up the alcohol in their system or just because they needed a place to go after the bars closed at 2:00 a.m.

"Hi, George." Danny nodded at the humorless proprietor, a muscular Greek in his early fifties with hawk-like features, dark penetrating eyes, and a flattop haircut.

George gave Danny the same stern, disapproving look he always gave him, most likely because Danny was typically stone drunk when he stumbled through the doors of the South Side Diner.

"How you doing, guy?" George replied in a thick Greek accent, as he always did. It was his standard greeting, delivered without the slightest hint of friendliness and with no expectation of a response.

For an instant, Danny thought about leaving, but resisted the temptation and moved toward a booth in the back. As he seated himself, he saw a big man with a shock of bushy white hair bustle into the restaurant. "What's up, Georgie?" the man called out in a loud voice to the proprietor, pumping his hand.

"Hello, Judge," George responded, flashing a smile Danny had never seen before. "You're here early today."

"I've got a meeting. I'll be back later with the boys."

"Okay, Judge."

The big man noticed Danny, waved, and walked purposefully across the restaurant. "Hello, Danny," he said in a cheerful voice, as if they were old friends. Danny was quite confident they had never laid eyes on one another before.

"You must be Andy," Danny replied, a bit uncertainly, standing and shaking the beefy hand.

"That's right—Andy Murray. It's great to meet you, Danny. I've been hearing your name for years. I think everybody in Chicago legal circles knows who Danny Moran is. Sorry I'm late. I'm in the middle of a trial, and we went a bit longer than I expected. Please, sit down."

A middle-aged waitress with red hair and far too much makeup approached their booth, a pot of coffee in hand.

"Trudy! You look great today! How's the world treating you?" Andy's voice boomed across the empty restaurant.

"I'm doing fine, Judge," she replied, batting her eyelashes and smiling self-consciously. "Coffee?"

"No, I think I'll go with hot chocolate today. How about you, Danny?"

"Coffee would be great," Danny replied, pushing his cup toward the waitress.

Andy waited quietly until Trudy had walked away. "I met your daughter a few nights ago, Danny. She and Jason stopped by for a visit. She sure has a lot of poise and confidence for a kid that age—wise beyond her years. You must be very proud of her."

"She's a great kid," Danny acknowledged. "So, you're a judge?" Danny asked, quickly changing the subject.

"Yeah, I was appointed a little over two years ago—Cook County Circuit Court—out in Markham. I cover the far southwest suburbs. Traffic court, mostly, but I get a smattering of criminal stuff, too. It's not the Supreme Court, but it's respectable, and I enjoy it."

Trudy returned with a cup of steaming hot chocolate. Andy pushed it aside, folded his arms on the Formica table, and leaned across toward Danny, lowering his voice. "Let's talk about you, Danny. Allie told me a bit about your situation. She's very concerned. I think you know that."

Danny looked at his coffee, nodding slowly.

"Look, Danny, I've been where you are. I was there for a long time, but I've been sober for eight years now, and my life is better than I ever thought it could be. I put my family through hell, and I'll never be able to really make it up to them, but they've been great, and I've reconciled with them. I've got a decent job, and I've got a real sense of purpose in my life." He paused. "I owe all that to AA, Danny. It changed my life, and it's worked for lots of other people, too. I'd love to see you give it a chance."

Danny picked up a spoon and stirred his coffee. "That's why I'm here," he said quietly, without looking up. "I need help. I don't think I can do this on my own." He looked up at the earnest face with the big gray eyes staring back at him. "Would you mind telling me a little more about it? I mean, I've heard about AA, and I know they hold regular meetings, but I don't really have a grasp on what it's all about and how it works."

"Sure thing, Danny. Partly, it's a support network. It's a group of people who all suffer from the same problem, and we're committed to trying to overcome that problem. But it's a lot more than that. It's a way of approaching life. It's a change of heart and mind. You acknowledge to yourself that the problem is bigger than you, that there's a greater power that can give you strength, and you turn to God for help, through prayer and meditation. You take a brutally honest look at yourself—your shortcomings, the errors you've made, and the people you've hurt. You try to live a new life with a new code of behavior, and make amends to those you've hurt. And you help other alcoholics deal with their problem. That's a big part of this. Another big part of the program is going to meetings on a regular basis."

"What happens at the meetings?" Danny asked apprehensively.

"People share their experiences. Sometimes there's a speaker or a specific topic that we discuss among ourselves. Usually people share stories about their struggles with alcohol and how it's impacted their lives. People share their successes, also—how long they've been sober, the difference it's made in their lives, the challenges and temptations they still feel, that kind of thing. It makes you realize that other people are going through exactly what you're going through, and that support and encouragement really helps, Danny. It inspires people to stay sober. You've probably heard the saying 'one day at a time.' It's a good approach."

Danny looked down and stirred his coffee again.

Andy continued, his deep voice gentle and encouraging. "The hardest part is walking through that door and making it through the first meeting. Let me take you, Danny. There's a meeting tonight at St. Martin's at seven thirty. I'll come by and pick you up. What do you say?"

Danny continued staring at his coffee, feeling paralyzed.

"It's all very confidential," Andy continued. "What's said in the meetings is kept in strict confidence. No one outside the meeting will know you're there. You can keep your last name to yourself."

Danny heaved a sigh and looked up again. "Okay, Andy. I'll try it." He sighed again and held his hand in front of his face. "Look at me. I'm shaking. I don't know why, but I'm terrified."

"Don't worry, pal. That's natural. You'll be glad you went, I promise," he said earnestly.

They got up from the booth and walked toward the cash register. George looked closely at Danny as he made change for Andy. "You a friend of the judge? That's good. That's very good." He smiled again.

Danny smiled back. "Yeah, it is good. Thanks, George."

***

Andy was right. Danny was glad he went to the Tuesday evening AA meeting in the basement social hall below St. Martin's Church. About twenty people attended the meeting, men and women, young and not-so-young, professionals and blue-collar types. A smattering of the faces were familiar, from church, from the train he used to ride downtown, from social functions and other places around the neighborhood he couldn't identify. Despite his trepidation, Danny found the atmosphere warm and welcoming from the moment he walked through the doors. He listened to others sharing their stories, some seeming completely at ease, others struggling mightily. More than once, he found himself trying to blink away tears as he listened to stories that mixed tragedy with hopefulness. Each story was different, yet they all hit close to home. They were different versions of his own story. He could understand each of them, with a kind of deep and personal understanding that comes only from common experience.

Before the meeting ended, Danny stood up. It felt right. He was ready to tell his story to a roomful of complete strangers with whom he felt a bond different from any he shared with his closest friends. "My name is Danny, and I am an alcoholic." He told of his twenty years of drinking: the blackouts, the all-nighters, driving his wife away, and being on the brink of driving his daughter away, too. He spoke of the accident, of the guilt and shame, and of prison and disbarment.

He wept unashamedly as he spoke. When it was over, complete strangers surrounded him and embraced him, sharing his tears. No one was angry or judgmental; no one was horrified. They knew that his story wasn't so different from theirs, and they wanted to help in whatever way they could, which was mostly just by being there, empathizing and offering words of encouragement.

Following the meeting, Danny joined Andy and six other men for coffee and dessert at the South Side Diner. They called themselves the "Dessert Club." They laughed a lot and told Danny stories about their drinking days, some funny, some outrageous, some sad, but all making the unstated point that they were just like him. There was a sense of camaraderie that reminded him of the old days, when he went out drinking with his college buddies, but now the drinks were coffee, lemonade, and hot chocolate. He couldn't wait until the next meeting.

***

The St. Martin's AA chapter held its meetings on Tuesday and Friday evenings. Danny found himself counting the hours between meetings. He was inspired and hopeful, yet he knew that his sobriety was precarious. The temptation to have a drink was ever-present, and at times, almost overwhelming. Andy called every afternoon to give him a pep talk. Danny was under standing orders from Andy to call him anytime, day or night, and to interrupt him even if he was in court, if he ever felt that he was on the verge of slipping and having a drink.

Danny found that trying to live by the "one day at a time" mantra was almost too much. He felt the need to live in more manageable units of time, so he would focus on just getting through the morning, then he'd face the afternoon and, finally, the most difficult challenge, getting through the evening without a drink.

He managed those time periods by forcing himself to schedule virtually every minute of every day. His schedules would include lists of chores, errands, and routine tasks, such as: *8:00—shower and shave; 8:20—breakfast; 8:45—read paper; 9:00—go to bank; 10:00—exercise walk.* Making it through the next task without having a drink was easier than telling himself he had to make it through the entire day without slipping.

He used drinks and snacks the same way, allowing himself six soft drinks and two snacks over the course of the day, trying to substitute those nutritional rewards for his alcohol craving. He was rigid in his schedule: Coke at 10:00 a.m., lemonade at noon, Dr Pepper at 2:30, root beer at 5:15, 7 Up at 7:00, then another Coke at 8:45. He would allow himself a late-afternoon snack of almonds or pistachio nuts; then at 10:30 he'd have a bedtime snack consisting of crackers and cheese—precisely six crackers and a different type of cheese each night. After that, he would sit in the old armchair in his living room and spend twenty minutes reading from a small devotional containing Scripture passages and inspirational messages. Then he would turn off the light and sit in the dark, meditating and praying, sometimes for twenty minutes, sometimes for hours.

Sometimes his prayers were a desperate plea for the strength to stay sober. Sometimes he prayed for the wisdom and courage to become a better father and a better person. Sometimes he prayed for the other struggling souls he had met through the AA program, and sometimes he prayed for the ability to accept his station in life and to be thankful for the blessings life had brought his way.

This routine had gotten Danny into the Christmas holidays without any close calls. The urge to drink was always there, but he kept his daily schedule in front of him, and with great focus and discipline, moved from one item to the next without getting sidetracked and yielding to the temptation to drink. He was always anxious—over the challenge of staying sober between meetings, over his future, over his divorce and the wrongful death lawsuit—but at least he was sober.

On Christmas Day, he and Allie exchanged gifts and went to Mass. They decided to cook a turkey dinner together, a first for both of them. Father and daughter felt a special joy to be spending the holiday together with Danny seemingly in a far better place—physically, mentally, and spiritually—than either of them could have hoped for six weeks ago. Just as they finished stuffing the turkey, the telephone rang, and Allie answered.

"It's someone named Pat," she said in a hushed voice, her hand over the telephone's mouthpiece. "I think he's drunk," she added, a look of concern clouding her face as she envisioned her father being lured away from home by some low-life in a bar. She handed her father the telephone and listened intently to the one side of the conversation she could hear.

"Pat? Where are you?" Pause. "Are you drunk?" Pause. "How many drinks have you had?" Another pause. "Okay, stay put, Pat. Start drinking coffee. I'm on my way. I'll be there in twenty minutes." He hung up.

"What was that about?" Allie asked, her voice tight with anxiety.

"Allie, I hate to do this, but can I leave this in your hands for a little while?" Danny asked, motioning to the turkey on the counter. "One of my new friends just fell off the wagon. He's drinking at a bar, and I need to get him out of there. I won't be long, I promise."

"Okay, Daddy," she said quietly, avoiding his eyes.

Danny sensed her apprehension. "Allie, I won't let anything ruin our Christmas together. I'm not going out drinking, okay? I've got a friend who needs help. I'm going to get him out of there, maybe take him for a cup coffee, and then I'll be right home—in plenty of time to carve the turkey!" He grabbed his coat and hurried out the door.

Kelly's Pub was a little over a mile away. Danny walked briskly, his rubber boots squeaking against the freshly fallen snow. This was a situation when having a driver's license would have made things considerably easier. Fortunately, his universe was now limited to the Beverly neighborhood—about two miles long from north to south, and a mile wide, east to west—so any place he needed to go was within walking distance. He had become accustomed to walking everywhere he went, and it no longer seemed like a hardship.

He thought about Pat Jordan. Pat was a regular at the Tuesday and Friday night meetings at St. Martin's, and also a regular with the post-meeting coffee and dessert crowd at the South Side Diner. Danny had liked him instantly. He was good company—smart, upbeat, and funny—and they quickly developed a bond based on their common experiences. Pat was an attorney, also. He and his father had once had a thriving neighborhood law practice, but after the elder Mr. Jordan had retired, Pat quickly made a shambles of the practice. His clients had quickly tired of the unreliability and unresponsiveness that resulted from Pat's long drinking benders. Like Danny, he was a capable lawyer who was now without a law practice.

Also like Danny, Pat's wife had gotten fed up with his drinking and left earlier that year, taking their six-year-old son with her. Apparently, facing Christmas Day alone in his small apartment was just too much for Pat.

Danny walked into Kelly's, stopping abruptly to allow his eyes to adjust from the brightness of the sunny, snow-covered world outdoors to the bleak dimness of the stale-smelling tavern. As his eyes adjusted, he saw three men sitting at the bar, together, yet each very much alone. Two of them were staring at the TV behind the bar. Pat Jordan gazed absently at the tiny Christmas tree with the flashing lights perched beside him on the bar.

"Hello, Pat," said Danny, taking a seat on the bar stool next to him.

"Merry Christmas, Danny. Thanks for coming," Pat replied, turning toward Danny and offering his hand, but not meeting his gaze.

Danny felt stunned at the sight of his new friend. In the short time they'd known each other, Pat Jordan had always looked like a man who had his act together, well groomed and well dressed, healthy, trim, and fit. At the moment, his hair was uncombed, he hadn't shaved in several days, and judging by the body odor, apparently hadn't showered, either. His eyes were swollen and bloodshot, either from drinking or crying, Danny couldn't tell which. Probably both, he surmised.

While walking toward Kelly's, Danny had decided that he'd take Pat to the South Side Diner for some black coffee, then take him home in a cab. After seeing Pat's condition, a wave of pity overtook him, and Danny couldn't bear the thought of his friend spending Christmas alone. "How about a nice Christmas dinner, Pat? At my place," Danny suggested.

"That would be nice, Danny," Pat replied meekly, "but look at me. I'm a mess."

"I've seen worse," said Danny, with an encouraging smile. "Come on, pal, you can shower up at my place. Allie and I are cooking Christmas dinner. It's just the two of us, but we've got enough food to feed an army. We'd love to have you."

***

Allie started at the sight of her father's companion when they walked through the front door thirty minutes later, but quickly composed herself and greeted their guest with cheerful enthusiasm. Pat was obviously embarrassed upon meeting Danny's daughter in the state he was in, but also clearly grateful to be spared the prospect of spending Christmas Day utterly alone. Danny provided Pat with a clean sweatshirt and a pair of jeans and guided him to the shower.

"I hope you don't mind the unexpected guest, sweetheart," Danny said when he returned to the kitchen to help with dinner preparations. "I know we planned on spending the day by ourselves."

Allie smiled and blinked away the tears in her eyes. "I'm so proud of you, Pops. Of course I don't mind." She hugged him tightly.

During dinner, Pat was haggard, but coherent, the shower and food lifting his spirits considerably. Allie showered him with attention, engaging him in conversation like a long-lost relative, quickly getting him past his embarrassment and self-consciousness and putting him at ease. Andy was right, Danny thought to himself. His confident, compassionate seventeen-year-old daughter was truly a special person, and Danny could not help but feel blessed on this Christmas Day.

After dinner, they watched *It's a Wonderful Life* together, all three of them wiping tears from their eyes during the final scene. Pat spent the night in the guest room and left at noon the next day, clear-eyed and clearheaded, if still a bit shaky.

Over the next week, Danny made a point of taking a long walk with Pat every morning, then checked in with him by phone several times each day. They attended the St. Martin's AA meetings together, where it became evident what a difficult time of the year the holidays could be for so many people.

On New Year's Eve, Danny, Pat, and a handful of others from their AA chapter gathered at Andy Murray's house for an alcohol-free evening of celebration and camaraderie, and to provide a means of avoiding temptation on one of the biggest drinking nights of the year. Danny felt a special closeness with the group of struggling souls gathered there. For many of them, their lives were in tatters, yet they felt a sense of hope and purpose, bonded by their collective effort to help each other conquer the biggest challenge life had thrown their way. The battle might never be over for them, but they took comfort in having comrades-in-arms and savoring the little victories that each day of sobriety represented.

"Thanks for being there for me, Danny," Pat Jordan said warmly as he drove Danny home shortly after midnight. "I feel like you're someone I can count on, and that means a lot to me."

"I'm glad I could help, Pat. Happy New Year." They shook hands and Danny went inside. He sat for a long time in the living room armchair, staring at the blue lava lamp on the adjacent table while he contemplated the events of the past year and the future that lay before him.

The back door slammed. Allie saw the wavering glow of the lava lamp emanating from the living room and knew that her father was waiting up for her.

"Hi, Pops! I'm home!" she announced cheerfully. She walked into the living room, leaned down, and kissed his cheek. "Happy New Year!"

"Happy New Year, little girl," Danny replied. "Let's make it a good one." He smiled at her, and then turned his gaze toward the strange, changing shapes silently erupting in the blue water of the lava lamp.

"What are you thinking about?" Allie asked.

"Oh, lots of things, but mostly I was sitting here thinking that for the first time in a long while, I'm doing something useful again. I was able to really help someone this week. And that really helped me. Strange, isn't it?"

"Not strange at all, Pops. That's what life is all about, isn't it? Good night!"

"Good night, sweetheart. Happy New Year!"

CHAPTER 26

It was a bright but bitterly cold morning as Danny Moran walked the sixteen blocks from his home to the law offices of Murphy & Murphy. He was wearing a suit and carrying his briefcase, feeling upbeat despite the assault of the icy January wind against his face. He was filled with a sense of purpose, partly because he was attending a legal meeting where he would be back in his element, but mostly because he was preparing to act in accordance with his new creed, making amends to someone he had hurt. It felt good.

The law office was at the end of a small strip mall, where it shared a parking lot with a currency exchange, a used bookstore, a pizza shop, and a beauty salon. The bell chimed as Danny opened the door and approached an empty reception desk. A boyish-looking young man in blue jeans and an oatmeal-colored sweater appeared from around the corner, walking slowly, a swagger in his step as he carefully surveyed his visitor.

"Are you Mr. Moran?" he asked in a tone that was all business.

"Yes, I have an appointment with Kevin Murphy," Danny replied amicably.

"That would be me," said the young man, offering his hand with no trace of a smile. "Let's talk in here," he said, leading Danny into a small conference room devoid of pictures, plants, or any other attempt at interior decorating. "Have a seat. My dad will be joining us. I'll get him."

A few moments later, the elder Mr. Murphy strolled into the office, his son trailing behind. Notwithstanding the gray hair and the fleshier face, the father's features were strikingly similar to his son's, although the elder Mr. Murphy was possessed of a quick smile and friendly eyes.

"I'm the other name on the letterhead," he announced in a chipper voice. "Paul Murphy. Nice to meet you, Mr. Moran," he said, shaking Danny's hand. "I've heard a lot about you. Hope you don't mind if I sit in."

"Not at all," Danny replied. He and the elder Murphy chatted briefly about neighborhood attorneys they knew in common until the younger Murphy brought the pleasantries to an abrupt halt.

"Well, let's get down to business, shall we?" Kevin said, doing his best to sound authoritative. "Mr. Moran, you called this meeting. What's on your mind?"

"Settlement," Danny replied matter-of-factly. "I'd like to see if we can settle the McGrath lawsuit."

"I'm not sure we have any interest in settlement," the young attorney replied, his tone confrontational. "This is a clear-cut case of wrongful death. Liability is a given. As I'm sure you can imagine, this incident has had a devastating impact upon Mrs. McGrath and her family. When we put our economic experts and medical experts on the stand, the jury will go crazy. There's not much reason for us to consider settlement when a substantial jury verdict is a certainty." He sat back and folded his arms, giving Danny a smug look.

For the briefest instant, Danny was tempted to walk away and teach this kid a few lessons in the courtroom. From the look of him, he couldn't have been more than a couple of years out of law school and probably had never tried a case in his life. But he had come to the office of this strip-mall lawyer with a purpose, and Danny would not let himself lose sight of that mission.

Danny looked steadily at the cocky young man across the table. "Look, Kevin, I don't want to fight you, and I certainly don't want to fight Mrs. McGrath. I'm here to make peace. Why would you wait years to go to trial and put yourself and your client through all that heartache and aggravation if it's not necessary? And I can assure you, it's not." Danny's voice was pleasant and agreeable, his face a picture of sincerity.

Kevin appeared taken aback. "Well, you may think it's not necessary, but Mrs. McGrath deserves her day in court," he said harshly.

The elder Murphy shot his son a quick glance, then interceded. "Well, Kevin, Mr. Moran took the time to come visit us this morning. Let's hear what he has to say." He smiled politely at Danny.

Kevin gave his father an irritated look. "Okay. If you've got a proposal, I'm all ears. I have an obligation to share any settlement offers with my client, so I'll pass along whatever it is you want to propose. I'll probably advise her to reject it, but I'll pass it along."

"Good," said Danny. "Then here's my proposal. First, I'd like you to explain to Mrs. McGrath that I'm truly sorry for what I've done. I understand that she may never be able to forgive me, and I'm not asking her to. However, I do want her to know that I stand ready and willing to do whatever she would like me to do, and that she doesn't need to go to court to make that happen, which leads to the second part of my proposal." Danny opened a manila folder and pulled out a piece of paper, which he handed across the table to the young attorney. It was an inventory of his assets:

House	$500,000
Cash	$120,000
Stocks and Mutual Funds	$1,350,000
Savings Bonds	$45,000
Retirement Plan	$200,000
Car	$80,000
TOTAL	$2,295,000

"This is everything I own, my entire net worth," Danny continued. "I'd like you to share that with Mrs. McGrath and tell her she can have whatever she wants. Tell her I want to make amends. I realize that I can't possibly compensate her for her loss, but I want to do whatever I can."

Kevin handed the piece of paper to his father and stared down at the table for a long time. Danny didn't know whether he was truly stunned and didn't know how to respond or whether he was attempting to calculate his share of the settlement.

"What about insurance?" Kevin asked gruffly.

"My auto insurance carrier will certainly deny coverage based on the DUI charges. We could litigate with them, but the prospects of recovery are low." Danny paused and stared first at the father, then at the son. "I'm trying to make this easy, gentlemen. Easy for you, and easy for Mrs. McGrath."

"How do we know this list is accurate?" Kevin asked suspiciously.

"I'll provide you whatever documentation you like—bank records, brokerage statements, tax returns. Just tell me what you want."

"The jury might award a lot more than this," Kevin pointed out.

"That's true," Danny replied. "But then again, they may not. Even if they do, that's all I've got, guys. I'm unemployed. I've been disbarred. Is there really any point in putting your client through a trial? Like I said, I'm trying to make it easy, and I'm trying to do the right thing."

Paul Murphy cleared his throat and scratched the back of his head. "This is quite a proposal, Mr. Moran. We certainly weren't expecting this. Can you give us a few minutes?"

"Certainly," said Danny. "Take all the time you need."

Father and son stepped out of the small conference room, closing the door behind them. Within five minutes, they returned, both appearing positive and upbeat. Kevin had clearly calculated his contingency fee by now, Danny surmised.

"Mr. Moran, we appreciate the visit, and we will communicate your proposal to our client," said Kevin. "I don't know how she'll react, and I don't want to give you any false hope, but we'll share it with her and get back to you."

Although the words were not encouraging, the looks on their faces were a giveaway. They were excited.

"Remember, guys," said Danny as he put on his coat, "it's very important to me that you explain to Mrs. McGrath how deeply sorry I am, and that I'm really trying to do the right thing here."

"We will, Danny," said the elder Mr. Murphy. "And for my part, let me say that I admire what you're doing. We'll be in touch."

At eight o'clock that evening, Danny's telephone rang. "Mr. Moran, this is Kevin Murphy. Here's where we stand. Mrs. McGrath will settle for $1.5 million. She doesn't want to force you to sell your home or wipe out your retirement plan. She also said to tell you that she appreciates your stepping up like this. Do we have a deal?"

Danny sighed audibly. "Yes, we have a deal, Kevin."

CHAPTER 27

Blair sat in the reception area outside the Oval Office, feeling important and slightly nervous, but most of all, curious. He had no idea why he'd been summoned by Arthur Courtright, the president of the United States. When Mrs. Richmond, the president's personal secretary, had called the week before to schedule the appointment, his own secretary had probed, but had been unable to learn the reason for the visit. "Just tell Congressman Van Howe that the president wants to have a personal visit," Mrs. Richmond had told her. "He doesn't need to do anything to prepare for the meeting."

Upon arriving for his appointment twenty minutes early, Blair had tried to use every ounce of charm he could muster to persuade Mrs. Richmond to give him some sort of clue about the purpose for the meeting. He failed miserably. "He just wants to chat," was all she would say.

Blair Van Howe was not in the habit of just chatting with the president of the United States. They had met on four previous occasions since Blair had arrived in Washington fifteen months ago. Three were formal receptions, attended by hundreds of other congressmen, senators, and other politically well-connected types. They had shaken hands and exchanged pleasantries at each of those functions, but none of those conversations lasted longer than sixty seconds. Blair's only other encounter with Arthur Courtright was at a meeting of the House Ethics Committee a week ago. Blair had been acting as co-chairperson for that committee, which had seemed like low-priority business to everyone until the president had made a personal appearance to let the committee know that ethics reform was a matter of significant importance to him. After making his pitch, the president stayed for the entire meeting as the committee discussed its priorities and debated the merits of various suggestions regarding campaign finance reform, conflict-of-interest disclosures, tighter controls on lobbying activities, and various other legislative proposals.

Mrs. Richmond picked up the ringing telephone. "Yes, Mr. President, I'll send him in." She turned to Blair. "The president will see you now."

Blair felt a tingle of excitement as he walked through the ornate doors into the spacious office that had been occupied by every president since Franklin Delano Roosevelt. The current occupant sprang up from his desk and walked briskly toward him. "Blair!" he called out in a booming voice with a thick Southern drawl. "Thanks for coming."

Arthur Courtright looked like exactly what he was—president of the United States and outdoor sportsman. He was fifty-eight years old and his well-coiffed hair was silver-gray, but his tall body was lean and hard. His face was weathered from years in the sun on his Texas ranch, yet ruggedly handsome, with a movie star smile. He had a presence, an aura of power and sophistication around him that Blair was certain would be equally evident whether he was meeting with heads of state in the Oval Office or deer hunting with a group of good old boys.

"Good morning, Mr. President," Blair replied, feeling quickly at ease as the president gripped his hand in a bone-crushing handshake. They sat opposite one another on matching white sofas situated on a deep blue oval rug bearing the presidential seal, as a waiter brought a tray of coffee, tea, and pastries. Blair's eyes darted quickly around the room as the waiter poured black coffee for both of them.

"First time here, Blair?" the president asked.

"Sorry, sir, I didn't mean to be gawking," Blair replied with an embarrassed grin. "Yes, it is my first time, and I must say it's pretty awe-inspiring." He glanced again at the portraits of Washington, Lincoln, and Jackson, as well as the oil paintings of Texas landscapes, a personal touch of the current occupant's.

"Well, it won't be your last," the president assured him. "This visit is long overdue. I've been wanting to get better acquainted for some time now. But I know a lot about you already, Congressman," the president said with a sly smile. "I have my sources, and I get reports."

"What do you hear, sir, if you don't mind my asking?" Blair inquired.

"Enough to make me want to know you better. I watched you during the Ethics Committee meeting last week. You were the junior-most person there, but you were in complete control. You clearly had a deep grasp of the issues and all of their nuances. You made your points eloquently and forcefully, without being bombastic. You were able to elicit involvement and support from the other committee members, and that ain't easy. Some of those guys are real pains in the ass, but you had them in the palm of your hand. It was a sight to behold. I know a political star in the making when I see one, and you're it, Blair. The real deal. A born leader. Hell, you remind me of myself when I first got here."

"That's kind of you to say, Mr. President. I'm flattered."

The president stared at him, a slightly amused smile on his face, and said nothing. After a long moment, Blair broke the silence. "So, what's the subject of our meeting this morning, sir? I feel a bit unprepared. I wasn't able to coax any information out of Mrs. Richmond."

Arthur Courtright laughed loudly. "Of course you weren't! I like tight lips around here, and no one's are tighter than Mrs. Richmond's. As for the agenda, it's pretty straightforward. You're the agenda."

Blair looked puzzled. "Sir?"

"As the leader of the Democratic party, I consider it my responsibility to help prepare our party for the future. A major part of that responsibility is identifying our future leaders, helping to groom them, helping them move their careers in the right direction. I think Blair Van Howe is someone who represents a bright future for our party and our nation."

Blair smiled modestly. "I'm honored, Mr. President, and I sure hope I can live up to your expectations. Any advice you can give me would certainly be appreciated."

Arthur Courtright leaned toward Blair, an intense look in his eyes. "Here's my advice, Blair. In Washington, you need to get along. You get things done by making friends and building alliances. Don't make enemies. No matter how much you dislike somebody or disagree with his ideas, don't make enemies. To do that, you need to leave your ego behind. It gets in the way. That's such an easy concept, but most senators and congressmen seem absolutely incapable of doing that. They're arrogant and pompous, and that makes them ineffective."

Arthur Courtright spoke forcefully, like a passionate professor lecturing a promising student. Blair listened with rapt attention, meeting the president's gaze and staring intently back at him. "Here's another thing to keep in mind," the president continued. "In addition to cultivating the right relationships, you have to be willing to make compromises. Quid pro quo, that's how politics works, but never, and I mean *never*, compromise your principles. You're developing a reputation around Washington as Mr. Integrity. In your short time here, people can see that in you, and they respect it. It's an intangible, but don't ever underestimate how valuable it is in terms of your ability to get things done, the relationships you have with other lawmakers, and most important, your future success."

"That sounds like good advice, Mr. President. I'll certainly take it to heart," Blair said in his most sincere voice.

"Well, I don't think anything I've said is news to you. You seem to be doing all of those things already, like it's second nature."

"I had a great mentor early in my legal career, sir. He was the most naturally gifted politician I've ever known, but he never got into politics. He was an attorney, and he was a master at everything you just described. Ever since I got here, when I faced a difficult decision, I would ask myself, 'What would Danny do?' It really helped me make the right decisions."

"That's great, Blair. Having a good mentor is invaluable. But you're in a whole different world now. If you'll let me, I'd like to provide whatever mentoring I can."

Blair almost choked on the coffee he was sipping, but outwardly maintained his composure. "Mr. President, I don't even know what to say. I'm humbled, and I'm honored, and I would be eternally grateful for whatever guidance you can provide, sir."

"It would be my pleasure. But remember what I just said. This is Washington, the land of backroom deals and quid pro quo. I'd like you to do something for me in return."

"Absolutely," Blair replied eagerly. "Just name it, sir."

The president walked across the room and picked up the calendar from his desk. He handed it to Blair, circling the date August 25. "Does this date mean anything to you?"

The date was four months off, and Blair's mind raced for a few seconds; then it clicked. "That's the start of the Democratic National Convention," he replied confidently.

"That's right. And, as you probably know, it's customary to have one of the party's shining stars give the keynote address. I'm afraid this election is going to be close, and you're the best person I can think of to energize and inspire the electorate and give my reelection campaign the boost it needs. Will you do that for me, Blair?"

Blair felt a surge of excitement race through his body. "Nothing would please me more, Mr. President. I'll make you proud."

"I know you will, Blair. There's not the slightest doubt in my mind."

CHAPTER 28

While Blair Van Howe visited with President Arthur Courtright in the Oval Office, Danny Moran inspected the first floor of his house with a critical eye, making sure it looked perfect for Allie's visit. He had always been tidy, but this occasion called for a thorough cleaning. He had just finished vacuuming the living room carpet, after dusting and polishing furniture, scrubbing sinks and counters, and cleaning the mirrors. He was determined to make sure that his daughter could see that he was surviving just fine on his own.

Allie was approaching the end of her second semester at Northwestern. As far as Danny was concerned, she could not have chosen a better place to attend college. Aside from the obvious benefit of a first-rate education at a world-class university, the location was ideal. Allie lived in a sorority house on the Evanston campus, so she was able to experience campus life at a major university and feel like she was an entire universe away from her former life on the South Side of Chicago. At the same time, she was only a little over an hour away, and therefore able to visit her father on weekends whenever she felt like it. Although she didn't have a car on campus, the city's public transportation system made the trip easy. She would take the elevated train, commonly referred to as "the El," from Evanston to downtown Chicago, and then take the Rock Island commuter train from downtown to Beverly. Her father's home was a ten-minute walk from the train station.

Allie had come home almost every other weekend during the fall semester. However, she was now working a part-time job on weekends, and therefore hadn't been home a single time since January. Although they spoke by telephone frequently, it'd been three full months since Danny had seen his daughter, the longest stretch of time they had ever been apart.

This morning's visit was prompted by a family tragedy of sorts. Scruffy, the cairn terrier who had been the family pet for the past twelve years, had passed away at Allie's sorority house the previous day. Allie was bringing her beloved pet home to be buried in the backyard of the family homestead.

As he returned the furniture polish and glass cleaner to the cabinet beneath the kitchen sink, Danny heard the front door open. He hurried into the living room, beaming in anticipation of the sight of his daughter. He stopped in his tracks when he saw her, his happy countenance quickly transforming into a look of bewilderment. Allie unceremoniously tossed her backpack on the floor and glared at him. She was livid, outrage and indignation written across her face and emanating from every inch of her body.

"You're not going to believe what just happened!" she said, her voice raised in anger.

"Allie, are you okay?" Danny asked, his imagination starting to conjure up visions of some scoundrel assaulting his daughter, snatching her purse, or perhaps robbing her at gunpoint.

"No, I'm not okay! I was just robbed! Some low-life scum-bag just stole Scruffy!"

Danny had rarely seen his daughter so angry, yet a wave of relief passed through him with that explanation, strange as it was.

"Calm down, Allie. Tell me exactly what happened, okay?"

Allie took a deep breath. "I was bringing Scruffy home, so we could bury him in the backyard, like we talked about. I didn't want to be seen carrying a dead dog on the train, so I wrapped him in his blanket and put him in a suitcase. Well, thirty pounds of dead weight is really heavy, and I was struggling with the bag as I tried to get on the train. Then some guy comes along and offers to help me with the bag and says, 'Jesus, this is heavy, what do you have in here, weights?' I didn't want to tell him it was a dead dog, so I told him I was carrying a few laptop computers in the bag. He seemed nice. He was polite and normal-looking, wearing an expensive jogging suit. He lifted the suitcase and put it on the overhead luggage rack for me." Her eyes were still blazing as she spoke.

"So, what happened?"

"When I got ready to get off the train at Ninety-first Street, he jumped up and offered to help. So he lifts the suitcase off the luggage rack and follows me off the train. The train pulls away and I start to thank him, then he looks around and sees that we're the only two passengers who just got off—and he bolts! He holds a suitcase under his arm like a big football and takes off running as fast as he can! I started screaming at him, but there's nobody around, and he disappears into the woods with my goddamn dog! Aaaargh! I'm so ticked off!" She shook both fists and stomped her foot.

Danny knew that he should be sympathetic and perhaps share in her outrage or offer some assistance in locating the remains of the precious family pet. He tried his best to look concerned, but found himself struggling mightily to suppress a smile. Allie could see the corners of his lips twitching as he tried to control them. She could see the look in his eyes was one of amusement rather than outrage.

"Daddy!" she protested. "I can't believe you think this is funny."

Danny exploded into laughter—loud, uninhibited, uncontrolled laughter.

"Daddy, I can't believe you're laughing at this!" she shouted, incrimination in her voice, but it was tempered with confusion and uncertainty.

Danny laughed harder as he doubled over, struggling to speak and forcing out broken sentences, a few words at a time. "I'm sorry, honey ... I just keep picturing that guy ... thinking he'd just scored some expensive laptops ... then opening the suitcase and finding a dead animal. That's priceless! He got what he deserved!" He roared.

"Daddy, it's not funny," Allie scolded, breaking into uncertain laughter herself at the sight of her father's reaction.

"I ... can't ... help it," Danny cried, struggling to force the words through his laughter. Tears streamed down his face as he bent over and put his hands on his knees.

Her father's reaction was contagious, and Allie's struggle to remain indignant yielded to her own fit of laughing, the two of them howling uncontrollably. Each time one of them came close to stopping, the sight of the other triggered a new round of hysterics.

Finally, worn-out, faces streaked with tears, they embraced. "Welcome home, kiddo. It's great to see you. And I really am sorry about Scruffy," Danny said, wiping the tears from his face and struggling to suppress another fit of laughter.

"It's great to see you, too, Pops," Allie replied, staring warmly into her father's eyes. "I've missed you." She took a deep breath, trying to compose herself. "I need a drink. Got any Coke around here?"

"In the basement fridge," Danny replied.

"Can I bring you one?" Allie asked as she headed toward the stairs.

Danny looked at his watch. It was 11:48. "Not yet, sweetheart. I'll wait another twenty-seven minutes, then it'll be time for my lemonade."

"Still sticking to your schedule, I see," Allie said with a smile.

"Like clockwork."

Allie returned with her drink, poured it over ice, and they sat down at the kitchen table, looking out at a group of robins gathered around the bird feeder in the backyard.

"You look great, Pops. You seem happier than you've been in a long time," Allie said, turning from the robins and looking closely at her father.

"I am, Allie. I've been sober for seventeen months now. Life is good again."

"And you're enjoying the teaching job at Loyola?"

"I really am. You know, I truly never even considered teaching before, but I actually enjoy it. I like the kids, I like the camaraderie with the other teachers, and I like having some connection with the law again. Besides that, it keeps me busy. That's really why I took the job in the first place. I was afraid if I didn't keep busy, I'd start drinking again."

"How busy does it keep you?"

"Well, last semester I taught just one business law class to undergraduates, and I spent a lot of time preparing for each class. This semester, I'm teaching two business law classes, but

I'm not working any harder because I taught the class before and don't have to prepare as much. The dean thinks there may be an opportunity to take on a full-time position in the fall, and maybe start teaching in the law school as well."

"That's fantastic, Daddy! Do you think you'll make a career out of this?"

"I don't know yet. Some other opportunities have come along recently. I've been approached by a couple of lobbying firms. They seem to think that, with my legal background and all of the business and political connections I've made over the years, lobbying work would be right up my alley. I've also been approached by several consulting firms. They tell me I'd be in high demand as a consultant to the corporate world regarding business strategies and transactions, and also to politicians, helping with campaign strategy, legislation, that kind of thing."

"Wow, that's great! You should really consider those opportunities. Sounds like you could come close to having the kind of career you're used to."

"You're probably right. I think I'd be good at it, and it would be pretty lucrative, but I'm not sure I want to get back into that world. The schedule would be demanding, and there'd be a lot of pressure. Teaching doesn't pay much, but the hours are great, and it gives me the time and flexibility to stay immersed in my AA world. That's a big part of my life now."

"It seems like you've got your drinking problems pretty well licked now. Do you still feel the need for AA?"

"It's the focus of my life now, Allie. Partly, that's because the temptation to drink is still there. I know I could slip very easily. But the other thing is that it's brought a purpose to my life. People count on me now. I'm making a difference.

AA absolutely turned my life around. It saved me, and now a big part of my life is helping others battle their problem. I often feel like an old-fashioned doctor or an emergency room. I get calls at all hours of the day and night. Sometimes guys are drunk and calling me from a bar. Sometimes they're on the verge of slipping, either because there's been some tragedy in their life or they're just battling their demons. And I can help. And do you know what else? These people have become my closest friends. I'm closer to a lot of these guys than I've been with any friends I've ever had. For the most part, they're not accomplished professionals. They're not hotshot lawyers or business leaders or politicians. They're drunks, or former drunks. Some are like me. They used to have good jobs, but they blew it. Some are lucky enough that they still have good jobs. AA saved them before they were too far gone. But a lot of the people I've met are people that the rest of the world would consider losers—people who never amounted to anything and probably never will. But we're friends. We have a common bond that others can never understand. We're there for each other."

Allie was touched by the passion and sincerity in her father's voice as he spoke. "Seems like you're in a good place, Daddy. I'm really happy for you—and proud of you. Speaking of your friends, do you still see Pat Jordan?"

Danny smiled wistfully. "Pat is one of my ongoing projects," he said, a trace of sadness in his voice. "He's one of the most charming, warm, and talented people I know, and it breaks my heart to see him struggle like he does. He just can't seem to stay sober for any length of time. He may stay clean for a couple months here and there, but then he slips and drinks hard for quite a spell. To his credit, he keeps trying. He keeps coming back to the meetings, but his life is a mess."

"Poor guy," Allie said, sharing her father's sense of sadness and compassion. "How does he get by? Financially, I mean?"

"He's pretty industrious when he's sober, and he doesn't mind doing menial work. He worked on a construction crew for a few months until he showed up drunk and got fired. He vanished for a while, and we later found out that he'd gone to Reno and was working as a blackjack dealer. He's back now, and sober. For how long, who knows? But he's good about staying in touch with me when he's sober. He calls and drops in a lot when he's around. He's training for a triathlon now and often stops by when he's out riding his bike. He always asks about you."

Allie looked up at the clock on the kitchen wall. "Ten after twelve, Pops. Ready for that lemonade?"

"Well, it's still a few minutes early, but this is a special occasion, so why not?"

Allie jumped up and bounded downstairs, returning with a can of pink lemonade. Danny waited until the clock struck 12:15 before popping it open.

"Speaking of my special projects, Allie, I've got a guest staying here at the moment. I hope you don't mind."

"Of course not. Who is he? Or she?" she asked, smiling suggestively.

"It's not a she," Danny replied quickly, looking embarrassed. "His name is Joe Jansen. I've known Joe for about six months now. He's a sweet, gentle kid, probably around thirty, but he's a real mess. He's drunk a lot more than he's sober. He comes from a wealthy family, but they've given up on him. He's been a raging alcoholic since he was in his teens. He's been in and out of rehab countless times, and recently wound up living on the street. He's been staying here for about a week now."

As if on cue, a scraggly looking man wearing jeans and a Grateful Dead T-shirt walked into the room in his bare feet. His face was thin and gaunt, with several days' growth of stubble, and his eyes had a hollow look about them. "Hello," he said, walking hesitantly into the kitchen. His harsh features seemed to soften as he approached Allie with a shy and slightly embarrassed smile. "My name is Joe. I'm a friend of your dad's."

Allie stood and shook his hand, flashing a welcoming smile. "Hi, Joe, I'm Allie. It's a pleasure to meet you."

She invited Joe to join them for lunch and busied herself making sandwiches. Joe appeared nervous and uncomfortable at first, but Allie had a way of putting people at ease. Danny watched with admiration as Allie led a lighthearted conversation, skillfully avoiding the subjects one would naturally discuss when getting acquainted, but which would undoubtedly be touchy subjects for someone in Joe's situation—jobs, schooling, and family.

By the time they finished their sandwiches, they had completely succeeded in bringing Joe out of his shell. He was not accustomed to engaging in a conversation where the other participants seemed so genuinely interested in him. His self-consciousness had faded away as he laughed and joked and seemed perfectly relaxed. Danny had rarely known his troubled friend to be this upbeat and animated and sensed a rare opportunity. "You two share something in common," he said, smiling brightly, looking from one to the other.

Allie and Joe looked at each other.

"Do you know what he's talking about?" Allie asked.

"Nope. I guess you'd better fill us in, Danny."

"Follow me," Danny instructed. They got up, mystified, and did as instructed, following him into the living room. Danny pointed at the Steinway baby grand piano.

Allie's face brightened. "Oooh, do you play, Joe?"

"Does he play? I've never heard anyone play like him! What do you say, Joe? How about a little concert?" Danny knew that Joe was a reluctant performer, but hoped that in his present ebullient mood, he'd be less inhibited than normal. His instinct was correct. Joe confidently strode up to the Steinway and took a seat at the keys.

"Okay, I'll go first, then I want to hear you, Allie!"

His scraggly face glowed with excitement as he moved the bench to just the right position and stretched his fingers. He started with Beethoven's "Für Elise," then moved on to Mozart, his fingers moving gracefully and effortlessly across the keys, his eyes closed, his body swaying gently to the music.

"He's fabulous, Daddy!" Allie whispered excitedly. "Look at him. Look how he feels the music, like it's coming from his heart."

Joe finished Mozart and launched right into Elton John and Billy Joel. Allie danced and clapped her hands to the music, while her father watched like a proud mentor, smiling and tapping his foot.

"Wow, you're unbelievable!" Allie gushed when he had finished. "You've got a real gift. They can't teach that! You ought to play professionally—in a studio or with a band or a symphony. Have you ever done that?"

"Nah," Joe replied. "I get nervous in front of crowds. And I'd never be able to stick to the practice schedule. That takes a lot more discipline than I'll ever have. I just play for fun. Your turn, Allie!" He stood and pulled the bench out for her.

"You're way out of my league, Joe, but I'll see if I can remember anything. It's been awhile." She gamely sat down at the keys and tried to think of a tune she could still play without sheet music. Her musings were interrupted by the ringing of the doorbell.

"Be right back," Danny said as he strode quickly toward the front door. Moments later, he was shouting excitedly from the front porch. "Allie, come look at this!"

She and Joe hurried after him. "Oh my God!" Allie exclaimed, as she saw her father unzipping an old suitcase.

"It's Scruffy!" Danny shouted. "Somebody left this at the door and drove off. Good thing our address is still on the suitcase."

"Who's Scruffy?" Joe asked.

Allie peered into the suitcase to confirm that the precious cargo was still there. The three of them sat on the front steps as Allie related the story of Scruffy's abduction. Her outrage had passed, and she focused more on how much her pet had meant to her and how important it was to bury him in the yard that he knew and loved.

Joe's eyes became misty as he listened intently. "There's a shovel in the basement. Let me dig the grave for you."

Allie started to protest, but caught her father's look and understood. It would make Joe feel useful, something that occurred all too infrequently in his life. "That would be very sweet of you, Joe," she said softly, wiping a tear from her own eye.

Father and daughter sat together on the front steps with the old suitcase as Joe went in search of the shovel. "Look who's here," Danny said, smiling and nodding in the direction of the street. A cyclist on a racing bike veered into the driveway at high speed and turned up the sidewalk, stopping abruptly in front of the steps. He was clad in yellow and black cyclist's attire, tight-fitting Lycra surrounding a lean, muscular frame. He wore a matching helmet and dark sunglasses, which he removed as he dismounted.

"How did such a gorgeous girl ever emerge from your gene pool, Moran?" Pat Jordan asked as he set the kickstand.

"Takes after her mother, I guess," Danny shot back.

"Hello, Allie girl. Jesus, look at you! You're so grown up! I'd give you a big hug, but I'm a little sweaty."

"Hi, Pat," Allie replied enthusiastically. "It's great to see you again. You look fabulous!" She meant it.

"Are you coming or going?" Pat asked, pointing to the old suitcase.

"I'm home for the weekend," Allie replied. "This is a long story," she said, pointing at the suitcase.

***

Allie and Danny sat at the picnic table in the backyard, watching as Joe and Pat labored with their shovels.

"I never realized that digging a little grave could be such a bitch," Pat grumbled. "This ground is like cement!"

Joe and Pat flailed away at the defiant soil, alternately laughing at each other and cursing as they made painstakingly slow progress.

"Maybe I should find a pet crematory, Daddy," Allie suggested as Pat flung his shovel aside after jolting his entire body striking a large rock. "I'm feeling guilty. These guys are killing themselves."

Danny smiled and patted her knee. "Nah, let them stay at it, sweetheart. I promise you, they're enjoying it." He looked at his two friends, sweating and cursing as they continued laboring. "Sometimes the best way to help someone is to let them help someone else."

CHAPTER 29

"You look lovely today, Mrs. R.," Blair sang out in a chipper voice as he approached Mrs. Richmond, the president's personal secretary. They had become friendly as a result of Blair's frequent visits, but she had scolded him when he had tried calling her by her first name, which was Jean. Such informality was not appropriate for the secretary of the most powerful man in the world. So, he began calling her "Mrs. R.," and she let him get away with it, since it seemed like a sign of affection from a man she was convinced was destined to go places.

"Thank you, Congressman," she said, beaming at the compliment. "Go on in, he's expecting you."

"What's this crap I hear about you wanting to leave Washington?" the president bellowed from behind his desk, leaning back in his chair, feigning shock.

Blair strode across the room, now comfortable in the surroundings as a result of frequent visits over the past twenty months. Some of those visits involved official business, but most were just casual chats at the invitation of the president, who had been true to his word about his desire to serve as a mentor to the talented young congressman from Illinois.

"Well, I'm just mulling it over, sir, and was hoping I could count on you for some advice and counsel."

The stern look on Arthur Courtright's face evaporated, replaced by a broad grin as he stood and shook hands with his protégé. "I'm all ears, Blair. Talk to me." The president motioned to the chair in front of his desk.

"Well, sir, you once told me to listen carefully when opportunity knocks, and that it may come from an unexpected direction. I think I hear some knocking, and it's not coming from here in Washington."

The president leaned back, put his feet up on the desk, and folded his arms. "Go on. I'm listening."

"I love what I've been doing since I arrived here," Blair began, "and I think I'm pretty good at it, but—"

The president sat upright and leaned across the desk. "Pretty good at it! For Chrissakes, you're the best I've ever laid eyes on! I've been around Washington for thirty years, and I've never seen anyone in Congress accomplish what you have in such a short time. In just three years, you've developed real influence, and that's our stock in trade around here. Your fellow legislators seek you out because they want you on their side. Having Blair Van Howe in their corner means something. You give them and their causes instant credibility. You can help them sell their agenda—not because you're a salesman, but because you're respected around here. You're Mr. Integrity." He leaned back again, his feet returning to their resting spot atop his desk. "Sorry, I interrupted you. Go on, please."

"Well, sir, here's the opportunity I see. The political scene back home in Illinois is in turmoil at the moment. The state is facing a financial crisis, largely because of runaway spending. The governor's office has been plagued by one scandal after another. First, there was the disclosure that he had a long-standing affair with a former stripper and may have fathered her child; second, there's talk about his dirty dealings with certain labor unions, promising generous contracts for state employees and pressuring the feds to back off their corruption investigations in return for the union's assurances of campaign contributions and votes; and third, there are all those allegations about the governor coddling special interest groups, which is contributing to the runaway spending. He's about to be run out of town on a rail, and if he had any sense at all or anything resembling a conscience, he'd resign. But the stubborn son of a bitch will never do that, and the voters are ready to revolt."

"So you want to be the white knight, riding to the rescue with your Mr. Integrity mantle, and then waltz into the governor's mansion as the man who can clean up the mess. And you'll be a hero when you do." The president folded his hands behind his head and nodded slowly as he considered the matter.

"Mr. President, you've often suggested that I consider my position in Congress as a stepping stone, a learning experience, but also a path to something bigger. I can win that election, and I can clean up that mess. I know I can! After that, maybe I can come back to Washington and get back into national politics."

President Arthur Courtright silently eyed his protégé for a long moment. "Let me be completely candid with you, Blair. When I took you under my wing, it was with one goal in mind—this goal, right here!" He pounded his desk with his index finger. "I want to see you in the White House. You've got what it takes. I sensed that as soon as you arrived here in Washington, and now that I know you better, I believe it more strongly than ever. It would be a great thing for our party and a great thing for our country. And if that's the goal, then your instincts are right on, as usual. It's rare for a congressman to be elected president. In the last fifty years, most presidents were either senators or governors before they were elected president. You got a lot of national exposure with your convention speech, so you've got good name recognition already. It'll only get better if you're successful as governor. This is smart, Blair! You're young, and you've got time. It's the perfect opportunity. You'll win, and you'll win big. You can be a hero when you turn things around. And that will set the stage perfectly for a presidential run. I say go for it!"

***

Arthur Courtright's prediction was correct. The following November, Blair Van Howe won the Illinois gubernatorial election in a landslide. He was thrilled to be going home with a new challenge in front of him. His wife was less than thrilled. Kimberly had made it very clear to her husband that, after four years in Washington, she did not relish the prospect of taking up residence in Springfield, Illinois. However, there was almost as much official business for the governor in Chicago as there was in Springfield, so she would be able to spend much of her time at their home in Beverly.

***

Just a couple of blocks from the Van Howe home, Danny Moran sat in his kitchen visiting with his daughter, Allie, and two college friends, Kristen and Lindsay, whom Allie had invited home for Thanksgiving dinner. Danny and Allie worked together preparing the stuffing according to the old family recipe, Danny tearing slices of bread into small pieces as Allie sautéed vegetables. Kristen and Lindsay spoke excitedly about the new governor upon learning that he lived nearby and that he and Danny had once been close friends.

"What's he like?" Kristen asked, trying hard not to sound like a political groupie.

"What you see is what you get," Danny replied. "He's smart, charming, charismatic. And he truly is a good, decent man. All that talk about integrity and ethics—those aren't just buzzwords. He really means it."

"How well do you know him?" asked Lindsay.

"We were best friends for a long time," Danny replied. "We were roommates all through law school. We went our separate ways for awhile after graduation, then we became law partners and worked closely together for ten years."

"Do you still keep in touch?" Lindsay asked.

"No, we went in different directions about four years ago. I stopped practicing law, Blair went into politics, and our paths just don't cross anymore. He still has a home right down the street, but he's almost never there except when Congress is in recess and during the holidays. He might be there now."

After the turkey was stuffed and placed into the oven, Kristen and Lindsay decided to jog around the neighborhood. Allie pointed them in the direction of the Van Howe house, so they could be sure to run past it and perhaps get a glimpse of the new governor. Allie stayed home and began setting the dining room table.

"Does it bother you that Blair has completely written you off, Daddy? It's hard to believe that someone who was your best friend could just abandon you the way he did."

Danny thought for a moment as he pulled dishes out of the china cabinet. "I have to admit that it does hurt when I think about it. We had a great friendship, and I miss our time together. I understand that he had to distance himself from me during his first election, right after the accident, but that was a long time ago. Anyway, I try not to dwell on it. Blair was part of my old life. I have a new life now, and I've come to grips with that."

After their Thanksgiving dinner, Allie took her friends on a tour of the Western Avenue watering holes, and Danny went to an AA meeting. The girls returned shortly after midnight, Kristen and Lindsay sounding giggly and tipsy. Danny was sitting in his usual late-night spot, in his living room armchair next to the window, the room dark but for the eerie glow of the old blue lava lamp.

"Goodnight, Mr. Moran!" the girls called out cheerfully as they bounded up the stairs, the sound of loud, clumsy footsteps echoing through the quiet house.

"Goodnight, Pops," Allie said, leaning over to hug her father. His face felt damp, and she pulled back and could see tears glistening on his cheeks in the pale blue light. "Daddy, what's wrong?" she asked, alarm in her voice.

Danny sniffled quietly and cleared his throat, struggling to find his voice. "Joe Jansen is dead. They found him in a hotel room in Yuma. He'd been dead two weeks when they discovered his body."

"Oh, Daddy, I'm so sorry." Tears of sympathy flowed freely down Allie's cheeks. "What happened?"

"We don't know yet. I'm sure it was drugs or too much booze, maybe both. He was such a sweet, gentle soul ... didn't have a mean bone in his body. And so talented. It's such a waste. I wish I could've been there for him. I wish I could have done something." He wept harder, openly and unashamed.

"But you did do something for him, Daddy. You were his friend. You were one of the few people in his life who cared for him. You can't save everyone."

Danny sighed deeply, his breath shaking from the quiet sobs. "I know that. It just breaks my heart that he was so alone. He was dead for two weeks, and no one even missed him. To the rest of the world, he was just another drunk ... a loser."

"But you know what he was really like, Daddy. Most people didn't know Joe like you did. You were able to see beyond the hopeless drunk and see him for the beautiful, talented soul that he really was. And he was better for that, and so are you."

Danny nodded slowly and wiped his eyes with the back of his hand. "You're right, sweetheart. He just had an adversary that was too much for him. Most people can't understand the brutal power that alcohol has over an alcoholic. Only another drinker can really understand it."

"That's why people like Joe need people like you, Daddy. You made a difference to Joe, and you make a difference to a whole lot of people, and I couldn't be more proud of you."

CHAPTER 30

B lair Van Howe stormed into the governor's mansion with a mandate from the populace. The State of Illinois was ready for a new leader, one who would bring ethics and accountability back to state government. Democrats and Republicans alike were ready for someone who could bring fiscal responsibility, jobs, and prosperity to the Land of Lincoln. The electorate saw that kind of leader in the inspirational congressman who had burst onto the national political scene just a few years earlier and had been thrust into national prominence through his captivating performance at the Democratic National Convention.

The people of Illinois were not disappointed in their choice. Blair Van Howe delivered exactly as promised. The mere absence of scandal during his administration would have been a vast improvement over prior regimes, but the Van Howe administration did far better than that. Governor Van Howe made ethics in government a top priority. He aggressively pushed an agenda that included campaign finance reform and real transparency and disclosure from elected officials and lobbyists. The goal was to reduce conflicts of interest and the sway of special interest groups, and by all accounts, he had succeeded in achieving major reform in these areas. Of even greater importance from the voters' perspective, economic prosperity had returned to the state. As he approached the halfway point in his second term as governor, Blair's approval ratings were higher than any Illinois governor in decades.

During the preceding presidential election campaign four years earlier, Blair had been approached by party leaders and asked to consider running as the vice presidential nominee on the Democratic ticket, alongside presidential candidate Colin Cooper, senator from the neighboring state of Wisconsin. Blair tactfully resisted the considerable pressure from the party's leadership and from Cooper himself. His stated reason was that he had made a commitment to the Illinois voters, and he intended to serve his full term as governor and possibly seek a second term to complete his unfinished business. His unstated reason was that he detested Cooper, whom he considered a blindly ambitious egomaniac who had no core values or beliefs and would take whatever position he believed would win him the most votes. Besides, he expected Cooper to lose handily and didn't want to tarnish his own name and reputation by being associated with that losing effort. Cooper got drubbed, and the Republican candidate, Jonathan Reese, took up residence in the White House.

Reese's tenure had been uneventful. He hadn't accomplished much, but he hadn't done anything foolish, either. To a large extent, his hands were tied by congressional infighting and inertia, and he had neither the forcefulness of personality nor the creativity of fresh ideas to break the congressional gridlock to make things happen. To make his plight even sadder, his wife had been diagnosed with breast cancer and her prognosis was bleak. President Reese had announced that he would forego the possibility of a second term to spend time with his family. That left the race for the White House wide open.

Governor Van Howe had thrown his hat into the ring and quickly become the front-runner. The primaries became a mere formality, and by early spring, it was a foregone conclusion that Blair Van Howe would be the Democratic candidate for president of the United States. By late May, it was becoming apparent that his Republican opponent would be Henry Hamilton, a three-term United States senator from California. Hamilton had made a fortune as an entrepreneur who had founded, developed, and then sold several fabulously successful software companies prior to embarking on his political career. He possessed a formidable intellect and was widely perceived as a brilliant businessman who did not readily suffer fools. He spoke his mind, even when it was politically incorrect to do so, but the media and his constituents found his candor refreshing. His drive to succeed, coupled with his aggressive personality, made him a ruthless but effective campaigner.

Arthur Courtright had stayed in regular contact with Blair Van Howe after Blair had left Washington and after Courtright had completed his second term as president. Courtright spent most of his time on the speaking circuit and writing his memoirs, but remained active in politics as the elder statesman of the Democratic Party. In that capacity, his contact with his star pupil had become much more frequent as Blair considered, and then announced, his run for the White House. For several months, he had been suggesting that Blair upgrade the caliber of his campaign team, and those suggestions had become much more forceful once it became apparent that Henry Hamilton would be Blair's opponent.

Following his mentor's advice, Blair had been conducting a weeklong series of intense interviews to fill the key positions on his team. He sat in his suite at the Intercontinental Hotel in downtown Chicago with his wife and father-in-law, having just finished his final interview. It was nearly 10:00 p.m. He flipped through the small handful of résumés, photographs, and crude scorecards on the coffee table in front of him, exhausted, yet determined to bring closure to the process of finalizing his campaign team.

"I want to finalize these decisions tonight," Blair announced, rubbing his bleary eyes. "Tell me what you think."

Kimberly spoke up, a tone of impatience in her voice. "I think it's easy," she said. "We're in agreement on almost all the key positions—policy director, finance director, chief media strategist. The only one we're still struggling with is the big one: campaign manager. And you're the only one struggling with that one, Blair. I think it's a no-brainer."

"I agree," Sam added decisively. "My only reservation is that nerdy little Indian guy who was just in here. Do we really need him?"

"Politics has changed, Sam," Blair replied. "You've got to have a professional pollster now, and those guys are usually computer geeks. Rama may not be the life of the party, but Arthur says he's the best there is. We need him."

"Well, I think you need to listen to Arthur's recommendation on the most important position, which is the campaign manager," said Kimberly, becoming even more insistent. "He used Bobby Rosensteel for both of his presidential campaigns, and the results speak for themselves. The guy knows what it takes to win."

"But so does Neil," Blair replied. "He handled both of my congressional campaigns and both gubernatorial races, and we did great. He's a winner, too, and as far as I'm concerned, there's something to be said for loyalty."

"Not in a presidential election, Blair," Sam growled. "All that matters is winning. Neil Miller is a nice guy, and we all like him. And you're right, he's done a fine job for you, there's no denying that. But he's got no experience with national elections. Kimberly's right. This one is a no-brainer."

Blair picked up a résumé from the coffee table and stared at the picture of Bobby Rosensteel. He had a thin face and sharp features; small, penetrating eyes that looked black as coal; and dark hair slicked straight back. He looked the part. "I don't know how else to say this, but I just don't like the guy," said Blair. "He's got about as much charm as a rattle-snake. He's an abrasive, arrogant bully, and if we take him, we'll have to take his entourage of assistants, too."

"I agree. He's a pompous little ass," Kimberly said curtly. "But he's not running for office, you are! And he's the right guy to get you there. What did Arthur say about him?"

"Arthur said I'd be a fool not to hire him. He said Bobby knows how to win, and he'll do what it takes. He also con-firmed all my suspicions and reservations. He said Bobby is sneaky and manipulative. He's been known to start rumors with the media when he sees an edge to be gained, and find underhanded ways to get intelligence on what the other side is up to. Hell, Arthur even said I'd be better off not knowing how Bobby does his job, that I should just let him do it. He also pointed out that Bobby's an expert in attacking the other guy, which we've all seen in previous campaigns. I reminded Arthur that I've never lowered myself to negative campaign-ing and I won't start now."

"Get real, Blair!" Sam snapped, a scornful look on his face. "This is the big time. You need a guy like Bobby. You may need to sling some mud before this is over. Even if you don't, the other guy will, and Bobby will know how to handle it."

Blair stood up and began pacing as he contemplated Sam's words.

"Look, Blair," Sam continued in a more accommodating voice. "Keep Neil involved. He's a good soldier and a good friend. You can make him deputy campaign manager if you want. But you need Bobby. He's a proven winner at this level. This may be a once-in-a-lifetime chance for you. You've got to do what it takes to win."

Blair threw up his arms in a gesture of surrender. "Okay, I give up. Politics is the art of compromise, right? It's against my better judgment, but I'll take your advice. Bobby's the guy. I'll call him in the morning."

"Good man!" Sam replied enthusiastically, getting up and slapping Blair on the back. "He's the right guy, Blair, you'll see. There will come a time in this campaign when things get nasty—you can count on it. When that happens, we need a guy like Bobby in our corner."

Blair looked from Sam to Kimberly. "I hope I don't live to regret this."

CHAPTER 31

Freddy Salazar and Martin Schwartz walked briskly through the Russell Senate Office Building toward the office of Senator Henry Hamilton, Republican candidate for president. The sound of their footsteps clicking in unison on the ancient marble floor echoed loudly through the deserted corridor. They were an odd-looking pair. Schwartz, the campaign's chief media strategist, was short, trim, and stylishly dressed, looking like he had just stepped away from a television anchorman's desk. Salazar, Senator Hamilton's campaign manager, looked like a former boxer, which is exactly what he was. There was a swagger in his step and an intense look in his dark eyes, as if he were ready for the next fight at any time.

Schwartz looked nervously at his watch. "What do you suppose this is about?" he asked. "When the boss summons us at 11:00 p.m., that can't be good."

"No shit," Salazar replied as they entered the senator's office.

Henry Hamilton sat behind his desk, shirtsleeves rolled up, reading glasses perched on the end of his thin nose as he studied a report containing a myriad of colorful pie charts and bar graphs. "Have a seat, gentlemen," he said in a brusque, no-nonsense voice.

Schwartz and Salazar seated themselves in the chairs in front of the senator's desk. Hamilton removed his glasses and unceremoniously thrust the report across the desk. "Have you seen this shit?" he asked, his tone turning sharp. He didn't wait for a reply. "These are the most recent polling results. It's a disaster! Van Howe has opened up an eight-point lead in the polls, and it's growing.

"Don't forget that there's a margin of error in those polls, Senator," Schwartz pointed out, trying to sound optimistic.

The senator waved his hand dismissively. "Any way you cut it, we're losing, and it's getting worse. We need to do something about this—now!"

Salazar eyed the senator coolly. They had worked together on three previous senatorial campaigns, and he knew his boss's moods, as well as his way of thinking. "Do you have something in mind, Senator?" he asked, knowing that was precisely why they had been summoned.

"You're damn right I do!" Hamilton slammed a fist into his desk, then pointed a long index finger at the polling results. "According to this data, one of the things people are saying about Van Howe is that they trust him. They're eating up his Mr. Integrity shit. Well, he can't possibly be as clean as he's holding himself out to be, and we need to prove that he's not. If the public sees that the Mr. Clean image is just a mirage, then he looks like a goddamn fraud, and his support will crumble like moldy cheese. We've got to find that dirt and get it out there fast."

Both advisers stared silently at the senator. "Well? Talk to me!" he demanded, raising his voice. "Does that make sense?"

"It makes perfect sense," Salazar responded, his lips curving upward, forming a trace of a smile. This was his kind of mission. He had handled similar tasks many times before with considerable success.

The senator turned toward his chief media strategist. "Martin?"

"It would be a great strategy, Senator, except for the fact that this guy has done an excellent job of keeping his nose clean. The fact is, we just don't have any dirt on him."

"Then find some, goddamn it!" Hamilton shouted. "We don't need a lot. Even the slightest indiscretion will help us show that this guy is a hypocrite and a phony! Even if he had one little fling years ago, we could make something big out of it."

"But, sir, there's no evidence of that," Schwartz pleaded. "Hell, look at his wife. Why would somebody fool around if he's got a wife who's that hot? He'd be crazy!"

"Maybe not," said Salazar. "By all accounts, she's a royal bitch. Their entire campaign staff is terrified of her."

"Well, then, maybe Van Howe is afraid of her, too," Schwartz replied. "But whether he's afraid of her or worships her, there's no evidence of infidelity or any other kind of misconduct since he arrived on the public scene."

"Shit!" Hamilton muttered. "What about before that?" he persisted, unwilling to relent. "Any problems when he was in college or law school? Did he represent any sleazy clients? Did he consort with shady characters? Come on, guys, there's something out there. There's got to be!"

"Well, there is this," said Salazar, pulling a copy of an old newspaper article out of his briefcase and handing it to Hamilton. "His former law partner and law school roommate is a convicted felon."

"Now you're talking!" Hamilton replied, rubbing hands together, a gleam in his eye as he perused the article. "We may have something here, some kind of guilt-by-association angle. Let's dig into this!"

Schwartz looked gloomy. "I hate to be pessimistic, Senator, but we've been down this path already. Van Howe was really smart about this. He actually turned it to his advantage during his first campaign for Congress. He threw his friend under the bus and publicly condemned him. He tied this into his law-and-order theme and used it as an example of the need for tighter laws and better enforcement. He came out completely unscathed. We've researched this thoroughly and didn't come up with anything useful at all."

Hamilton glared at his media adviser. "Then dig deeper," he demanded, his voice ominous. "Did you do anything other than read old newspaper articles? Things are not always what they appear to be, Martin. I shouldn't have to tell you that. I don't believe for one minute that Van Howe is the Boy Scout he pretends to be. We need to prove that. Start with that accident and keep digging until you find something. It's out there!"

CHAPTER 32

Danny Moran lifted his champagne glass and tapped it with his fork. For an instant, he flashed back to the last time he had held a champagne glass during a toast. It was the night of the Champions HealthCare banquet, a night that ended in tragedy and changed the course of his life. Things were different now. His champagne glass was filled with water. This occasion marked a joyous new beginning. He looked at the crowd of happy faces in front of him as an echo of silverware clinking against glass drowned out the lively chatter.

"I'd like to thank all of you for coming and for sharing in this special occasion," he began. "It's one of life's great joys to see those we love so happy. And it's also a great joy to see them embark on the most exciting and rewarding adventure life has to offer. As a father, I've always wanted the very best for my daughter. Now, as I look at the two of you, I know, beyond any doubt, that you are perfect for each other, and I couldn't be happier for you. You are two very special people, and you will accomplish great things over the course of your lives, but your greatest accomplishment, and your greatest gift, will be the love you have for each other."

He turned toward the stunning newlyweds seated to his left. "To Allie and Jason, all the best, and all our love."

He raised his glass, and the room burst into a spirited applause. Allie stood up and embraced her father tightly. Then she stepped back, and they stared at one another, both of them misty-eyed, but beaming.

"I love you, Pops," she stammered through her tears.

"I love you, too, Allie-Baba."

Danny turned toward Jason, and they shook hands warmly. "Congratulations, Jason. Take care of my little girl."

Jason smiled and looked at his bride. "You can count on it, sir."

Danny looked from one to the other. "I knew you two were right for each other the very first time I saw you together," he said, still glowing with unabashed pride and joy.

Allie gazed lovingly at her new husband. "So did I, Daddy."

That had been ten years earlier, when they were seniors in high school. They had been dating ever since, although for much of that time, it had been a long-distance romance. As a result of his disciplinary suspension during his senior year in high school, Jason had lost his scholarship opportunities with all of the big-time, Division I schools that had been eagerly recruiting him to play football. Not to be deterred, he attended a small Division III program in southern Indiana, where he was light-years ahead of the competition on the football field, and also distinguished himself in the classroom. That record, coupled with enthusiastic recommendations from his teachers and coaches regarding both his talent and his character, provided him the opportunity to transfer to a Division I school his sophomore year. Half a dozen schools offered him admittance, although none of them offered an athletic scholarship or even a guaranteed spot on the football team. He was required to try out as a walk-on and prove himself.

Jason opted to enroll at the University of Michigan, both because of its status as a collegiate football powerhouse and because it was close enough to Chicago that he and Allie would be able to see each other on weekends with some regularity. Through his drive, determination, and extraordinary talent, Jason quickly became a standout linebacker for the Michigan Wolverines. He was named to the All Big Ten team, both sophomore and junior years, leading the entire conference in tackles as a junior. A professional football career seemed like a real possibility until he suffered a serious neck injury in practice just before his senior season was to begin. Just like that, his football career was over.

Rather than feeling sorry for himself, Jason shifted gears and focused on his backup plan, which was medical school. That was the direction that Allie had chosen for herself, as well. Allie wound up at the University of Chicago, and Jason enrolled at Baylor in Houston. Their long-distance romance continued all through medical school. Following graduation, they were finally able to settle in the same city, as they both entered residency programs at Northwestern University Medical Center in Chicago. Despite the grueling hours, they made their time together a priority. Their shared residency experience served as a bond that drew them even closer together. Now, two years out of medical school, they were husband and wife.

The reception was held at Ridge Country Club, in the heart of the Beverly neighborhood. Danny was in a state of euphoria, and the evening passed as a happy blur. He tried his best to chat with each of the guests at some point during the evening, but with over two hundred friends and relatives in attendance, he found it impossible to have a meaningful conversation with anyone. But there was one serious conversation he needed to have.

The evening was getting late, and most of the crowd was either dancing to the upbeat music played by the energetic rock-and-roll band or watching the dancers. Danny looked around the room until he saw her, sitting at a table near the back, as far from the din as one could get. He took a seat next to her. "Our little girl looks beautiful tonight, doesn't she, Karen?"

She smiled at him. "She certainly does. And happy, too."

They looked at each other in silence for a long moment. Except for Allie's graduation ceremonies, Danny hadn't seen his ex-wife since she had left him ten years ago. To his eyes, she hadn't aged a bit. Her fair skin was still flawless, with barely a trace of a wrinkle. Her blonde hair still looked natural and radiant. She looked as alluring to him as she always had, but something about her was different. There seemed to be an air of serenity about her, which certainly had never been there during their marriage.

"You look good, Karen."

"Thanks. So do you, Danny."

"Allie tells me that Bill is a great guy, and she's never seen you happier. I'm glad things have worked out so well for you."

"Thanks, Danny. I am happy. Life is good again."

Danny stared down at the table. "I have to admit, when I heard that you and Bill were getting married, it hit me hard. It hurt—partly because it was a painful reminder that I'd lost you, but also because it got me thinking again about why I lost you. I know how badly I must've hurt you when I was drinking the way I was. I tried to apologize in that letter I sent you right after I joined AA, but I really need to say this to your face."

He looked up into her pale blue eyes, which stared back with a kindness and understanding he had not seen in them for a long time. "I am truly sorry for what I put you through, Karen. It was cruel and selfish of me to treat you the way I did. I just hope you can understand that the way I behaved was never a reflection of my feelings for you. I honestly loved you and cared for you more than I can ever say, but I know I didn't act that way. I was out of control. Alcohol had a grip on me that I couldn't break, and you suffered because of it. Thank God, I finally was able to break that grip, but I know it was too late." He took a deep breath and let it out slowly. "I want you to know how deeply sorry I am and that I don't blame you in the least for leaving me. I gave you no choice. And I'm truly happy that you've been able to build a new life and that things have really worked out for you. You deserve to be happy."

Karen's clear blue eyes had become red and misty. "I never doubted your heart, Danny. I knew it was your addiction that caused you to do the things you did. You've always been the most kindhearted, compassionate man I've ever known. That's why I fell in love with you, and that's why I married you. And I'm so proud of the way you've turned your life around. Allie keeps me posted. She talks about you all the time, and I love hearing it."

There was a long silence between them. Karen glanced toward the dance floor and saw Bill walking in their direction. She picked up a napkin and wiped her eyes. She bit her lip to keep her voice from breaking. "Have a great life, Danny," she whispered in a soft voice, smiling at him warmly through watery eyes. She squeezed his arm affectionately as she rose from her seat and walked toward her husband.

***

Late that night, Danny sat in his living room armchair, the house dark but for the wavering blue light emanating from the lava lamp. He thought back over his daughter's life, trying to conjure up as many memories as he could—from her birth, through her childhood and teenage years, up to the present. It was a pleasurable exercise, one that filled him with a sense of well-being as he reflected upon what a happy life she had lived and what a promising future lay ahead of her.

His ruminations took him back to other aspects of his past. He thought about his ruined marriage. He thought about the promising career that never panned out the way he had envisioned. Then he thought about his life as it was today. He felt an overwhelming sense of joy as he reflected upon the special relationship he enjoyed with his wonderful daughter, who was embarking on an exciting new life. He thought about his conversation with Karen. He felt a comforting sense of closure, knowing that he had made his peace with her and that she had succeeded in making a fresh start and was genuinely happy. Then he thought about his own station in life. He was sober, he had good friends, and he was doing something that mattered. He drifted off to sleep in his chair, a feeling of peace and contentment settling over him as he realized that he, too, was in a very good place.

CHAPTER 33

Vic Slazak blinked several times as his eyes adjusted to the dim light of the Acey Deucey Bar. Outside, the sun was shining brightly at the beginning of what was certain to be another blistering hot day in Las Vegas. Inside, it was cool and dark. The smell of stale beer reminded him of the dive bars he'd frequented on the South Side of Chicago. The patrons also reminded him of home. Their accents were different, but for the most part, it was an assemblage of the working class and unemployed—some quiet, some friendly—lost souls seeking respite and shelter from their struggles with the outside world through the elixir of the alcoholic beverage.

That's where the similarity with Chicago's drinking establishments ended. This was clearly Las Vegas, as evidenced by the colorful slot machines scattered around the premises and the fact that a dive bar could draw a crowd at eight o'clock in the morning. That was not a reflection of the fact that boozers were more plentiful in Vegas; it was simply a natural consequence of the fact that days and nights were reversed for many in Sin City. Nighttime was prime time at the casinos, and many of the all-night gamblers wound up at places like this early in the morning, not quite ready to call it quits. Also, an entire element of the working population, like Slazak, lived a nocturnal existence, working the night shift and then finding their way to local drinking establishments like the Acey Deucey Bar when most of the rest of the world was having breakfast.

Slazak found a seat at the bar and ordered a shot and a beer. This had become his routine. He'd been working nights as a security guard for one casino or another since he'd landed in Vegas ten years ago. It was a depressing existence. He had no real friends, but then he had gotten by without any real friends throughout most of his adult life in Chicago. The difference was that he had loved his work then. He was a born investigator and considered himself as good as any in the business. That work gave him a sense of pride and a sense of purpose, both of which were sorely lacking now.

Slazak didn't need the money, since he had "retired" with his full pension from the Chicago Police Department. He worked because it gave him something to occupy his time, but he could never escape the feeling that the work was demeaning and beneath him. His primary responsibility was escorting patrons off the premises when they were unruly, either because they were drunk or because they had lost their shorts gambling. His other duty was shooing away hookers who didn't understand the concept of subtlety. The good ones were discreet and well behaved, and management was more than happy to have them around, because they were good for business. Slazak had gotten to know most of them and had become friendly with a few, which he considered perfectly natural, since he and they walked the same floor night after night, performing their respective jobs.

This morning, Slazak's mood was even more sour than usual. His boss, a foul-tempered, self-important bully who could never have held a job with any respectable police department, had just chewed him out for spending too much time consorting with the working girls. It took every ounce of self-restraint Slazak could muster to keep from punching out the pompous little shit, and he was still seething as he flung back the shot of whiskey and chased it with a long swallow of cold beer.

Slazak's eyes drifted to the television behind the bar, where he saw footage of Illinois Governor Blair Van Howe waving to the crowd at a Chicago White Sox baseball game after throwing out the ceremonial first pitch. The sound was turned off, so he couldn't hear the commentary, but the caption at the bottom of the screen read "Van Howe Widens Lead in Polls."

Perhaps it was the homesickness triggered by the image of his beloved White Sox; perhaps it was the scolding from that incompetent little prick of a boss; or perhaps it was a sight of a man whom he considered a liar, a hypocrite, and a despicable scoundrel on the cusp of being elected to the most powerful position on the planet. Whatever the reason, his mood transformed from sullen and irritable into a simmering rage.

Slazak glared at the smiling visage of the Democratic candidate for president. "You lying scumbag!" he said in a venomous voice. "I've had it with this shit. It's time to finish what I started!"

***

It was 9:00 p.m. in Washington, D.C., and Freddy Salazar sat alone at campaign headquarters, looking at the mountain of mail and stacks of telephone messages on his desk. It was Wednesday, and he'd been on the road for ten straight days, with campaign stops in St. Louis, Kansas City, Chicago, Milwaukee, and Detroit. He needed some late-night catch-up time.

Salazar flipped through the dozens of phone messages, placing them into two stacks, one for the calls he would return himself, and the other for calls he would delegate to staff members. Most of the names he recognized. They included well-known political figures being considered as a possible running mate; influential business leaders, usually calling in connection with fund-raising activities they were sponsoring; reporters with major newspapers or television networks; and politicians of all types from around the country, seeking favors or offering assistance.

One name he didn't recognize: Victor Slazak. Mr. Slazak had left messages on three consecutive days, the last two bearing notations from his secretary indicating that Mr. Slazak wouldn't explain who he was or the nature of his business, other than to say that it was extremely urgent and that he didn't want to talk with anyone other than Mr. Salazar. Freddy crumpled the messages and tossed them into the wastebasket. He was far too busy to waste time with a caller who wouldn't even explain the nature of his business.

It was close to midnight by the time Salazar had finished going through his mail and fine-tuning his schedule for the next several days. His cell phone rang as he was packing up his briefcase. He answered instinctively on the first ring.

"Hello?"

"Mr. Salazar, I'm glad I reached you. My name is Vic Slazak. Got a few minutes?"

Salazar glanced at his watch, irritated that a complete stranger would call him on his cell phone so late at night.

"It's almost midnight," he responded, making no attempt to conceal his annoyance. "What's this about?"

Slazak got right to the point. "I have information about Blair Van Howe that I think will interest you."

"What kind of information?" Salazar asked impatiently.

"Information that will blow this campaign wide open. Information that will demonstrate that he's not as squeaky-clean as he makes himself out to be. There's some dirty laundry in this guy's closet."

"Listen, mister, I don't know who you are. We get calls from crackpots and attention-seekers all the time. Unless you have something specific to tell me, I'm going to hang up."

"I understand, Mr. Salazar. That's fair enough. I'll be brief. Here's the story. There was an auto accident involving Van Howe's former law partner about ten years ago. It happened just as Van Howe was running for Congress for the first time. You can research much of what I'm about to tell you to confirm its accuracy."

"So what has that got to do with Van Howe?" Salazar snapped. His voice was impatient, but his interest was keenly aroused, since his own staff had spent considerable time and effort researching the incident, trying in vain to find some basis to use it against Van Howe.

"It has everything to do with him—Van Howe was driving the car. He was responsible for killing the other driver. He fled the scene and framed his partner, letting him take the rap and go to jail."

There was a long silence on the other end of the line. "Listen, Mr. Slazak. I know about the accident. The other guy confessed. Why would he do that if Van Howe had been driving?"

"The guy who confessed was an alcoholic who was prone to blackouts. He was good and drunk that night and had absolutely no recollection of what happened, so it was easy for Van Howe to frame him. The poor bastard had no choice. He had to cop a plea or he'd have gotten massacred at trial and sent to prison for a long time."

Salazar was silent for another long moment, trying to evaluate what he had just heard. His mind was racing at the implications, and he desperately wanted to believe the story, but this was explosive, and he couldn't afford to be duped. "It's an interesting story, Mr. Slazak, but frankly, it sounds pretty far-fetched. Why should I believe you?"

"Because I was the cop who investigated this. You can check the Chicago Police Department records. When I started getting close to the truth, I got pulled off the case. My life was threatened, and I was run out of town. I've kept this to myself for ten years because I didn't think it was worth dying over. But now he's running for president, and people should know what I know."

"Then, as a cop, you can understand that I need more than a good story. I need evidence. Can you back up what you're telling me?" Salazar asked, his voice beginning to sound hopeful.

"I've got plenty of evidence. Let me tell you the whole story and you can evaluate it for yourself.

"Okay, Mr. Slazak, but not over the phone. I'd like to meet you in person, the sooner the better. When can we meet?"

"I'm planning on heading back to Chicago tomorrow afternoon. That's where the evidence is."

Salazar walked over to his desk and looked at his calendar. He drew a diagonal line through the entire next day's appointments. "When are you getting in?"

"Two o'clock, at Midway Airport."

"I'll meet you there."

***

Six hours later, Henry Hamilton's cell phone rang as he walked briskly on the treadmill in his Georgetown home. Few people had his private cell phone number, and those who had it knew better than to interrupt his morning workout. "What?" he shouted into the phone without breaking stride.

"It's me," said Freddy Salazar. "Sorry to bother you so early, but I wanted to let you know I won't be attending the strategy session this morning. Something has come up."

"Damn it, Freddy, I need you there! Our campaign is in the shitter, and we need to get it on track in a hurry. Whatever just came up will have to wait."

"I don't think so, Senator. Listen to this," Freddy replied, and then he briefed his boss on the late-night phone call from former detective Vic Slazak.

"I knew it!" Hamilton exclaimed triumphantly. "I knew there was something not right about Van Howe. I could just smell it! This could be exactly what we need, Freddy. Get on it right away, and keep me posted!"

"I'll do that. I'm meeting with Slazak this afternoon. I'll check in as soon as I have anything to report."

"Excellent! Good man, Freddy! Keep a tight lid on this for now, okay? If it turns out that there's something to this, we'll get the whole team together and decide how to play it. If that story's true, it'll blow this thing wide open!"

CHAPTER 34

To Vic Slazak, walking through the bustling summer crowds at Midway Airport felt like a visit with a long-lost friend. The airport had expanded considerably since he'd last seen it ten years ago on his hurried trip to Las Vegas; however, the aura felt the same. He was surrounded by Chicago faces, Chicago accents, Chicago sports jerseys, and Chicago baseball hats. Even the profanity he heard was distinctly Chicago. He hadn't heard anyone called a "jagoff" during the entire time he'd been in Vegas—and plenty of people there were deserving of such a title. These were his kind of people, and this was his kind of place. He was home, and he felt alive again.

Slazak stopped at the airport food court and ordered a bratwurst with mustard and onions. He ate slowly, savoring every bite of the hometown delicacy. He felt invigorated, partly from being home again, but mostly because he was embarking on a mission that mattered. He was there to bring closure to the last investigation he had handled for the Chicago Police Department, an investigation he'd never finished. He was determined to finish it now. There was a chance that his enemies, whoever they might be, were long gone, or that they had no further interest in his business. But if he encountered resistance, so be it. He was ready for combat.

Slazak walked outside and again was immediately reminded that he was home. It was a typical summer day in Chicago, warm and muggy, but refreshingly different from the blast furnace effect he experienced whenever he set foot outdoors in Las Vegas on a summer afternoon. He looked around and dialed a number on his cell phone. "I'm right in front, outside the baggage claim area," he said into the phone. "I'm wearing a white shirt and carrying a black duffel bag."

"I see you," came the reply. "I'm pulling up right now— the black Town Car."

Slazak hopped in and exchanged greetings with Freddy Salazar.

"Let's talk as we drive," Salazar suggested. "Nothing personal, but for the time being, I think we should avoid being seen together in public."

"Fine by me," Slazak replied. "Where shall I start?"

"Just tell me everything you know about the accident. You gave me the big picture on the phone last night. I want to know the details. Tell me everything that makes you think Van Howe was involved."

Slazak stared intently at Freddy Salazar for several moments. "Okay, here's what I know. First, when I arrived at the accident scene, the guy who confessed, Moran, was behind the wheel, so drunk that he was passed out. But thirty minutes earlier, a call was placed from his cell phone to 911. He wouldn't have made that call and then passed out, still buckled into his seat. Someone else called from his phone. Second, there was a witness at the scene, the victim's daughter. She told me that a man approached her and spoke to her before the police arrived. The police claimed that no one was on the scene when they arrived.

I think someone was there, and then fled before the police arrived. Here's why I think that. The valet at the restaurant remembers Moran getting into his car to head home, but he said that someone else was driving. He was positive about that."

"And you think that person was Governor Van Howe?"

"Absolutely. They drove to the restaurant together, and they live just two blocks apart, so it stands to reason that they would have gone home together. But I'm basing this on more than just logic and supposition. Like I said, the valet told me someone else was driving the car. Besides that, there was blood in Moran's car, and he didn't have a scratch on him. And, the very next day, Van Howe is walking around with a big bandage on his finger."

"Anything else?"

"Yeah, when I started chasing down these leads, I was pulled off the case. I kept sniffing around on my own time, and the next thing I knew I was attacked in my own house and told to leave town or I'd be a dead man. I've been a cop for twenty years, and I know the difference between scare tactics and a real threat. Those guys meant business. I left town because I knew I'd be dead if I didn't."

Freddy Salazar pulled into the parking lot of the Mid-America Inn, a low-budget hotel a few miles from the airport. He parked the car and took a long, hard look at his passenger. "You tell a good story, Mr. Slazak, and I'm inclined to believe you, but this will rock the world if it goes public, so I need more than just a good story. I need evidence."

"That's why I came back to Chicago," Slazak replied, meeting Salazar's steady gaze. "I've got some hard evidence that will be very compelling. I entrusted it to one of my former colleagues here for safekeeping. I intend to get my hands on it right away, and once I do, I'll share it with you."

Salazar's eyes narrowed. "What kind of evidence are we talking about?"

"A couple of things that are pretty damn incriminating. The first is the lab report analyzing the blood collected from Moran's car that night. The second is a recording of the 911 call."

"And who's got this evidence?" demanded Salazar.

"I'll have it within the next day or two, so where it resides today is not your concern," Slazak said coolly.

"It *is* my concern," Salazar insisted. "For all I know, you could be fabricating this evidence yourself. I need to be able to assess its reliability."

Slazak stared hard at Freddy Salazar, trying to decide whether he was trustworthy. "Look, Salazar, I'm sure you can understand that I need to protect my sources. Somebody went out on a limb for me, and I'd be putting him in a tight spot if I revealed his identity."

"I understand that, Mr. Slazak, but you need to understand the significance of this information. You're talking about serious allegations against the man who is the leading candidate to become president of the United States. I can't make allegations like this without having complete confidence in their accuracy, and I can't be confident without knowing where this evidence is coming from."

Slazak hesitated. It was contrary to all of his principles to betray a colleague who had risked his own neck to help him out, yet he had to weigh that against the need to gain Salazar's trust, since Salazar was his vehicle for publicizing the truth. "I asked a colleague of mine in the evidence lab to keep copies of those things for me," Slazak said, with obvious reluctance.

"What's his name, Slazak?"

"Why does that matter?" Slazak asked, irritation in his voice.

"Because I need to know that this guy is real, and that he is who you say he is."

Slazak hesitated again. "Can you assure me you'll keep his identity to yourself? I don't want anyone contacting him—not you, not the media, or anyone else for that matter. I need your commitment on that."

"You got it. What's his name?"

"His name is Mike Nolan. Check the Chicago PD's records, if you want. Check their records on me while you're at it. They'll show that I left the force within a week of the Moran accident. They'll show that I retired with a full pension, even though I had only twenty years of service rather than the thirty it takes for full benefits. That was supposed to give me another reason not to make waves, in case the risk of getting my head blown off wasn't enough!"

Freddy Salazar looked steadily at Vic Slazak. "That leaves me with just one question."

"Which is?"

"What do you want out of this? Money, I presume?"

Slazak shook his head, giving Salazar an indignant glare. "*What do I want?* Jesus Christ, you people are jaded. I don't want a goddamn thing! I'm just trying to do what's right. That bastard has no business running our country. He belongs in jail! I want him to get what he deserves."

Salazar nodded slowly, then held out a meaty hand. "Thanks, Slazak. You're doing your country a real service. Call me when you have that evidence."

***

Senator Henry Hamilton answered his cell phone on the first ring. "Talk to me, Freddy," he ordered, a sense of urgency in his voice.

"I think this guy is for real, boss," Freddy blurted out, his normally dour and skeptical demeanor giving way to unadulterated excitement. "And his story will absolutely destroy Van Howe!"

"I don't want to discuss this by phone. Get your ass back here right now. I want you to brief me tonight, as soon as you get back in town. I don't care how late it is. I'll call a staff meeting tomorrow to discuss how we play this."

"I'm on my way."

"Good man, Freddy!"

CHAPTER 35

Danny Moran took a special interest in the presidential campaign solely because of his history with the front-runner, Illinois Governor Blair Van Howe. There was something exciting about the possibility of having a close personal connection with the president of the United States, even if that connection and their friendship had come to an abrupt halt years ago. Aside from his interest in this one particular candidate, politics was no longer part of Danny's life. Years ago, while he was still practicing law, he had been an adviser and confidant of many local politicians, and therefore was closely involved and keenly interested in politics at all levels, local, state, and national. Now, that life was but a distant memory, and the world of politics was of little concern to him.

Danny had been presented with opportunities to reestablish himself in that universe. He'd been approached on multiple occasions by prominent lobbying and consulting firms that believed his legal and business acumen, coupled with his political instincts and connections, made him a valuable commodity, even without a law license. The offers were lucrative, and the work would have been a natural extension of his prior professional life. He was intrigued and appreciative of the offers, but he politely rejected every one of them. He was living a different lifestyle now, and was quite content.

For the past eight years, Danny had been a professor at Loyola University near downtown Chicago, where he taught business law to undergraduates and MBA students. He liked teaching, and he genuinely enjoyed the interaction with the impressionable young students, but what he liked most was the fact that it was not all-consuming. The hours were manageable, which left him time for what had truly become the central focus in his life: his involvement with Alcoholics Anonymous.

The AA program had worked for him. He'd been sober for almost ten years now. However, the program had become far more than just a means of avoiding the bottle. Danny had completely immersed himself in it and found that it had given his life meaning and purpose. Over the years, he had helped countless people as their AA sponsor—a guide, mentor, resource, and friend, someone who helped them fight their battle against alcoholism and live by the AA creed. Some made it and some didn't. Many were still works in progress, like his friend Pat Jordan, whom he had met at his very first AA meeting, but who had been dropping in and out of the program for years. To Danny, Pat was a special project, and he never gave up on him.

Even after nearly ten years of sobriety, Danny still craved routine in his life, and the flexible job hours enabled him to live that way. He made his to-do lists every day and followed them with uncompromising discipline. He drank his soft drinks and ate his snacks precisely in accordance with his schedule. The St. Martin's chapter of AA still held its meetings on Tuesday and Friday evenings, and he attended them religiously. Coffee and dessert at the South Side Diner afterward continued to be part of the routine. Some of the faces were the same—Judge Andy, for example—however, there had been a steady stream of new participants over the years. Some of them became regulars and others abruptly vanished from the program.

Aside from Tuesdays and Fridays, Danny purposely left the other evenings unscheduled. During his first few years of sobriety, he had sought out AA meetings at other locations to fill most of his evenings. That had changed over the years, partly because he felt a greater level of security about his sobriety, but also because he was frequently in demand by members of the program who needed companionship or encouragement. Sometimes those visits were casual and relaxed; other times, he was responding to desperate cries for help.

Over the past several weeks, Danny had been spending a considerable amount of time with a young man by the name of T. J., who had shown up at a meeting looking scared and uneasy, as most first-timers did. Danny had made a point of trying to put the young man at ease during the meeting, and invited him to join the coffee and dessert crowd at the diner afterward. T. J. accepted, but despite the best efforts of the group to make him feel comfortable and welcome, he was obviously ill at ease. Danny sensed that the young man was painfully shy and perhaps socially inept, and that the large, boisterous crowd was just too much for him. He walked T. J. out of the restaurant and offered to meet him for coffee the following evening, alone. T. J. gratefully accepted, and for the next two evenings, they met at the South Side Diner for coffee and blueberry pie.

During those visits, T. J. divulged little about himself or his situation, other than the fact that he was twenty-two years old and had been drinking and doing drugs since he was fourteen. T. J. continued attending regular AA meetings, although he declined Danny's invitation to pick him up and drive together. Danny understood. It was clear that T. J. did not want others to know where he lived, as that might reveal his identity and more about himself than he was ready to share. They met privately for coffee and pie several more times, until T. J. confided that he really wasn't a coffee drinker and was trying to watch his weight.

Exercise had been part of Danny's routine since he became sober. He walked precisely three and a half miles every day, regardless of the weather. He had five different walking routes through the neighborhood, each of which he had measured precisely to confirm the mileage. Upon learning of T. J.'s desire to lose weight, Danny invited the young man to join him on his exercise walk rather than going out and consuming calories. T. J. happily agreed, and they began walking together at four thirty every afternoon.

As with many who were new to the program, the "anonymous" aspect of AA was critical to T. J.'s willingness to participate in it. He had never divulged his last name, nor anything about his family, the kind of work he did, if any, or where he lived. He purposely avoided asking other AA members personal questions out of fear that they would ask about his life. That tended to make conversation stilted and difficult.

After three weeks of walking together, Danny had developed a genuine fondness for his young walking partner. T. J. was awkward and nervous in a crowd, but he loosened up considerably during their walks. He was clearly a lost soul who had lived a tough life, but there was a quiet warmth, a good sense of humor, and an undeniable intelligence that had become increasingly evident through their conversations. Danny sensed that a level of trust had clearly been established and that it was just a matter of time before T. J. would really open up and talk about his life. Danny awaited that time patiently, knowing that it was much easier to help someone once you truly knew and understood him.

"Let's stop and rest for a few minutes," Danny said to T. J. as they approached the playground at Beverly Park, the halfway point on their walk. "I thought I was in decent shape, but I'm feeling a little winded today."

T. J. looked amused. "Now, there's a switch," he said. "I'm the one who's fat and out of shape and always slowing you down. Are you feeling okay?"

"I never thought that just walking could wear me out," Danny replied, taking a seat on the nearby swing. "I must be getting old."

T. J. sat on the adjacent swing. "Well, you're still in much better condition than I am, even if you are an old coot." T. J. smiled and began swinging slowly back and forth, just a few feet in either direction. "You're whipping me into shape, though, Danny. I haven't had regular exercise like this in I don't know how long. It feels good. I actually look forward to these walks. In fact, it's the highlight of my day."

Danny looked at his young friend and returned the smile. "I'm glad to hear that, T. J. I look forward to it, too."

Danny started swinging, also, matching T. J.'s easy pace. T. J. looked at him and grinned as he began pumping his legs, swinging faster and higher. Danny began pumping, too, trying to keep up. It became a competition, each pumping furiously, trying to swing higher than the other. Danny glanced at T. J. and saw a competitive fire in his eyes and a huge, open-mouthed grin, the first time he had seen anything resembling joy on the young man's face. Their swings rose until they were parallel to the ground.

"We look like damn fools!" Danny shouted.

"I don't give a shit! This is fun!" T. J. yelled back. "Yeeeee-haaaaa!" he hollered like an exuberant cowboy. They looked at each other and burst into wild, unrestrained laughter.

To anyone passing by, it would have been an odd sight: a trim, dignified-looking, middle-aged man and a large, overweight kid half his age swinging furiously and laughing uproariously as if they were small children. Eventually, they slowed to a stop, because their laughter had them doubled over, at risk of falling off of the soaring swings. They looked at each other again and were seized by another laughing fit, knowing how ridiculous they must have looked.

When the laughter subsided, Danny noticed that, for the first time since they had met, T. J. seemed truly relaxed and uninhibited. Danny sensed that a breakthrough might be imminent. He had been in similar situations with other alcoholics struggling to get a grip on their lives, and he recognized the signs of progress: the ability to trust another person, to accept friendship, and to stop punishing oneself and accept small doses of happiness.

They resumed their walk and were silent for a long while, but it was a comfortable silence. "Thanks for being there for me, Danny," T. J. said after they had walked several blocks. "It means a lot to me," he said softly, but without embarrassment, staring at the sidewalk.

"You're welcome, T. J."

"For the first time in years, I feel like I'm on a good path," T. J. explained. Danny said nothing, sensing that T. J. wanted to say more and not wanting to interrupt. "My life has been a mess for a long time," T. J. continued. "I've had some bad breaks, and they became my excuses for the booze and the drugs. I gave up, and I've been wasting my life away. And do you know what? Nobody cared. That made it so much worse, until you came along."

"What about your family?" Danny asked.

"My dad died when I was twelve. That's what started the downward spiral. It destroyed my mom. She got remarried about a year later, to a real jerk, and she's on husband number four now. She drinks a lot. I guess that runs in the family. Anyway, we don't keep in touch much."

"Do you have any brothers or sisters?"

"One sister, four years younger than me. She's got Down syndrome and lives in a home for people with special needs. I try to visit her as often as I can, but it's not like she can help me get my act together. She's got her own issues."

"Sounds like you've had it pretty rough, T. J., but I'm glad you're focused on the here and now rather than dwelling on your past. That's what you really need to do." Danny thought for a long moment, some part of him telling him not to probe deeper. "So, how did your dad die?" he asked with some hesitation.

"He was killed in a car wreck, by a drunk driver," T. J. replied matter-of-factly.

"When was that, T. J.?" Danny asked, a sense of anxiety gripping him.

"Well, I'm twenty-two now, so that would make it ten years ago."

Danny felt a cold chill overtaking him. "By the way, what does *T. J.* stand for?" he asked, trying his best to sound nonchalant.

"Thomas Joseph," T. J. replied. "I used to go by Tommy when I was little, but I just felt like I wanted to change my identity when my mom remarried for the first time. So I became T. J. T. J. McGrath."

Danny's stomach did a somersault. He walked in stunned silence, trying to process the information he had just received. T. J. chatted happily, more open and talkative than Danny had ever seen him. He talked about being ready to build a new future, about going back to school, maybe even applying to law school eventually. He talked about job prospects that he might pursue while he went back to community college. He talked about ramping up his exercise program and really getting into shape so he'd feel as good physically as he did mentally.

Danny barely heard him. He was grappling with the undeniable reality that had just sunk in: he was the drunk driver, the one responsible for killing T. J.'s father and destroying his family. Could he possibly confront T. J. with that harsh reality? For what purpose? Should he make that confession now, when T. J. had at last seemed ready to pull his life together, when he finally felt that there was someone he could trust and confide in? How could he tell him that? It seemed so cruel. Yet his conscience tortured him. Knowing what he now knew, how could he conceal this information? Friendship and trust were based on honesty. How could he expect T. J. to believe he was trustworthy if he kept such a secret?

They reached the end of their trek, T. J. having chattered virtually the entire way since they left the park.

"Same time tomorrow, Danny?" he asked.

"Yeah, sounds good, T. J.," Danny replied, looking and sounding distracted.

T. J. looked at him closely. "Are you okay, Danny? You don't seem like yourself."

Danny stared at his young friend for a long moment, looking troubled. "T. J. ... there's something I need to tell you."

"Sure, what is it?" T. J. responded, starting to tense, based on the anxious look on Danny's face.

"That car accident ten years ago ... the one that killed your father ..." Danny began, his voice trembling. "It was me. I was the drunk driver who drove him off the road."

T. J. stared at him blankly, his mouth hanging open, unable to speak.

Danny continued. "My full name is Daniel Moran. Ten years ago, I was in a car accident with a man named Terry McGrath, who lived at Ninety-first and Hamilton. He died shortly after the accident. I went to prison—"

"It was *you?*" T. J. broke in, looking incredulous, his voice shaking. "*You* killed my father?"

"I'm afraid so, T. J. I didn't know until just now. I can't tell you how sorry—"

"You killed my father?" T. J. asked again in a loud voice, his shock quickly transforming into rage. "I can't believe this! You ruined my life!" he shouted angrily, tears streaming down his face. "You ruined my mother's life! You destroyed our family!" He stormed away, turning around after he'd gone ten feet. "Screw you, man! Stay the hell out of my life!" He ran off.

***

That evening, Danny sat in his living room armchair, feet up on the ottoman, flipping through his devotional like he did at the end of every day. The Scriptures and inspirational thoughts almost always brought him comfort and peace of mind. Tonight, he couldn't focus on the words or the thoughts. He was consumed by misery and remorse. He had known for years that he had grievously harmed the McGrath family, and that guilt would always be with him. But learning of the consequences firsthand brought back a harsh sense of reality and renewed pain.

His heart broke for T. J. and the difficult life he had endured for the last ten years. He felt a profound sense of anguish as he imagined what T. J. was going through at that moment as he confronted the possibility of his world crashing down around him again, just when there'd been some glimmer of hope.

He turned off the reading lamp and sat in the darkness. After a while, he flipped on the lava lamp and stared absently at the molten wax, amorphous, contorted shapes rising and falling in the blue water as he tried to blink back the tears. The effort was too much for him, and he gave up trying, weeping bitterly until he drifted off into a fitful sleep.

CHAPTER 36

Vic Slazak awoke feeling exhilarated, now that he was back in investigative mode again. It had taken a little creativity and a healthy dose of bullshit to coax a reluctant campaign staffer into providing Freddy Salazar's private cell phone number, but he had gotten it. Likewise, it took a bit of effort to locate Mike Nolan, who had left the Chicago Police Department nearly five years ago, but he had succeeded.

Nolan and a colleague had launched their own investigation and forensic testing company, where he was able to parlay his considerable skills into a growing and lucrative business. Their clients included private companies, county coroners' offices, and an expanding list of suburban police departments that found it more economical to outsource non-routine evidence work than to try to maintain a staff with the necessary expertise, which was hard to find.

"Nolan? This is Vic Slazak." Slazak was genuinely pleased to hear an old familiar voice answering his phone call.

There was a long pause on the other end of the line. "Vic Slazak? Jesus Christ, it's been a long time. I figured you were probably dead, finally pissed off the wrong guy or something."

Slazak chuckled. "No, I'm not dead. I just moved away for a while, but I'm back now. Just got into town."

"Well, welcome back, Slazak." Nolan sounded cheerful and friendly. "So, I'm sure you're not calling to invite me to a ball game. What can I do for you?"

Slazak laughed again. "You're right on the money, as usual, Nolan. I'll get right to the point. I'm here because I'm finishing up some old business. Do you remember, right before I left, I was working on an auto accident case involving a drunk driver who ran somebody off the road and killed him?"

"How could I forget? You asked me to hang onto some evidence for you and told me I'd be in deep shit if anything ever happened to it."

"You've got a good memory, Nolan. Were you able to get that stuff and put it somewhere for safekeeping?"

"It was against my better judgment, but I did it. I've got it in a safe at home. At least I don't have to worry about getting fired by the police department anymore."

"Excellent! Mind if I take it off your hands?"

"I've been hoping you would, but once you have it, you have to promise to leave me out of whatever it is you're up to. I don't want any part of it," Nolan said sternly.

"You have my word. And I can assure you, I'm not up to anything devious. I'm just trying to make sure that an old case gets handled the right way."

"I believe you, Slazak," Nolan said agreeably. "I didn't always agree with your methods, and sometimes you were a real horse's ass, but I never questioned your motives."

"Thanks, Nolan. Hey, if you've got a minute, I'd like to test your memory. Mind if I ask you a couple of questions?"

"Not at all. Fire away."

"Good. First, I know it's been a long time, but I was wondering whether you might recall the content of that blood analysis report?"

"Yeah, there wasn't much to it. It was just a preliminary screening, no DNA testing. All it shows is that the blood recovered from that vehicle was Type B negative."

"Like I said, you've got a great memory. What about the 911 recording? Is the quality good?"

"As I recall, it's perfect. I remember the caller saying he'd been in an accident and that the guy in the other car was hurt pretty bad. That's about all there was to it."

"Did the caller sound drunk?"

"Hmmm ... Not that I remember, but it was ten years ago. I seem to recall him sounding a bit panicked, which is pretty normal, but I don't remember thinking that the guy sounded drunk."

"Did you recognize the voice?" Slazak asked, trying hard to sound nonchalant.

"No. Should I?"

"Probably not. I was just curious."

"Well, like I said, it's a good quality recording, so it may be fairly easy to recognize the voice if you think you know who it is."

"I'd like to get my hands on that stuff as soon as I can. When can I come by and get it?"

"I'll be home about seven o'clock tonight, so any time after that is fine. I live in Oak Lawn now." He gave Slazak the address.

"Thanks, Nolan. I still owe you."

"Yes, you do, Slazak, and don't think I'll forget it."

Slazak was about to hang up, but caught himself. "Hey, Nolan, how's everything with you?" he asked in a voice that was softer and sincere. "Has life treated you okay since you left the force?"

"Life is good, Slazak. Thanks for asking. I'll see you tonight."

CHAPTER 37

Like sharks sensing blood in the water, the inner circle of the Hamilton campaign organization was in a frenzied state, eager to launch into attack mode. Freddy Salazar had just briefed the team on his meeting with the former Chicago cop whose story could dramatically alter the course of the presidential election campaign. In addition to Hamilton and Salazar, the inner circle consisted of George Raines, director of campaign strategy; Susan Nash, deputy campaign manager; and Martin Schwartz, chief media adviser. Due to the nature of the issue, Schwartz's two assistant media advisers, Derrick Woods and Tina Witherspoon, were also present.

The entire group seemed to be talking at once, as soon as Salazar finished sharing his report. Henry Hamilton raised his arms and whistled loudly. "Okay, listen up, team. We need to work together closely on this one, and we need to work fast. Let's talk about how we get this story out. There are lots of options. We could leak it to the media. We could call a press conference. We could have Slazak call a press conference. Or we could turn him loose with a single reporter, as long as it's the right one. There are probably plenty of other avenues as well. Tell me what you think."

George Raines spoke up first. "We need to keep our distance on this, Senator. If it comes from our camp, then some people will be skeptical, and it looks like we're fighting dirty. There's no need to go there. Let it come directly from the source, which is the cop."

"That's a good point, George, but I think we need to take a big step back before we go there," said Susan Nash. "Let's make sure that this guy is for real before we go off half-cocked with this thing. What do we know for certain? What evidence is there to back up this guy's story?"

Freddy Salazar spoke up. "I called our sources with the Chicago PD. Slazak left the force abruptly, right after the accident, just like he said. And I was able to confirm that he's been getting a full pension even though he was ten years short of qualifying for it, so that part of his story checks out, too. He also told me that he left incriminating evidence in the custody of a crime lab guy by the name of Nolan. My source tells me that there was an evidence technician on the force by the name of Michael Nolan, who left the department and went into private business about five years ago."

"That's not much," Nash replied curtly. "So, we know who this guy is, but exactly what evidence does he have?"

"I was just getting to that," said Salazar. "I spoke with Slazak by phone less than an hour ago. He confirmed that Nolan does have hard evidence, and that it will be in Slazak's hands tonight. More specifically, he's got a blood analysis report showing that the blood found in the car is Type B negative, which is fairly rare. Less than 2 percent of the population has that blood type. Van Howe made his medical records public, and guess what: he's Type B negative. Moran, the guy who was convicted, is Type O. And it gets better. There's a recording of the 911 call that was made from the accident site.

The quality of the recording is said to be excellent, and Slazak is convinced the voice will be recognizable as that of Blair Van Howe. I'd say that's pretty compelling stuff!"

"It may be, but let's not get ahead of ourselves," cautioned Schwartz. "Let's wait until we can examine the evidence for ourselves."

Again, multiple voices began chattering at once. Senator Hamilton allowed the animated and sometimes heated discussions to continue for several minutes; then he again raised his arms, gesturing for silence.

"Here's how I see this," he spoke over the crowd, which abruptly came to the attention. "Time is of the essence. We need to act fast. This is a once-in-a-lifetime opportunity, and we can't miss it. If this guy Slazak gets cold feet or disappears, we have nothing. He's ready to move, so we need to move now."

Martin Swartz looked doubtful. "But if his evidence doesn't pan out—"

Hamilton abruptly cut him off. "Slazak should have that evidence tonight, and he's agreed to share it with Freddy. We won't make any decisions until that happens, but in the meantime, let's get our plans in place. Hell, even if his evidence isn't as solid as we hope it'll be, the strongest evidence is Slazak himself. It doesn't matter whether he can prove his case beyond a reasonable doubt. He doesn't have to. The mere fact he comes forward with this story will raise all kinds of questions about Van Howe."

"And those questions themselves may cause Van Howe's lead in the polls to evaporate overnight," Freddy Salazar pointed out in a confident voice. "The court of public opinion doesn't require proof beyond a reasonable doubt."

Henry Hamilton paused for a long moment and stared at his advisers with a look of newly found confidence. "Ladies and gentlemen, elections are unpredictable. They can turn on a dime. Unexpected developments can dramatically alter the course of events. It looks to me like the outcome of this election may very well be in the hands of an ex-Chicago cop by the name of Victor Slazak."

CHAPTER 38

The late-August sunshine beat down on his face, and the sounds of summer surrounded him—lawnmowers, sprinklers, and the ubiquitous cicadas—as Danny Moran trudged along Longwood Drive, a gently winding street at the base of the city's only real hill. Perched atop the hill were stately old mansions built during the early part of the twentieth century by some of the most renowned architects of the time. Spacious, well-manicured lawns sloped downward toward the street, creating a scenic backdrop for a morning exercise walk.

Danny's walks had always invigorated him, physically and mentally. Until this past summer, he'd always walked alone and found it to be a good time for reflection and meditation. Therefore, it was with some reluctance that he had given up that solitary time to allow T. J. McGrath to join him in his daily exercise routine. Despite his reservations, Danny soon found that he enjoyed having T. J. accompany him, both because he felt it was doing T. J. some good and also because he truly enjoyed the company of his young friend. He hadn't seen or heard from T. J. since his startling and tragic revelation, and his walk now felt lonely.

For years, Danny's three-and-a-half-mile walk had taken him precisely one hour. The exercise had typically left him feeling clearheaded and energized, even when the elements were not cooperating. Today, the weather couldn't have been more pleasant, yet his legs felt heavy and his breathing labored before he got halfway through his route. The walks had been getting progressively more difficult over the past few months. He had tried to shrug it off as a natural part of the aging process, but he was only fifty-one years old. Then there was the persistent nagging pain in his abdomen and the sporadic vomiting for no apparent reason, as well as the fact that his friends had been telling him that he looked tired.

Danny sat down on a fire hydrant, not because it looked inviting or comfortable, but because he felt like he couldn't go on without stopping for a rest. "Crap," he muttered to himself. "I've got to do something about this."

He knew that, on some level, he'd been in denial. Life was so good for him now. He remembered telling Allie when he turned fifty that he felt better about himself than he ever had and that he was certain the best years of his life were right in front of him. He couldn't allow some pesky health issue to interfere with that. Yet he couldn't go on like this anymore, either. His daily walk had become a dreaded, grueling ordeal, rather than the invigorating highlight of his day that it used to be. He changed course and walked toward the office of his good friend, Dr. Rich Carroll, on Western Avenue, hoping that Rich would be able to see him without an appointment.

CHAPTER 39

Bobby Rosensteel was in his element as he scurried around the San Diego Convention Center. In three days, the place would be overrun with thousands of delegates, politicians, and reporters. This morning, the advance guards were doing their things: television crews setting up their equipment, security details receiving their briefings, facility personnel making sure that the seating and festive convention décor were just right.

Bobby had his own reasons for being there early. He wanted to personally ensure that the accommodations for his boss and the staff were suitable and that the setup of the stage and the convention floor was to his liking. In addition, he had scheduled meetings with party leaders and convention organizers to ensure that every aspect of the carefully choreographed program was precisely as he wanted it. He had also arranged pre-convention meetings with elected officials from key states where he needed those officials to be vocal and visible in their support of the Democratic nominee to get the vote out.

Bobby had attended every Democratic National Convention for the last twenty-eight years. Some were memorable and some were not. He was determined to leave nothing to chance and to make this one the most memorable yet. There would be no suspense this time, no surprises and no dissension within the party ranks. He could not remember going into a convention when the presidential nominee had generated such universal and enthusiastic support throughout the party. It was more than just party loyalty and support—it was unabashed excitement, an infectious exuberance generated by a candidate whose charisma sparked comparisons to our greatest presidents. His popularity was soaring, as evidenced by an ever-widening gap between him and the Republican candidate, Henry Hamilton. This would feel like a coronation. It would be a celebration and a preview of the inauguration festivities that would surely follow when Blair Van Howe was elected president of the United States in sixty-nine days.

Bobby's cell phone rang as he chatted with the television engineers, checking out the various camera angles on their monitors. He looked at the caller ID, excused himself, and walked away from the television technicians to answer the call.

"Bobby, it's me. Can you talk?"

Bobby Rosensteel felt a rush of adrenaline at the sound of the voice. It was Derek Woods, his mole inside the Hamilton camp. He had given Woods strict instructions not to contact him by phone except under the most urgent circumstances.

"Hold on, Woodsie, let me get to a quiet place." Bobby stepped outside and walked along the expansive concourse overlooking San Diego Harbor, blinking as his eyes adjusted to the brilliant sunshine sparkling off the blue waters. "Okay, talk to me," he ordered.

"Hamilton's team is about to drop a bombshell," Woods said in a voice that was low and urgent. "They've come into some information that implicates Van Howe in a messy situation that happened ten years ago. If it's true, this could blow Van Howe right out of the water."

***

Sam McIntire awoke to the sound of loud pounding on his hotel room door. "Hold on, I'm coming," he bellowed irritably. He opened the door, and Bobby Rosensteel rushed past him into the room.

"You haven't been straight with me, Sam!" Bobby shouted, flailing his arms. "I need you to come clean right now!"

"I don't know what you're talking about," Sam shot back, looking surprised and angry.

"When I accepted this assignment, I told you and I told Blair, no surprises! I told you that if there were any skeletons in the closet, I needed to know about them up front. Remember that?"

Sam glared at him. "What's your point?"

"You've been holding back on me, both of you!"

Sam drew himself up to his full height and glowered at the agitated little man in front of him. "What the hell are you talking about, Bobby?"

"Here's what I'm talking about: Hamilton's camp has information about a car accident that happened ten years ago. My sources tell me that they believe Blair was driving home from a party late one night, and he ran somebody off the road. The guy was killed. Blair's former partner was with him, but he was drunk and passed out. They claim to have evidence that Blair fled the scene and framed his partner, who wound up in jail. Please tell me that's not true, Sam!"

"Shit!" Sam muttered angrily, turning his back on Bobby and walking toward the window.

"Sam?" Bobby's voice rose with alarm at the lack of any denial.

"That's bullshit," Sam replied in a steady voice after a long silence. "At least, most of it."

"Tell me what part of it is *not* bullshit," Bobby demanded.

"Here's what happened," Sam said slowly, still staring out the window at the sailboats darting around the harbor. "Blair and his partner, Danny Moran, were at a reception late on a Saturday night. Moran drove home, but he was pretty loaded. He passed out at the wheel and drove a guy off the road, into a tree, and the guy died a few days later. Blair did what he could. He tried to help the guy out of the car, but he couldn't get him out. He was really wedged in there. Moran wasn't hurt, but he was passed out. Blair called 911, and when they got close, he took off. It was stupid as hell, but Blair had just announced his candidacy for Congress. He was afraid that if word got out that he was there at the accident scene, the public would find fault with him—you know, guilt by association." Sam turned around and shrugged. "That's what happened," he said meekly. "Blair didn't cause the accident. There was nothing he could have done to save the guy other than what he did."

"So Blair wasn't driving?"

"Hell, no! Whoever is telling that story is crazy. Moran confessed, for Chrissakes!"

"So why didn't you tell me all of this before?" Bobby asked, his voice still harsh.

"We thought it was a nonissue," Sam replied. "It happened ten years ago. No one pointed any fingers at Blair then, so it just didn't seem to matter," said Sam, his tone almost apologetic.

"Well, Henry Hamilton is going to try to convince the world that it does matter. And they claim to have evidence putting Blair at the scene."

"Evidence?" Sam sounded puzzled. "What evidence could they possibly have?"

"For starters, they claim to have a recording of the 911 call you just mentioned."

"Son of a bitch! What else?"

"There's a police report showing that blood was found in Moran's car—blood that matches Blair's blood type and not Moran's. They also claim there was a witness, the daughter of the driver who was killed."

"Does Hamilton's team have this evidence?"

"Not yet. It sounds like their source doesn't have it yet either. He's a former cop who's been in Vegas for the past ten years. He claims that he left the evidence with somebody inside the Chicago Police Department for safekeeping. He's on his way to get it."

Sam rubbed his big right hand vigorously over his face, up and down. "Look, Bobby, if they don't have this evidence, then all they have is the word of some crazy ex-cop who's just trying to get some attention, right? Like I said, Moran confessed."

Both men were in action mode now, past their anger, trying to formulate a plan. Bobby paced across the room, hands behind his back. "I know somebody who's got some contacts with the Chicago PD. They might be able to take a look at that evidence to see what's really there. With a little luck, it just may happen to get lost."

"Let me handle it, Bobby," Sam insisted. "It's my town, and I can assure you, I've got the right connections. I shut this down the first time, and I can do it again!"

Bobby eyed Sam skeptically. "Okay, but listen to me, Sam. Don't do anything stupid, got it? We can't risk drawing attention to this. If we can't make this go away quietly, we'll just need to be prepared to respond when Hamilton attacks. We'll point out that this is ten years old, the driver confessed, and it's just a desperate attempt to smear a good man's name, based on a wild, uncorroborated story from an attention-seeking, has-been cop."

"I'll take care of it," Sam said resolutely.

"Who else knows about this little incident, Sam?" Bobby asked, looking worried.

"Nobody except me, Blair. and Kimberly."

"Is there anything else you haven't told me, Sam?"

Sam glared again. "No, Bobby. There's nothing else."

"I need to have a serious talk with Blair," Bobby said. "But if it looks like this may blow over, I'll wait a few days. We can't have him rattled going into the convention. He needs to be focused and at his best."

***

Kimberly Van Howe looked at herself in the bedroom mirror in her upscale Georgetown townhouse. She'd been trying on various outfits that she was considering for the convention. She smiled smugly at herself in the mirror, knowing full well that she looked great in all of them. Her phone rang, and she ignored it until the answering machine clicked on and she heard her father's voice. "Kimberly, pick up the phone. It's important!"

"Hi, Daddy," she said sweetly. "I was in the shower. What's up?"

"I need to talk to Blair right away. Is he there?"

"No, he just left. He's having lunch with Senator Couch."

"See if you can get him on the phone, okay? I need him right now!"

"What is it, Daddy? Something's wrong—tell me."

Sam hesitated, then told his daughter about the conversation he'd just finished with Bobby Rosensteel.

"Oh, my God, not now! How can this be happening?" she stammered through tears of rage and frustration.

"Kimberly, I'm dealing with it, but I need Blair now. Find him!"

Within ten minutes, Blair Van Howe called his father-in-law in his San Diego hotel room and listened as Sam recounted the story he had just heard from Bobby Rosensteel.

"Blair, I'm telling you this because I didn't want you to get blindsided when Bobby confronts you. But for now, you need to forget about it and focus on the convention. Bobby and I have some ideas for handling this. Leave it in our hands. You just focus on the convention, and we'll deal with this when it's over." There was an urgency and forcefulness in Sam's voice.

"How can I forget about it, Sam? This could be an absolute disaster! What does Bobby say?"

"He didn't even want you to know yet because he wants you focused on the convention, which is precisely what you need to be doing. But remember, when you do talk to him, your story is that you just left the scene—you weren't driving. That's what I told him, and no one can ever prove any different."

"I don't know about this, Sam," Blair said doubtfully. "Bobby is my campaign manager. I have to trust him. Maybe we should tell him everything."

"Not a chance!" Sam said emphatically. "He might resign, then there'd be all kinds of questions and rumors and innuendo, even if he kept his mouth shut. We need to stick to our story, Blair. There's a big difference between leaving the scene of an accident when you can't do anything to help compared with driving the car and ... what actually happened. Anyway, the situation is contained. I just wanted to be sure you knew what I told Bobby."

"One more question," Blair asked, sounding dazed and despondent. "How do we know what Hamilton's got?"

"Bobby's got a source in Hamilton's inner circle."

"My God, Sam, what kind of people are we dealing with?"

CHAPTER 40

The timing would work out nicely. Nolan had suggested that Slazak stop by his home sometime after seven o'clock that evening, which gave Slazak the entire day to pursue the other loose end he needed to tie up: Ashley McGrath.

Slazak knew that if Nolan came through with his evidence, he would have a pretty compelling case. However, it would be far more compelling if Ashley McGrath supported his story. There was nothing like an eyewitness to move a case from the realm of conjecture and possibility to the realm of certainty. He had told Freddy Salazar that his eyewitness could put Blair Van Howe at the scene of the accident. He needed to tell Salazar that to be sure that he got his attention. Now he had to find her and determine what kind of witness she would really make.

During their only other encounter, Ashley had been adamant that there was a man at the scene before the police arrived. She had been convincing, too. Ten years ago, Slazak had intended to follow up with Ashley to show her pictures of Van Howe and ask whether he was that man, but he never got that opportunity. That was a long time ago, and it was entirely possible that Ashley wouldn't remember now. Also, she clearly had some type of mental disability and was probably in shock following the accident. Van Howe's people would surely raise all of those points if Ashley came forward as a witness. But Slazak didn't need to prove his theory in a court of law. He just needed to raise serious questions, and the media would do the rest. There was plenty of solid circumstantial evidence, even if he couldn't find Ashley or her memory had faded, but having her as an actual eyewitness would be powerful.

Slazak had been unable to find a telephone number for Nancy McGrath, which didn't surprise him. He realized that there was a good chance she had remarried and changed her name. He drove his rented Ford to the North Beverly home where the McGraths had lived at the time of the accident. The young woman who answered the door didn't know the Mc-Graths or their present whereabouts. She explained that she had purchased the house four years ago from another family, so the McGraths must have moved well before that. She suggested that Slazak visit Mr. or Mrs. Patton across the street, who had lived there for over twenty years and were very active in neighborhood affairs.

As Slazak walked across the street, Mrs. Patton emerged from her house with her cocker spaniel on a leash. She had been friendly and happy to share what she knew about the McGraths, although her cheery disposition darkened as she told her story. Nancy McGrath had married within a year of Terry's death and had been divorced at least twice that she knew of. The boy, Tommy, had turned into a bad sort, into drugs and alcohol from an early age. As for the little girl, Nancy McGrath couldn't manage to keep her own life together, so she had Ashley moved to an institution for children with special needs. She thought it was somewhere in the south suburbs.

Armed with that information, and with some help from the Internet and the Beverly Library, Slazak made several phone calls and confirmed that the home in question was called Concordia, and that Ashley McGrath was indeed a resident. It was located in Blue Island, just a few miles south of Beverly. Thirty minutes later, Slazak drove through the front gate and pulled into the visitors' parking lot, in front of a large, red brick building.

Slazak walked through the glass doors and found himself in a spacious entryway with portraits of priests and nuns hanging on the walls. To his left was an office, identified by a sign that read "Administration." He walked into the office to find two women seated at side-by-side desks, conversing in quiet tones as they busied themselves with some sort of paperwork.

"Good afternoon," Slazak greeted them in the most pleasant voice he could muster. "I was hoping you might be able to help me. I'm looking for a young lady by the name of Ashley McGrath."

"Hello, I'm Sister Therese," said the older of the two, standing and shaking his hand. She was a pleasant-looking woman wearing no makeup, who appeared to be in her early sixties. "Are you a relative of Ashley's?"

"No, Sister, actually I'm a police officer, and I just need to ask her a few questions. It shouldn't take more than ten minutes." He pulled out his badge and his ten-year-old ID card that he'd never relinquished.

"Is there a problem, Officer?" Sister Therese asked, a concerned look crossing her face.

"No, nothing to worry about, Sister," Slazak assured her, trying his best to sound nonchalant and put her at ease. "She was a witness to an incident that happened a long time ago. I interviewed her then, and I just need to confirm a few things. You know how the legal system is," he said with a smile and a shrug. "Sometimes it takes years before a case finally works its way through the system."

"I understand, Officer," the nun replied. "Kara, would you take this gentleman out to the grounds and find Ashley for him? I imagine she's at the track."

"I'd be happy to," replied Sister Therese's office mate, a fresh-faced girl in her late teens with flaming red hair. "Right this way, Officer."

The campus included an array of similar-looking red brick buildings, old but well maintained, surrounded by spacious, well-manicured grounds. Kara explained that the larger buildings were residence halls that provide living quarters for over five hundred residents of all ages with a variety of special needs. There were also classrooms, a cafeteria, a bakery, a library, and a gymnasium. A beautifully landscaped path wound through the campus toward a large athletic complex, which included a soccer field, a swimming pool, a baseball diamond, outdoor basketball courts, and a running track. Teenagers and young adults in powder-blue T-shirts were everywhere.

"There's a lot of excitement around here today, Officer," Kara said. "The Windy City Olympiad starts tomorrow—it's an Olympic-style competition for special needs kids from all over the tri-state area. Quite a few of our residents are participating."

Slazak stared in amazement at the hordes of young athletes scattered around the area. Several dozen kids were engaged in drills at various stations around the soccer field. A field hockey match was in full swing on the basketball court. The track was crowded with runners of all types: sprinters racing against a stopwatch, long-distance runners tirelessly circling the track, and others jumping hurdles.

"Wow, do all these kids live here?" Slazak asked.

"No, not all of them. A lot of them do, but others come from all over the area because we have the best athletic facilities around. This event is really a big deal for these kids."

They reached the track. "That's Ashley there," Kara said, pointing to a short, stocky girl running past them with a determined look on her round face. "She runs several of the long-distance races—the four-hundred-meter and sixteen-hundred-meter, I think."

Slazak watched the little figure as she rounded the track. Her form was odd, as if she were running with baby steps, but she moved pretty fast. She completed her lap, then walked toward the bleachers, limping slightly, and took a long gulp from a plastic water bottle, spilling most of it on her shirt.

"You were flying, Ashley!" Kara called out enthusiastically as they approached the little runner. "You're going to bring back that gold medal, I just know it!"

Ashley gave her a wide, open-mouthed grin. "Hi, Kara-Bara," she said in a low voice, wrapping Kara in a sweaty embrace.

"Ashley, this is a police officer. His name is Detective Slazak. He'd like to talk to you for a few minutes, okay?"

"Okay," she said, still smiling.

Slazak looked around for a place they could talk privately, yet still be out in the open, so Ashley wouldn't feel threatened. "Let's sit over there in the bleachers, okay, Ashley?" Slazak suggested.

"Okay."

A few athletes and spectators sat in the lower rows of the bleachers facing the track, so they climbed past them and sat together in the top row.

"We met once before, Ashley, a long time ago," Slazak said gently. "You probably don't remember."

"I remember," she said matter-of-factly.

Slazak stared at her, unsure whether she did or not. "Then you have a very good memory." He smiled at her. She smiled back, obviously proud of herself.

"That's Ricky," Ashley said, pointing to another young runner sprinting past them. "He's fast."

"He certainly is," Slazak replied. "But I bet he's not as fast as you," he added, smiling at the young girl. "I'd like to ask you a couple of questions, Ashley." He pulled out a wrinkled envelope and extracted two pictures. He showed her the first one, a photograph of Blair Van Howe taken from one of his presidential campaign posters. "Have you ever seen this man before?"

She looked at the picture, then turned her eyes to the track, without responding.

"Here's another picture of him, taken a long time ago." He showed her the picture taken during Van Howe's run for Congress ten years ago, the same picture he had intended to show the valet at Chez Pierre before he vanished. "Have you seen him before?"

"I see him on TV sometimes," Ashley replied.

"Do you remember him from anywhere else?" Slazak asked.

Ashley stared at the runners speeding past them. "Yes." She continued staring straight ahead.

"Where?" Slazak asked, his voice becoming intense.

"At the car crash, when Daddy got killed. He was there."

"Are you sure about that, Ashley? Are you absolutely sure?"

Ashley nodded vigorously. "I have a good memory."

CHAPTER 41

The words sucked the air out of his lungs: hepatocellular carcinoma—liver cancer. Danny Moran stared at the pained expression on the face of his friend and physician, Dr. Rich Carroll.

"Are you sure, Rich?" Danny asked weakly.

"I'm sure, Danny," he heard Dr. Carroll respond in a faraway voice. Dr. Carroll explained something about blood counts and alpha-fetoproteins, but the explanation was just a jumble of words without meaning, as a flurry of scattered thoughts raced through Danny's mind. Dr. Carroll showed him the MRI and ultrasound images, and proceeded to explain them. Again, the words were beyond his grasp, but Danny understood the pictures: the large dark masses all over his liver were cancer.

"How bad is it?" Danny asked, staring at the images and fearing that they spoke for themselves.

"It's not good, Danny. To be honest, I'm surprised that you're even able to walk around and that your body is still functioning somewhat normally. We call this Stage Four HCC. That means the cancer is very advanced. I'm not going to sugar-coat this for you, Danny. When we see this kind of cancer this far along, it's almost always fatal in a very short period of time. I can't tell you how sorry I am."

Danny looked at the floor, hoping to hide the fear that he knew was plastered across his face. "What are my options, Rich?" he asked.

"It's inoperable, Danny. It's too far advanced. There are things we can do to control the pain and discomfort, and we can probably slow it down a bit with some aggressive treatments, but the treatments will be hard on you. They'll make you sick, and they'll wear you out, but they may prolong your life for at least a little while. How long, I can't say, but even in a best-case scenario, you probably don't have much time. As your doctor, I want to fight this and buy you as much time as we possibly can, and I'm willing to do that if that's what you want. As your friend, I should tell you that my honest opinion is that there's something to be said for making the most of the time you have left. To me, that means spending as much quality time with your family and friends as you can and doing your best to enjoy the quality of life you still have, rather than embarking on a brutal course of treatment that can only prolong the inevitable for a short time. There are some experimental treatments, but there's no record of success yet and frankly, given your condition, it would take a miracle, Danny."

"Miracles can happen, Rich. My life is a testament to that," Danny said softly, still looking at the floor and trying to fight through the daze that had possessed him. "I need to think about this. I'll call you tomorrow."

***

Danny decided to skip his regular Friday night AA meeting that evening. He was in no frame of mind for casual visiting and was not ready to share his grim news with his friends. He was struggling to come to grips with it himself.

He spent the evening hours alternating between pacing aimlessly around the house and sitting in his living room armchair, seeking wisdom and solace in his devotional, but they would not come. His thoughts were scattered. What should he do about treatment? How should he break the news to Allie? Should he call Karen? Was his will up-to-date? He couldn't focus. His efforts to think rationally were thwarted by two overpowering emotions. The first was a profound sense of sadness at the prospect of leaving his daughter and his friends behind. The second emotion was even more powerful: fear—pure, unadulterated, primal fear.

The stillness in the house was pierced by the shrill ringing of the telephone. "Danny? It's Pat Jordan. I was hoping you could help me out."

"Are you drinking again, Pat?" Danny knew the answer before he asked the question. Pat's slurred speech and the bar noise in the background left no doubt.

"Yeah, I've slipped again, Danny," Pat replied in a shaky voice, thick with embarrassment and remorse. "I need your help before I get too far gone. I'm at Harrigan's Pub. Can you come get me?"

"Okay, stay there, Pat. Order some black coffee. I'm on my way."

CHAPTER 42

Mike Nolan had said that he typically returned home from work at around 7:00 p.m. Slazak was so anxious to get his hands on Nolan's information that part of him wanted to be waiting on Nolan's front steps. He resisted that temptation and decided to give Nolan a little time to get settled and have some dinner before dropping in on him.

Nolan lived in Oak Lawn, one of the larger suburbs southwest of the city, approximately halfway between Slazak's airport hotel and his old Mount Greenwood neighborhood. As Slazak pulled his rented Ford onto Massasoit Avenue shortly before eight thirty, he thought that this was exactly the type of place he envisioned Nolan living. There was nothing exciting about the area—no bars, nightclubs, or elegant restaurants—just street after street of neat, tidy little brick houses built during the 1950s and 1960s. The homes and their tiny front lawns were meticulously well maintained. The streets and sidewalks were immaculate and in perfect condition, unlike the dirty, pothole-ridden streets within the city limits.

Slazak drove slowly down the street, straining to see the addresses on the houses, as darkness was rapidly descending. Halfway down the block, he found the correct address. Immediately, he sensed something was amiss. The house was dark, but the front door was wide open.

Slazak raced up the walkway and pounded loudly on the open door. "Nolan! Hey, Nolan, you in there?" There was no response.

He stepped inside and looked around. In the dim light, Slazak could see that the place had been ransacked. Lamps, pictures, drawers, and their contents were strewn all over the living room. Shattered plates and glasses littered the kitchen counters and floors. Cabinet doors were flung open, revealing empty interiors. "Jesus Christ!" Slazak whispered to himself as he surveyed the damage. "Nolan!" he shouted.

He heard movement from the second story, grabbed a kitchen knife and bounded up the stairs. At the top of the stairs, he stopped, listening carefully. He heard a muffled groan coming from the front bedroom. He walked quickly in that direction, looking around cautiously as he did so. He peered into the front bedroom and gasped at the sight.

Mike Nolan was sitting on the floor, back against the wall, holding a grossly misshapen left wrist in his right hand. Blood streamed down his face from a gaping wound on his forehead, just below the hairline. His left eye was bright red and swollen shut.

"Jesus, Nolan, what happened?" Slazak rushed to his old colleague and wiped the blood from his face with a handkerchief.

Nolan glared at him through his one good eye. "What the hell does it look like, Slazak?" he shrieked. His voice was harsh and accusatory. "I was attacked and robbed! They got here first!"

"Calm down, Nolan! Who got here first? Tell me exactly what happened," Slazak asked in a steady voice, trying hard to mask the confusion and rage he was feeling.

Nolan took a few deep breaths, trying to calm himself. He was shaking all over. "I got home and came in the front door, probably about an hour ago, and someone grabbed me from behind. There was another guy going through all my drawers, throwing things everywhere. The guy who grabbed me said, 'We're here for Slazak's package. Where is it?'"

"What? He used my name?" Slazak asked, a look of disbelief on his face.

"Yes, he used your name, Slazak! But I knew you hadn't sent him because they were ransacking my house. I told him I didn't know what he was talking about. Then he started hitting me." Nolan put a hand over his swollen eye and began sniffling.

"Let me help you up, Nolan," Slazak said, his voice softening. "Damn, that arm looks bad." Slazak put his arm around Nolan's back and under his arms, and gently guided him to a standing position, then walked him over to the side of the bed, where he gingerly helped him sit down. Slazak crouched so that he was at eye level with his old colleague. "Then what happened, Nolan?" he asked, his voice intense.

"They said they wanted the package or they'd break my arm. I told them I didn't have it. Then one of them grabbed my arm and held it out in front of me, and the other smashed it with his nightstick."

Slazak looked at Nolan's wrist, limp and crooked where it should have been firm and straight. "Those bastards!" he said, menace in his voice. "They won't get away with this, Nolan, I promise you!"

"They got the stuff, Slazak!" Nolan wailed. "I gave it to them. After they broke my arm, they stuck my finger inside a cigar cutter and threatened to cut off my fingers one-by-one until I gave them what they came for. It was in that safe in the closet." Nolan nodded to a small safe visible through the open closet door. "I opened it for them." He hung his head as if ashamed of himself and began whimpering again.

"You did the right thing, Nolan. You didn't have any choice. Now let's get you to a hospital. Have you called the police yet?"

"No! No police!" Nolan shouted through his tears. "These guys said that if I reported this to anyone, they'd know about it and they'd come back and finish the job. They said I'd be a dead man. Besides that, I think they *were* cops. They were wearing Chicago PD uniforms."

Slazak froze momentarily. "Did you see what they looked like?" he asked.

"No, they had nylon stockings over their faces. One of them was huge, probably six foot five and built like a brick shithouse. These are bad guys, Slazak. I mean really danger-ous. I don't want the cops involved," he said adamantly.

"Okay, Nolan. But let me get you to a hospital."

"No, just leave me alone, Slazak! I can take care of my-self." His voice was shrill and thick with recrimination. "My life has been nice and peaceful since you left town, and as soon as you show up again, this happens. I don't know what you're involved in, and I don't want to know. Just get the hell out of here, okay? Stay out of my life!"

Slazak climbed back into his car, his emotions vacillating between rage and despair. He was enraged over the fact that a harmless soul like Nolan had to endure what he just had, and even angrier at himself for putting Nolan in that position. He was overcome with despair because the evidence that could prove his story was now gone, and there was no hope of recovering it.

The message light on his cell phone was flashing. He retrieved the message and heard Freddy Salazar's recorded voice. "Do you have it yet?"

Slazak dialed Salazar's private cell phone number. Salazar picked up immediately. "Where do we stand, Slazak?"

"You prick!" Slazak shouted into the phone. "You told someone about Nolan, didn't you?"

There was a long pause on the other end of the line. "Is there a problem, Slazak?"

"Answer my question!" Slazak demanded.

There was another long pause. "When I briefed Hamilton and his inner circle, I mentioned that a cop was holding some evidence for you. I might have mentioned his name. I had to give them some details or they would have thought you were just another wack job, and we wouldn't be proceeding with this."

"You son of a bitch," Slazak shouted. "You could've kept Nolan out of this or just waited until I had the evidence. There was no need to blow his cover!"

"What happened, Slazak?"

"Someone just kicked the living shit out of Nolan. And they took the evidence, Salazar!" The accusation in his voice was unmistakable.

"Are you suggesting that I had something to do with this?" Salazar asked, his voice rising.

"You're goddamn right I am! As of last night, only two people on the planet besides Nolan knew that he was holding that evidence—you and me. Then you told your cronies and this happens!"

"Shit!" Salazar muttered. "Goddamn it!" He paused, and let out a deep breath, obviously struggling to maintain control. "Okay, let's think this through, Slazak. We need to figure out where to go from here. The prospect of having a mole on my campaign team is absolutely unthinkable, but I'll deal with my staff issues. You and I need to figure out how we take this story forward. The facts haven't changed. It will just be a bit more of a challenge convincing the rest of the world without that evidence."

"A bit of a challenge?" Slazak roared. "The evidence is gone, Salazar! We can't prove shit now! It's over!"

"It's not over. We still have you, Slazak. You're the evidence now. And we have the girl."

Slazak felt a surge of panic. In all the commotion, he'd forgotten about Ashley McGrath. "Did you tell your team about the girl, Freddy?" he asked, his voice filled with dread.

"Damn! I think I did mention her," said Salazar, realizing the implications. "I didn't say much about her. I was more focused on the recording and the blood analysis, but I did mention her. You don't think—"

"Son of a bitch!" Slazak hung up and sped off into the night.

CHAPTER 43

"Come on, Sister, answer the goddamn phone!" Vic Slazak shouted to himself as he drove as fast as he dared toward Concordia. He heard the click of an answering machine, and then a recorded message advised him to call back during regular business hours. "Shit!" he yelled. He glanced at his watch. It was nine o'clock, and trying to confirm Ashley McGrath's safety via telephone at this time in the evening was clearly futile.

Thirty minutes later, he brought his car to a screeching halt in the Concordia visitors' parking lot, leapt out of the vehicle, and raced to the front door, only to find it locked. Peering inside, he saw no signs of life. He rattled the door and banged loudly. After a few long minutes, an elderly security guard came into view, walking slowly in his direction. The guard approached the door, pointed to his watch, and mouthed the words *We're closed. Come back tomorrow.*

"Open the door!" Slazak yelled, holding his badge against the glass. The guard studied it carefully, then pulled a large key ring off his belt and complied.

"What can I do for you, Detective?" he asked, looking unsure of himself.

"I think one of your residents may be in danger," Slazak replied in an urgent tone. "I need to make sure she's okay."

The guard looked even more nervous. "Which one?" he asked.

"Ashley McGrath. Can you check on her?"

"She's in the women's residence hall, next building over. I'll call the guard over there and ask him to look in on her."

The elderly guard radioed his counterpart in the other building and explained the situation.

"He's checking on her, Detective. He'll call back in a few minutes."

"Can you take me over there, Curtis?" Slazak asked, reading the name from the guard's uniform.

"I'm not supposed to leave my post," Curtis replied nervously.

"It'll take just a few minutes, right? Come on, Curtis, this is really important."

The elderly guard reluctantly accompanied Slazak to the women's residence hall, where they met the other security guard at the door, a stocky young black man with a sincere face and a nameplate that read "Marvin."

"I just checked on Ms. McGrath," said the young guard. "She's asleep in her room. I'm not surprised. She's got a big day tomorrow, with the Olympics and all."

"What kind of security do you have around here, Marvin?" Slazak asked, doubt evident in his voice.

"You're looking at it," Marvin said proudly. "I'm on duty all night. These doors are kept locked. No one can get in or out between now and 7:00 a.m. And, we have an alarm system in case anyone tries to break in. We keep these residents safe, sir. Nothing to worry about."

"Well, be alert, guys," said Slazak. "I've got reason to believe Ashley may be in danger. Keep a close eye on her room tonight, okay?"

Curtis looked less confident than his young colleague. "What kind of danger are we talking about here? Should we call the police?"

Slazak's mind flashed back to his final night in his Mount Greenwood home, vividly recalling that the intruders with the nylon stockings over their faces were wearing uniforms of the Chicago Police Department. Nolan's description of his assailants was identical. "No, I don't think that's necessary," Slazak said, trying his best to sound confident and reassuring. "I am the police, remember? Anyway, you guys seem to have things under control here. Like I said, just be alert. If anything strange happens, call me right away." He jotted his cell phone number on a piece of paper he ripped from his small spiral notebook and handed it to Marvin, then did the same for Curtis.

Slazak left Concordia feeling less panicked but still uneasy about Ashley McGrath. His thoughts then returned to Mike Nolan. He was haunted by the vision of the prissy, harmless little geek sitting on his bedroom floor, face bloodied and battered, holding a grossly contorted broken wrist. It was his fault. Nolan had trusted him and gone out of his way to help, and this was what he got for it.

Slazak's guilt turned to rage as he thought about Freddy Salazar. Everything would have gone perfectly if Salazar hadn't mucked up the works by broadcasting his story to who knows who. It served him right for trusting a politician. Now he had to rethink his strategy. Should he set his wrath aside and continue working with Salazar, or should he go it alone? If he could find the right reporter, he might be able to achieve the desired result without having to collaborate with politicians.

It was past ten o'clock, but Slazak was in no mood for sleep. He needed to regroup and sort things out. Besides, after the day he'd had, he could use a couple of drinks.

He found himself instinctively driving toward Western Avenue, where he would have his choice of former drinking haunts. During his years in Vegas, one of the things he missed most was the neighborhood bar scene, not because there was anything remarkable about Chicago's South Side bars, but just because they were full of his kind of people.

The Celtic Lounge had been his favorite spot on Western Avenue. As Slazak approached the nondescript tavern, he noticed the name on the marquee was now Harrigan's. It seemed inviting nonetheless. Slazak stepped inside and could see that the tavern was just as he remembered it, tables and chairs spread around the front part of the bar, two pool tables and a dart board attracting a crowd in the back. It was crowded and noisy, but the noise had a fun and upbeat feel to it.

Slazak found an empty bar stool and ordered a shot and a beer, both of which he slammed down instantly. Then he ordered another beer. He looked sideways at the man on the bar stool next to him. He was scruffy and disheveled, and looked like he'd been drinking heavily, although the beverage in front of him at the moment was hot coffee.

Slazak was not normally inclined to strike up a conversation with a stranger at a bar, particularly one who seemed to be withdrawn and keeping to himself. He was one to respect boundaries. However, despite the troubles he had encountered earlier that evening, he felt his spirits lifting, through some combination of the alcohol and the feeling that he was home again on the South Side of Chicago, where he belonged.

"My name's Vic," he said, turning to the coffee drinker and offering his hand. "How's it going?"

The man looked at him with bloodshot eyes and offered a weak smile. "I'm Pat," he replied, shaking hands.

"Do you live around here?" Slazak asked.

"Sometimes," Pat responded. "I grew up around here, and I've moved away a few times, but I seem to keep finding my way back." His speech was slurred, and it was evident that he hadn't been drinking coffee all evening.

"Me, too," said Slazak. "I'm from Mount Greenwood, but I've been living in Vegas for the past ten years. Miserable place."

Pat looked past Slazak and waved to a man in a dark blue windbreaker who had just walked in. The man returned Pat's wave and approached them.

"Hi, Pat," the man said in a somber tone, a troubled look on his face.

"Thanks for coming, Danny." Pat took a closer look at Danny Moran. "Jesus Christ, you look like shit!"

"So do you, Pat," Danny replied.

"*Touché*, pal. I need to take a leak, then we can get going." Pat rose from his bar stool and walked unsteadily in the direction of the men's room. Danny seated himself on the stool Pat had just vacated.

Vic Slazak stared intently at Danny Moran. "My name's Vic," he said, extending his hand. "You look familiar."

"Danny Moran," Danny replied, shaking hands and barely glancing at Slazak, his eyes darting around the bar nervously. He'd visited many a bar on missions like this one over the years, and they always unnerved him. Even after ten years of sobriety, some part of him still feared that he could give in to the temptation at any time.

Danny noticed that the man he'd just met seemed to be staring at him. He focused and returned the look.

"Do you live in North Beverly, on Hamilton?" Slazak asked.

"Yeah, I've lived there for twenty years now," Danny replied, realizing that the man he'd just met looked familiar to him, too.

"We've met before. My full name is Vic Slazak. I used to be a cop. I was the one who investigated your auto accident years ago."

Danny's sense of discomfort with the surroundings immediately escalated. "That was a long time ago," he said. "I've tried to put that behind me."

"Listen, Danny, I'd really like to talk to you about that accident," Slazak said, urgency in his voice.

Danny looked confused, as well as a bit annoyed. "Look, Mr. Slazak, this is something I don't like to talk about. I'm not proud of what happened. It was a dark time in my life, and like I said, I've tried to put it behind me."

"Let me tell you about my investigation. I think you'll be interested in what I have to say. I'm convinced that what actually happened is very different from what most people think."

"Okay, Danny, let's get out of here," Pat Jordan stepped between them. "Nice meeting you, pal." He nodded at Slazak.

"I can explain some things. You really need to hear this!" Slazak said in a loud voice as Danny began walking away, a bewildered look on his face. "Can I call you tomorrow?"

"Sure, I'm in the phone book," Danny replied in a reluctant voice, without looking back.

"What did he want?" Pat asked.

"Who knows?" Danny replied. "I think he's just a drunk with some wild story he wants to tell."

CHAPTER 44

Slazak slept uneasily, his rest disturbed by unsettling dreams of Ashley McGrath lying in a casket. He awoke with a start, his head pounding and his stomach feeling queasy. He looked at the alarm clock next to his bed: 7:42. "Shit!" he yelled, a feeling of panic quickly overtaking him. He splashed cold water on his face, swallowed three aspirin, then threw on his clothes and raced out of the hotel. There was little traffic at that hour on Saturday morning, so he made it to Concordia in a little over twenty minutes.

He sprinted from the parking lot to the front office, where he found Sister Therese calmly talking on the telephone.

"Where's Ashley McGrath?" Slazak blurted out.

Sister Therese gave him a cross look and held up an index finger, signaling for him to be patient.

"Sister, this is important!" Slazak shouted. "Where's Ashley?"

Sister Therese put her hand over the mouthpiece and said, "Try the athletic field. The buses are meeting the kids there and taking them downtown for the Olympics. You might've missed them," she said, glancing at the clock.

"Thanks, Sister," he said hurriedly, turning and making for the door.

"Wait, Detective!" Sister Therese called after him. "Is everything okay with Ashley? You're the second person asking about her this morning."

Slazak froze.

"Who was the first one?" he asked as a chill shot down his spine.

"The other policeman, the one in uniform. He was here about ten minutes ago."

"What did he look like, Sister?"

"He was a giant. Tall, big shoulders, dark complexion. I sent him down to the field, too. Is everything okay?"

Slazak raced out the door without answering and sprinted through the winding paths toward the athletic field. As he approached, he saw the last few stragglers in their powder-blue T-shirts boarding an old yellow school bus. A young man in his late teens with curly blond hair stood outside the bus, checking names off the list on his clipboard as the excited young athletes boarded the bus.

"Hey, is Ashley McGrath on this bus?" Slazak shouted to the young chaperone.

"No, she caught the earlier bus. It left about twenty minutes ago."

"Where's it going?" Slazak asked, breathing hard from his sprint.

"Downtown. Grant Park. That's where they're holding the opening ceremonies. After that, the athletes go their separate ways for their events. Some are in the park, some are at Soldier Field, and some of the swimming events are in the lake."

"Are you sure she was on that bus?"

"Positive. She gave me a big hug before she got on."

The young man hesitated, his expression becoming worried.

"There was a policeman here looking for her just a few minutes ago. Is something wrong?"

"Can you reach that bus driver?"

"Maybe. I can try Annie's cell phone. She's one of the chaperones on that bus."

"Call her!" Slazak demanded. "Tell her not to let Ashley out of her sight!"

Slazak raced back to his car, grabbing his cell phone as he screeched out of the parking lot. "Son of a bitch!" he yelled, realizing he had no one to call.

CHAPTER 45

Bobby Rosensteel answered the knock on his hotel room door at six thirty. "That was fast," he said as he opened the door, expecting the room service attendant with the breakfast he had ordered ten minutes earlier.

He found himself facing the massive frame of Sam McIntire. "Morning, Bobby," Sam said cheerfully, handing Bobby the newspaper that had been lying outside his door. "I've got some news."

Bobby looked down the hall in both directions, then closed the door.

"Well, is our boy ready for the big show next week?" Sam asked casually.

"You know Blair," Bobby responded. "He thrives on this. He'll be at his best. So, you've got some news?"

Sam smiled smugly. "You bet your ass."

"Out with it, goddamn it," Bobby ordered impatiently.

"Relax, Bobby, everything is good. In fact, we can all relax. Remember that evidence in Chicago we were concerned about? Well, there ain't no more evidence."

"Are you telling me there wasn't any evidence in the first place, or that there was, but now it's gone?"

"Oh, there was evidence, all right, but it's been taken care of. Damn good thing, too. It was exactly as advertised."

"And it was handled discreetly?"

"With the utmost professionalism, I can assure you. You won't hear a peep out of anyone. Now we just have one more loose end to tie up, and I've got those wheels in motion."

"What loose end?" Bobby asked. "What are you talking about?"

"The girl—the witness," Sam replied, as if stating the obvious.

"Leave her alone, Sam," Bobby said sternly. "The evidence is gone. We don't need to worry about her."

"Like hell we don't! This is too big—we can't take any chances. Don't sweat it, Bobby. I'm handling it."

"Do you mind telling me exactly how you intend to handle this?" Bobby asked, an edge in his voice.

"You don't need to concern yourself with that," Sam replied curtly.

"Bullshit! I'm responsible for this campaign, and I need to know exactly what you're up to. We can't afford any messes, Sam! Tell me exactly what you have in mind."

Sam eyed Bobby skeptically for a long moment. "Okay, here's what I'm thinking. The kid's got mental issues. She's participating in some sort of Olympic event in downtown Chicago, right on the lakefront. There'll be mobs of people there. It would be easy for a kid like her to get lost in the crowd. If she shows up floating in Lake Michigan, nobody will think twice. A lot of those kids can't swim. Everybody will think she just wandered off and fell into the lake. It happens."

"Have you lost your goddamn mind?" Bobby exploded. "This campaign won't have any part in something like that. I can't believe you're even suggesting it. No way, no goddamn way, Sam! Making some evidence disappear is one thing, but nobody gets hurt here, got it? Whatever you've put in motion, call it off!"

"Look, Bobby, the campaign isn't involved in this. You're not involved in this, so cool your jets! Just leave it to me. I won't do anything stupid."

Bobby stepped to within inches of Sam. "Call it off, Sam. Right now!"

Sam glared at him. "You coward," he sneered scornfully. "You shitty little coward."

"Pick up your cell phone and call it off, Sam," Bobby said in a low, threatening voice, carefully enunciating every word. "I mean it. That's an order!"

Sam shook his head in disgust as he turned away from Bobby and slowly pulled his cell phone from his pocket. He punched in a number.

"Hey, it's me," he said in a low voice. "Abort the mission. That's right. The mission is off."

Sam listened as the answering machine at his home beeped on the other end of the line.

"Satisfied?" He glared at Bobby contemptuously as he stormed out of the room.

CHAPTER 46

Thirty-four young athletes from Concordia were packed into the old yellow school bus as it made its way from the Far South Side toward Grant Park in downtown Chicago. The two young chaperones made a halfhearted attempt to keep some semblance of order, but they had little inclination to stifle the exuberance among their charges.

The level of excitement and anticipation escalated as the bus rolled up behind a long row of other buses parked along the curb on Jackson Drive, adjacent to the park. The young athletes poured out of the bus onto the wide sidewalk, joining the throng of participants and spectators making their way toward Pritzker Pavilion, the site of the opening ceremonies. Eric and Annie, the two young chaperones, shouted instructions, mostly about staying together and not wandering off, as they cheerfully led the parade of young Olympians toward the Pavilion. Their cheerfulness was quickly put to a test as they made the half-mile trek across the park. Their team seemed to have little desire or ability to maintain the same pace. Some were compelled by their eagerness to race toward their destination, while a few stragglers maintained their own leisurely pace, more interested in taking in the sights and sounds of the big city than in getting to the opening ceremony. Between their concern about their charges wandering off and dealing with requests to find restrooms or water, Eric and Annie soon found themselves frazzled and wishing they'd recruited another half-dozen volunteers to help maintain order and keep the group together.

"Hey, are you the group from Concordia?" Vic Slazak called out to Eric as he approached the swarm of athletes in their powder-blue T-shirts. He was sweating and winded from scurrying around the Pavilion area in search of a group wearing that color.

"That's us," Eric said, also sweating from the exertion of keeping his team together.

"Are you in charge?" Slazak asked.

"I guess you could say that. I'm one of the chaperones."

"Is Ashley McGrath in your group?"

"Yeah, she's with us," Eric replied, looking over the sea of faces in front of him. "Hmmm ... I don't see her ... Hey, Annie," he called out to his fellow chaperone. "Where's Ashley?"

"She went to the bathroom," Annie replied, looking harried and distracted. She pointed toward a row of about two dozen bright-blue portable toilets across the park, about two hundred yards away.

"Alone?" Slazak asked, his concern turning to anger. "Didn't the kid from the other bus call you guys and ask you to keep an eye on her?"

"We've got thirty-four kids to keep track of. We're doing the best we can!" Annie replied testily. "Anyway, there's no need to worry. We found a policeman to walk her over there."

Slazak looked at her with stunned disbelief. "When? What did the guy look like?" The urgency in his voice was not lost on the young chaperone.

"Just a few minutes ago. I didn't look at him all that close-ly. He was wearing his uniform. He was big and had kind of a dark complexion."

Slazak bolted in the direction of the portable johns. When he reached them, he walked hurriedly down the row of rectangular blue boxes, staring at each one as if he were willing his eyes to see through the closed doors. He stopped at the midpoint of the row, bent over and put his hands on his knees, struggling to catch his breath. From that vantage point, he could see everyone going in or out. As he looked toward the far end of the row, his eyes were drawn to a sight several hundred feet beyond, a tall man in what appeared to be a policeman's uniform, next to a diminutive figure in a pale blue shirt, limping slightly, walking away from the park.

Before that morning, Victor Slazak hadn't run a step in years, yet he immediately broke into a sprint like a well-conditioned runner, his mind fixated on just one thought: *Get to the girl!*

"Ashley! Ashley McGrath!" Slazak yelled as he neared them. They were stopped at a traffic light, waiting to cross Lake Shore Drive. Simultaneously, the girl and the uniformed figure at her side turned around and stared at Vic Slazak as he slowed to a fast walk and approached them.

"Who are you?" Slazak asked the massive officer, noticing that there was no nameplate where one should have been.

"I'm a police officer. Who are you?" the uniformed man shot back in a belligerent tone.

"Where are you taking her?" Slazak demanded, ignoring the officer's question.

"She's running the track events. Those are at Soldier Field. I'm taking her over there."

Slazak looked hard at the officer, then looked at the girl, crouching to speak to her on her level. "Ashley, you need to go back to your group, okay? Come on, I'll take you." He held out his hand. Ashley hesitated, then reached for it. The officer stepped between them.

"Get lost," he said in a threatening voice. "You're not her father. You must be some kind of pervert, chasing little girls around like this. Beat it or I'll arrest you right here and now. *Capisce,* amigo?"

Slazak felt the hair on the back of his neck stand up. He had heard that voice before, asking that same simple question, mixing the foreign languages, sounding both sarcastic and threatening. He straightened up and stared coldly at the giant in front of him, who was at least half a head taller and probably outweighed him by sixty pounds.

"You're not taking her anywhere, *amigo*," Slazak replied, venom in his voice. "Ashley, let's go. This man is not your friend!"

The officer quickly thrust both arms forward, striking Slazak squarely in the chest, knocking him backward and leaving him struggling to stay on his feet. Slazak steadied himself and approached his adversary, his body language cool and calm, in stark contrast to the burning intensity in his eyes. Slazak knew he was no kid and that, physically, he was no match for the monster standing in front of him, but several years of amateur boxing had taught him how to use his fists. Besides, he didn't need to overpower this behemoth; he just needed to distract him long enough for Ashley to make a break and run back to the park.

Slazak stared coldly at the uniformed giant, but spoke to the girl. "Ashley, when I say 'go,' you run back to the park as fast as you can, just like it's a track meet."

In the next instant, his left fist shot forward in a lightning quick jab that caught the big man flush on the nose, knocking him backward.

"Run, Ashley, run!"

"You son of a bitch," the cop bellowed as he advanced on Slazak, both arms flailing.

Slazak backpedaled, blocking the torrent of blows.

"Run, Ashley! Go, go, go!"

The girl was frozen where she stood. As he continued to ward off his assailant's blows, Slazak shot a glance in Ashley's direction. It lasted just a fleeting instant, but it distracted him enough that he lost focus and felt a devastating blow crash into the left side of his face. He felt himself hitting the ground as if in slow motion. He heard onlookers shouting. He heard someone yell, "Call the police!" although the voice seemed distant and muted.

"I am the goddamn police!" he heard the big man roar.

As Slazak struggled to his knees, he saw his adversary approaching him, pulling back his leg, preparing to deliver a vicious kick. Slazak rolled away and the kick missed its mark. As the big man tried to regain his balance, Slazak lunged at him, grabbing both legs in a clean tackle, sending the officer sprawling to the pavement. They rolled around on the sidewalk, inches from the curb, as a city bus whizzed by. In his dazed state, Slazak was quickly overpowered and found himself face-down on the pavement. A powerful hand yanked the hair on the back of his head and slammed his face into the concrete sidewalk. He felt his cheekbone shatter and blood spurt into his right eye, and he began slipping toward unconsciousness. Then he felt hot breath on the back of his ear as he heard a menacing voice that he remembered all too well. "I told you before that if you ever set foot in Chicago again I'd kill you. You should have listened, Slazak."

Slazak felt his arms being pulled behind his back and heard the click of handcuffs. He felt the weight lift from his body as the big man stood up. Slazak lifted his head sideways and saw the man walking along the curb back toward the intersection. Ashley McGrath stood there like a statue.

The inside of his skull ached, and his entire face was a mass of pain. Slazak felt the pull of unconsciousness slowly overtaking him. Then he thought of the taunting, sarcastic voice, the assault in his home, and the ten years of exile in Vegas. For a man who had never let anyone push him around, he had allowed this thug to rob him of a big part of his life— his job and his home. Now the same man had just beaten him almost senseless and was about to walk off with Ashley McGrath, taking her to what was certain to be a tragic fate.

"Get up," he whispered to himself. He rolled onto his back, raising himself to a sitting position, the pain is his skull almost knocking him down again. He tried to stand and fell over, partly because his hands were cuffed behind his back and partly because he was dizzy and disoriented.

He looked toward the intersection. The cop was leaning over, saying something to Ashley. They both turned toward the street, their backs to him, as they waited for the traffic light to change.

Slazak saw a tree several yards away and rolled toward it, his arms straining behind his back as he rolled over them. He raised himself to a sitting position, placing his back up against the tree, and slowly pushed upward with his feet, forcing himself into a standing position. He took a deep breath to steady himself and began walking toward the intersection, approaching Ashley and the cop from behind. He was unsteady at first, walking slowly and listing badly to his right side as he fought to regain his equilibrium. He stopped momentarily to allow his sight and his head to clear.

Then a surge of panic overtook him. The light would turn green in a few seconds, and the cop and Ashley would move on. Slazak staggered to a position directly behind them, about twenty feet away. He looked at the intersection and saw a bus rapidly approaching. It would cross the intersection, the light would turn green, and his enemy would hurry across the street with the young girl.

Panic and uncertainty yielded to rage and determination. Slazak lowered his head and began running directly at the cop, who was staring straight ahead, oblivious to his presence. The cop took a step back from the street as a speeding bus approached. Slazak let out a ferocious yell like that of a marauding warrior. The cop spun around. His eyes widened at the sight of Victor Slazak three feet away, charging at him like a deranged, armless linebacker. The cop grunted loudly as Slazak's shoulder hit him squarely in the midsection, sending him reeling backward into the street, Slazak following, carried by his own momentum. Ashley McGrath stared in horror as the bus did the rest.

CHAPTER 47

Bobby Rosensteel climbed out of the hotel pool and toweled himself off. Life was good this morning. Governor Blair Van Howe had a commanding lead in the polls. The convention would begin tomorrow, and he felt supremely confident that it would be an event to remember. He planned to allow himself the luxury of an hour of relaxation, soaking up the Southern California sun, before diving into his last-minute preparations. He sat down in a poolside chair and began perusing the newspaper with a sense of self-satisfaction.

Bobby looked up as a large figure moved between him and the morning sun, casting a shadow across his face. Sam McIntire stood there, looking oddly out of place, wearing a dark suit among the crowd of sunbathers lounging around the hotel swimming pool in the early morning San Diego sunshine.

"Mind if I sit down?" Sam asked.

"Be my guest," said Bobby agreeably, motioning to an adjacent lounge chair. "I was just reading the latest polls results. We're pulling away, and the convention is bound to give us another big boost."

"Well, here's a report from the Chicago paper that I just pulled off the Internet," said Sam, handing Bobby a short article from page fourteen of the *Chicago Tribune*. The article read:

Bus Kills Two on Lake Shore Drive

A Chicago police officer and another man were struck and killed by a city bus at the corner of Lake Shore Drive and Monroe Street yesterday morning. According to witnesses, Officer Frank Capetta, a fifteen-year veteran of the Chicago Police Department, was assaulted by a man identified as Victor Slazak, 54, who at one time also was a Chicago policeman. One witness reported that Slazak appeared to be deranged and instigated an altercation with Capetta. During the ensuing fight, both men tumbled into the street and were struck by a passing bus. Both men died at the scene."

"Is there more to this story?" Bobby asked, looking concerned.

"Shit, Bobby, it speaks for itself. We caught a break! This Slazak guy was apparently a nut job. Anyway, this mess is behind us now. There's no evidence, the cop is dead, and there's no one else to tell the story. It's over. We're completely in the clear. The only thing between Blair and the Presidency now is time—sixty-six days, to be exact!"

CHAPTER 48

The doorbell rang, and Allie answered. "Hi, Kristen." She embraced her former college roommate. "Come on in."

"It's great to see you, Allie," Kristen replied, looking at her friend with compassion in her eyes. "How's your dad?" she asked as she stepped inside and removed her coat.

"He's having a pretty good day today. Like I mentioned on the phone, he's completely bedridden now, but mentally he's all there. And he's still himself. I'm grateful for that."

"I'm looking forward to seeing him again," Kristen said. "And I really appreciate the fact that he's allowing me to interview him about the early days of Governor Van Howe. Is he still up to it?"

Allie smiled. "Absolutely. He considers it an honor to be working with the *Tribune*'s most promising reporter."

Kristen reached into an oversized purse and pulled out a handheld digital recorder and a small notepad. "Oh, I brought this thing, too," she said, pulling out what looked like a walkie-talkie and a small plastic blue-and-white radio. "This is the baby monitor I used when my kids were newborns. You put the base in your dad's room, near his bed, and you can put this receiver anywhere in the house, or you can carry it around with you. Whenever he talks, you'll be able to hear him. The sound quality is great. Even if he's just whispering, you'll hear him loud and clear."

"Thanks, Kristen, this will really help," Allie said in a quiet voice.

"How are you holding up?" Kristen asked sympathetically.

"Not so good," Allie replied softly, looking down as tears filled her eyes. "This is so hard, Kristen," she stammered, as she began to weep quietly. The two friends embraced again, sharing tears of sorrow.

Danny Moran had been diagnosed with liver cancer in late August. He'd seen several doctors, all of whom expressed the same grim opinion: nothing short of an absolute miracle could stop the spread of the insidious disease. The most advanced, cutting-edge treatments might prolong his life for some period of time, but it would not be long, and it would be at the expense of his quality of life.

It was November first, barely two months since the diagnosis, and the cancer had ravaged his body at a merciless pace. Allie had taken a leave of absence from her residency position beginning in early October to move in with her father and act as his caretaker. She was determined to be there for whatever time he had left, which wasn't likely to be much. She could see that his vital body functions were showing signs of shutting down. Blessedly, he was not in great discomfort. He slept a great deal, but when he was awake, he was lucid and peaceful.

Danny was sleeping as Allie and Kristen walked into his room. "Don't wake him," Kristen whispered. "I'm in no hurry. I'll go ahead and set up the monitor." She plugged in the base and set it on the bedside table, then checked the frequency to make sure its setting matched the receiver. "There you go. We're all set," she said in a hushed tone, handing the receiver to Allie.

They walked into the kitchen, and Allie put a kettle on the stove. As she poured hot water over their tea bags, the doorbell rang again. Allie opened the door to find a burly young man with long brown hair hanging over large, sad-looking brown eyes. "Hi, Allie," he said hesitantly. "My name is T. J. I'm a friend of your dad's. I was hoping I could see him."

"Hi, T. J.!" Allie said, warmly shaking his hand. "It's so nice of you to come by. Daddy's told me a lot about you, and I'm so glad to finally meet you. Come on in."

She introduced him to Kristen and offered him a cup of tea.

"How's he doing?" T. J. asked, looking uncomfortable and self-conscious, avoiding eye contact.

"He's doing okay," Allie said in a comforting voice. "He doesn't have much time left, but he's peaceful and he's lucid. He'll be delighted to see you."

"Allie?" Danny's voice came through the monitor, sounding a bit hollow and metallic, but otherwise loud and clear.

"Perfect timing!" Allie said. "He's awake now. I'll take you in there, T. J."

They walked out of the kitchen and down a narrow corridor adorned with old family photos to the master bedroom. Allie peeked in. "Daddy? You have a visitor."

T. J. peered in over Allie's shoulder. "Hello, Danny," he said, his voice breaking just a bit as he beheld former mentor. Danny looked like an old man, shriveled and pale, with sunken eyes and hollow cheeks.

"T. J.!" Danny exclaimed, his voice sounding weak and tired, yet upbeat. "What a wonderful surprise!"

T. J. lumbered across the room and shook Danny's frail hand with his meaty paw.

Danny smiled at his young friend. "You look good, T. J. Are you still sober?"

T. J. chuckled softly. "You never were one to beat around the bush. Yes, I'm still sober, Danny." He seated himself in the wooden desk chair next to the bed, and Allie retreated to the kitchen. "How you feeling?" he asked quietly.

"Tired ... weak ... I'm dying, T. J.," Danny answered with a matter-of-fact shrug.

"Judge Andy told me you're not doing chemo or radiation ... or anything. Can't you fight this, Danny? You've helped so many of us fight to straighten out our lives. Can't you fight for yourself?"

"I wish I could," Danny replied. "I'm afraid this is a fight I just can't win."

T. J. began sniffling and wiping his nose with his hand. "I'm sorry I walked out on you, Danny. I shouldn't have done that. You're the best friend I've got. I don't want to lose you ..." He pulled out a rumpled handkerchief and blew his nose loudly. "I would have come sooner, but I didn't know. I stopped going to the meetings at St. Martin's. I go to the one in Blue Island now, so I've been out of touch. I just found out you were sick yesterday when I saw Andy at the mall. I'm so sorry. I should have been a better friend." He wiped his eyes with his handkerchief.

"T. J., you had every right to be upset with me, after all the pain I caused you and your family. I don't blame you a bit."

"I don't care what happened ten years ago, Danny. That's in the past, and we can't do shit about that. All I know is that, when you came into my life, you made a difference. No one's cared about me in forever, until you came along. You didn't treat me like a loser. You treated me like a friend, and you helped straighten me out. You actually cared. You'll never know how much that means to me."

"And it means a lot to me that you're here now, T. J.," Danny replied, reaching out and putting his frail hand on T. J.'s bulky forearm. "Don't feel sorry for me. I've had a good life. Having real friends, friends who are there for each other, making a difference in each other's lives, that's what matters. I've been blessed to have you for a friend, T. J. And you're going to have a good life, too. I just know it. You're on the right track now."

T. J. smiled through his tears. "I owe that to you, Danny."

CHAPTER 49

For a presidential candidate four days before the election, Blair Van Howe was remarkably relaxed. He had good reason to be, as all the polls indicated that he was on the verge of the biggest landslide victory in decades. There was no need for the usual frenzy of last-minute campaigning in key battle-ground states. He had just one final stop on the campaign trail, a speech in Chicago, where he launched his career, on the day before the election. Until then, he intended to relax and spend time working on his victory speech, out of the limelight, at his home in North Beverly, free from the ubiquitous cameras and microphones he would encounter at any downtown hotel.

Kimberly had stayed behind at campaign headquarters in Washington, and Blair was relishing the prospect of a few days of quiet solitude. Solitude was, of course, a relative thing for a presidential candidate, since a small army of Secret Service agents would be hovering nearby. An around-the-clock detail was stationed on his property and others blanketed the surrounding area.

It was late Friday afternoon, as Blair looked out his front window and saw his next-door neighbor, Mrs. Hubbard, lifting grocery bags from the trunk of her Buick. Mrs. Hubbard had lived there when Blair moved into his house fifteen years ago. She was well into her seventies now. Blair felt an urge to reconnect with the old neighborhood and bounded down his front steps into the chilly November air without his jacket.

"Hi, Mrs. H.," he called out brightly as he hurried across the lawn toward the Hubbards' driveway, followed by one of his Secret Service agents. "Let me help you with that."

"Blair, what a surprise! Or should I call you Mr. President now?" She beamed at him like a proud parent and gave him a warm embrace.

Blair and the agent each hoisted several grocery bags and carried them into the kitchen. Blair listened with genuine interest as she brought him up-to-date on the lives of each of her four children and proudly showed off her most recent pictures of her six grandchildren.

"So, what's new around the neighborhood, Mrs. H.?" Blair asked when she completed the update on her family.

She thought for a moment. "Well, I assume you've heard about Danny Moran," she said, a trace of sadness in her voice.

"No, what about him?" Blair asked.

"The poor chap has cancer. It was just diagnosed a couple of months ago, but it spread really fast. Nothing they could do about it. It was just too far along when they found it." She shook her head sadly. "Such a shame. He's always been such a nice man."

"Is he in the hospital?" Blair asked, trying to conceal his sense of shock.

"No, he's at home. Probably doesn't have more than a few days, from what I hear."

Blair left the Hubbard house pale and shaken. Over the years, he'd managed to compartmentalize his life very well. Danny Moran was a subject he'd tried to keep locked away somewhere in the distant recesses of his memory. Whenever he thought about Danny, he felt besieged by guilt and sadness, so he did what Sam and Kimberly repeatedly told him he must do: put Danny out of his mind. Danny Moran was part of his past, and there was simply no place for Danny in his present life. It wasn't right, and he knew it, but that was his coping mechanism—doing his best to stay oblivious to Danny's existence. The guilt and sadness flooded back.

He sat on the leather sofa in his living room and flipped on the television. He stared at a football game with unseeing eyes for a long time. He thought about Danny: their time together in law school, their early years in the legal profession, all the fun they'd had together. He thought about the selfless mentoring and encouragement Danny had always provided. He thought about Danny's efforts to bring him into the fold at the city's premier law firm and Danny's tireless efforts to use his influence and connections to pave the way for Blair's political career.

Then he thought about the accident. He had always banished those thoughts when they ambushed him at inopportune times. But he could not banish them now—or would not. His conscience tortured him. That piece of unexpected news from Mrs. Hubbard had jolted him, instantaneously transforming his mindset and his self-image. He no longer felt like a man of supreme talent and confidence on the threshold of greatness. He felt like a regular guy who had egregiously harmed his best friend.

He stood and walked to the front window. In the gathering darkness, he could see a Secret Service agent standing on his porch, a car with two agents inside parked on the street in front of his house, and another Secret Service vehicle parked farther up the street. He turned and walked toward the back of the house, determination in his footsteps. He exited the back door, strode past an agent posted there, and hurried across the yard, scaling the four-foot wrought-iron fence and landing in his neighbor's yard. The Secret Service agent hustled after him.

"Sir, where are you going?"

Blair stopped and looked at him. "I'm taking a little walk, Tony. Visiting an old friend, and I don't want to attract a crowd. Come on, I guess you'd better come along."

"How far are we going?" the agent asked nervously, hurrying to keep up as Blair walked briskly across the neighbor's yard.

"Not far. We just need to cut through a few yards, and we'll be there." Blair stopped and stared at the young agent. "Don't call this in, Tony. This is just you and me, got it? We won't be gone long."

"Yes, sir."

***

Allie and Kristen sipped their tea in the kitchen. They could hear T. J.'s halting voice coming through the baby monitor as he read from Danny's devotional.

"Thanks for waiting, Kristen. You can meet with Daddy as soon as T. J.'s finished."

Kristen gave her friend an understanding smile. "No problem. I'm in no hurry." She swallowed the last of her tea and said, "I think I'll step outside for a smoke."

"I could use some fresh air, too," Allie replied. "I'll join you."

Allie grabbed their jackets, and they sat on the cement stairs leading down from the kitchen door to the backyard. They sat in silence, enjoying the cool night air and the companionship. As Kristen took a drag from her cigarette, the stillness was interrupted by the rattling of the chain-link fence. Two dark figures scaled the fence and walked purposefully toward them. Allie pulled her cell phone from her pocket, ready to dial 911 if necessary. The dark figures stopped in their tracks when they noticed the two women sitting on the steps. The taller figure approached first, the other man lingering behind. Halfway across the yard, a motion-activated floodlight bathed the visitors in a bright light. The tall man stopped momentarily and held a hand in front of his face, shielding his eyes from the harsh glare.

Allie's eyes grew wide. "Blair?"

"Is that you, Allie?"

Kristen dropped her cigarette and stared in stunned disbelief as the unmistakable figure of Governor Blair Van Howe approached them.

"What are you doing here?" Allie asked, a look of bewilderment on her face.

"I heard about your dad, and I was hoping I could see him. Sorry to sneak up on you like this, but the Secret Service is all around my place, and I didn't want to attract a crowd. They don't know I'm gone. It's just me and Tony here."

Allie stood up and said in a cool voice, "Kristen, this is Blair Van Howe. He *used to be* a good friend of the family." She purposely avoided calling him "Governor Van Howe," fully intending that to be a sign of disrespect.

"It's a pleasure to meet you, Governor," Kristen stammered, still looking stunned.

Allie turned toward her friend. "Would you mind giving us a few minutes alone, Kristen?"

"Not at all," Kristen replied, quickly retreating into the house.

The back door slammed, and Allie folded her arms, staring defiantly at the governor of the State of Illinois, a man who would certainly be elected the next president of the United States in just a few days. "You've got a lot of nerve!" Allie began, her voice trembling. "After all these years ... you were like family ... I used to call you Uncle Blair ..." Her voice broke, and tears of anger ran down her cheeks. "Why did you abandon us?"

"Allie, I'm so sorry. You've got every right to despise me. I wish I had a good explanation—"

"He was your best friend, Blair!" Allie yelled. "I want to hear your explanation—whatever it is! You owe us that much at least!"

"I was a coward, Allie, and I can't tell you how ashamed I am. And you're right, you deserve an explanation. It's not a good one, but here it is. After the accident, my advisers told me it would hurt my political career if I associated with your dad. They told me I could do a lot of good for a lot of people if I could get elected, so—"

"So you sacrificed my father—after everything he did for you!"

Blair hung his head and took a deep breath, then looked up at Allie with pain in his eyes. "I'm sorry, Allie. I know I've done you and your father a terrible wrong. I wish there was some way I could make it up to you."

"It's a little late for that," Allie said bitterly through her tears. "He's dying, Blair," Allie shouted, her voice thick with hostility.

The anguish was evident on the governor's face. "I don't deserve your forgiveness, Allie, and I certainly don't deserve your father's. But it sure would mean a lot to me if I could see him."

Something about the sincerity in his voice and the look of genuine remorse in the governor's face touched her. She stared at him for a long moment, her countenance softening as anger transformed into sadness. "I've missed you, Blair," she said, looking up at the man she once loved almost as much as her own father.

"I've missed you too, little girl," Blair replied, wrapping his arms around her. "And I've missed your father—more than I can say."

***

Allie stepped inside her father's bedroom. "Daddy, you have another visitor. Blair's here." T. J. McGrath dropped the devotional he was reading and stared in astonishment at the visitor standing alone in the doorway.

"Hello, Dano," Blair said in a voice thick with emotion.

Danny smiled a peaceful smile. "Blair! What a surprise!"

"I'll let you two visit," T. J. stammered as he stood up hastily and began walking out of the room, avoiding eye contact with the governor.

"Stick around awhile, T. J.," said Danny. "I'd like to read some more in a little while, if you don't mind."

"Sure thing, Danny," T. J. replied, looking embarrassed.

Allie shut the door behind her and left the former law school classmates to themselves.

"You look like shit, pal," Blair said with a strained smile as he looked at the ravaged body lying helplessly before him.

Danny stared at his former partner for a long moment. "It's really good to see you, Blair," he said sincerely. "I'm so proud of you. I hope I can hang on long enough to see you win the election. And I really wish I could be around to witness all the great things you're going to accomplish. You've become a hero to a lot of people, and I know you won't let them down."

"I'm no hero, Dano," Blair said sadly. "After the way I

treated you, I'll never feel like a hero."

"Don't be hard on yourself, Blair. I know how politics works. I know how the media works. You did what you had to do, and it turned out great. Look at you! The next president of the United States!"

***

Allie, T. J., Kristen, and Tony the Secret Service agent sat in the kitchen, lost in their thoughts. The room was silent, except for the sound of teacups occasionally striking saucers and the muffled voices of Blair and Danny coming through in quiet tones over the baby monitor. They stared at their tea, trying to act as if they weren't listening, but no one made any effort to strike up a conversation or to turn off the monitor.

***

"Yes, but at what cost, Dano?" Blair continued, an anguished look coming over his face. "You're the best friend I've ever had. You were just flat-out the most honest, selfless, kindhearted person I've ever met—the most loyal friend I've ever had, and I betrayed you."

"I don't look at it that way, Blair. Politics is a tough business, and you had to distance yourself from me—*because of what I did*. You're not responsible for that. You didn't betray me."

Blair stared down at the floor. "But I did betray you, Dano," he said in a voice full of self-reproach. "I built my entire political career on my reputation for honesty and integrity. Ethics reform was a major part of my agenda in every office I've held, but it's all built upon a lie."

***

In the kitchen, T. J., Allie, and Kristen looked up from their tea and gave each other a curious glance. Tony looked down the hall at the closed bedroom door. Kristen subtly flipped on her handheld recorder.

***

"Built upon a lie? What are you talking about, Blair?" Danny asked.

"Dano ... the accident ... I let you take the fall for it." Blair looked up at the ceiling, sighed deeply, then looked directly at his old friend. "You weren't driving that night, Dano—I was."

Danny stared at him uncomprehendingly.

"*I* drove home that night, Dano. *I* drove Terry McGrath off the road. *I* killed him. You didn't! You were passed out in the passenger seat. I panicked. I figured my political career would be dead if anyone found out, so I strapped you into the driver's seat, called 911, and then I ran home. When I got there, I had a change of heart. I was going to go back to the scene and make it right, but I let Sam and Kimberly talk me out of it."

***

Kristen, Allie, and T. J. huddled around the monitor, stunned looks on their faces. Kristen turned up the volume and placed her recorder adjacent to the monitor. The young Secret Service agent stared over their shoulders at the monitor, looking equally stunned.

***

"I wasn't driving that night?" Danny asked incredulously.

"No, Dano, it was me. And I let you take the fall. Jail, disbarment, the lawsuit, all the public shame and humiliation. You didn't deserve any of that! It should have been me!"

"So I had nothing to do with Terry McGrath's death?" Danny asked quietly.

Blair shook his head. "No, Dano," he said in a voice that was barely above a whisper.

"That's such a relief, Blair. I've carried that guilt around for so long. To be free of that burden ... I can't tell you how much that means to me. Thanks for letting me know."

"You're thanking me?" Blair asked, a look of disbelief on his face. "I've ruined your entire life, and you're thanking me?"

"You didn't ruin my life, Blair. In fact, my life turned out to be very good. I think that, in the end, we mostly live the kind of life we deserve. My life took an unexpected turn after the accident, but I truly believe I've lived a richer and more meaningful life as a result. I was able to make a real difference to at least a few people. I made good friends. I have a great relationship with my wonderful daughter. My life has been good, Blair. I hope that, when you're in my position, looking back over your life, you'll feel the same way."

They stared at each other in silence for a long moment. "What do I do now, Dano?" Blair asked, his voice shaky and tinged with despair. "I should have come clean with this a long time ago, with you and with everyone else." He shook his head sadly, then put a hand over his eyes and began weeping quietly. "I made a terrible mistake," he said, his voice breaking. "I've tried to justify it by telling myself I could serve the greater good ... that I could help a lot of people in public office ... our state and our country ... and I honestly think I have ... and that I can continue to do that. That's how I've rationalized it. But now ... sitting here talking to you ... I feel like a coward and a fraud. I don't know if I can live with myself if I don't make this right. I should come clean with this, shouldn't I? That's what you would do."

Danny looked steadily at his old friend, compassion shining through his sunken eyes. "That's something you need to figure out on your own, Blair," he said gently.

They sat in silence for a long time, lost in their thoughts, until Danny's eyelids began drooping. "Thanks for coming,

Blair," Danny said in a tired voice. "It means a lot to me. And thanks for telling me what you did. I can leave this world with a much greater sense of peace now." Danny heaved a deep sigh. "I'm really tired, Blair. I'm going to close my eyes and rest."

CHAPTER 50

Sam McIntire, Kimberly Van Howe, and a handful of tired but elated campaign staffers sat in the Washington hotel suite that had been used as media central by the campaign team over the past few weeks. It was the Saturday before the election, and they were relaxing, talking football more than politics as they watched the University of Illinois Fighting Illini battle the top-ranked Ohio State Buckeyes on national television.

Late in the fourth quarter, the Illini were down by six points and staging a valiant comeback drive against the heavily favored Buckeyes. With thirty seconds to play and the ball on Ohio State's ten yard line, the Illini quarterback dropped back to pass. The crowd in the room let out a collective shout as the screen went momentarily blank. Within seconds, the face of the local anchorman appeared on screen.

"We are interrupting our regularly scheduled programming to bring you breaking news regarding the upcoming presidential election, and more specifically, front-running Democratic candidate, Blair Van Howe. The *Chicago Tribune* is in possession of an audiotape of Governor Van Howe admitting that he was the driver in a fatal car accident ten years ago that was blamed on his former law partner, Daniel Moran. In a dramatic confession made by Van Howe to Moran on his deathbed, Van Howe acknowledged that he was actually driving that night, and that he framed his friend and left the scene of the accident. According to the recording, Van Howe's wife and father-in-law, longtime Chicago powerbroker Sam McIntire, assisted in the cover-up."

Sam stared in stunned silence at the television as every head in the room turned in his direction. His eyes bulged. He gasped for air, then clutched at his chest. Kimberly shrieked as he fell like a giant oak, crashing into the glass coffee table, sending snacks, drinks, and glass flying in all directions.

***

Sam McIntire did not live to see the media firestorm that followed, nor did he live to see his son-in-law withdraw in disgrace two days before the presidential election. He did not see the shock and consternation that swept the nation or the resulting political upheaval. He did not live to see the chaotic congressional hearings convened to consider postponement of the election, nor the Democratic party's decision to elevate Paul Richardson, the stunned vice presidential candidate, to the top of the ticket once it became clear that the election would not be postponed. Sam McIntire did not live to see the Republican candidate, Henry Hamilton, swept into office in a landslide victory of historic proportions. Neither did Danny Moran.

CHAPTER 51

The wake was scheduled to start at 5:00 p.m. Allie and Jason arrived at the funeral home an hour early for a "private viewing," as the funeral director called it—an opportunity for them to spend time alone with Allie's father one last time before visitors began arriving. It was also an opportunity to make sure that Allie was pleased with the arrangement of the visitation room and her father's appearance. In keeping with the customary practice within the Chicago Catholic community, it would be an open-casket visitation, with her father's remains on display for those who came to pay their final respects.

Allie and Jason were guided to the visitation room by Chuck, the young funeral director who had assisted them with the arrangements with the utmost kindness and compassion. Jason tenderly put his arm around his wife as Chuck escorted them to the casket. To Allie's surprise, she remained completely calm. She thought her father looked good; at least as good as a departed soul can look with the help of the modern-day restorative techniques and the cosmetics skills of the funeral home staff. A large photograph of Danny as a young man—smiling, handsome, and vibrant—was displayed on an easel several feet away, so that people would remember Danny in life as well as in death as they approached the casket.

Chuck politely excused himself and quietly closed the door, leaving Jason and Allie alone with her father in the empty room. Allie put her hands on her father's. They were cool and stiff, but that didn't bother her. She smiled at him as a collage of happy memories flooded back. She bent over and kissed him on the forehead. "I love you, Pops," she whispered, still smiling. Her eyes were misty, but she did not weep. She'd had plenty of time to grieve during her father's illness and upon his passing three days earlier. Now, she felt ready to honor and celebrate his life with those whose lives he had touched.

She turned away from the casket and surveyed the visitation room. It was large, probably too large, she thought, upon seeing it empty. The casket was at the front of the room, a good hundred feet from the entrance. Despite the size, however, the room felt comfortable and warm. Pictures of her father at various stages of his life were tastefully scattered around the room, along with a multitude of flower arrangements that had been arriving all day. Rows of neatly arranged folding chairs stretched from the front to the back, with ample space around the perimeter to allow guests to congregate and visit comfortably.

Allie and Jason spent several minutes casually wandering around the room, reading the notes that accompanied the flower arrangements; then they went in search of Chuck to confirm that all of the arrangements had been completed for the funeral mass and the burial the next morning. A few minutes before five o'clock, Allie left Jason to finalize the arrangements, and returned to the visitation room, where she saw three men standing together in front of her father's casket. Their backs were to her, and from the opposite end of the long room, she could not make out who they were. As she approached, Allie recognized them as three of Danny's longtime pals from the post-AA-meeting dessert club: Judge Andy Murray and two other men she knew only as Paul and Wayne. The judge embraced her, unable to speak, as his eyes turned to faucets. The other two awkwardly shook her hand, muttering inarticulate but heartfelt condolences.

"Thanks for coming, guys," Allie said warmly. "You were all very special to Daddy."

"He was special to us," Judge Andy replied, finding his voice and wiping his eyes. "The three of us here and everybody in the program."

His two companions nodded silently.

"The program changed his life, and you guys were a big part of it for him," Allie replied, looking kindly at the three distraught men standing before her. "You were his closest friends."

Andy cleared his throat, struggling to find his voice. "I can't imagine how painful this is for you, Allie, but we want you to know that we're all thinking of you and praying for you. We're here for you, okay? Tonight, tomorrow ... anytime."

"Thanks, Andy," Allie replied, giving the judge another embrace. Then she stepped back and looked at the three of them. "You know, I'll miss him terribly, but I really believe he had a great life. He was happy. He was doing something that was important to him and making a difference for people. When I think about how his life could have turned out, I'm truly grateful for the life he had. He was blessed, and I was blessed to share that life with him. We all were."

All three men nodded in agreement. Wayne finally found his voice. "He did make a difference. Your father saved me. I want you to know that. If it hadn't been for him, I'd be dead, or I'd be a drunk living on the street."

"Danny Moran was … a great guy," said Paul, his voice shaking. "I've never met a better man … and like the Judge said, we're here for you. If you need anything at all, just let us know. We'll be here all night."

"Thanks, guys. Thanks for coming. It means a lot to me."

The three friends walked slowly toward the back of the room, seating themselves on the folding chairs in one of the rear rows. While she'd been visiting with them, Allie noticed that a line was forming along the wall as people waited their turn to approach the casket to pay their respects. One by one, they filed by, some kneeling at the casket to say a quiet prayer, others stopping and standing respectfully. After filing past the casket, they stopped and offered their condolences to Danny Moran's only child. It quickly became apparent to Allie that, although she was poised and in control, many of the visitors were overcome with emotion as they greeted her. They had come to offer their condolences, and yet she frequently found herself trying to comfort them. It was a role she was happy to play.

By six o'clock, the line stretched from one end of the room to the other. By seven o'clock, the line extended out the door; how far, Allie couldn't tell. By eight o'clock, every one of the folding chairs was occupied, the crowd overflowed into the corridors, and the line continued out the door. Allie looked at the mass of people who had come to pay their respects to her father. There were neighbors and relatives, and lots of Allie's friends. There were teaching colleagues from the university. There were lawyers and business leaders and politicians, looking well-dressed and important. They had been friends of her father's before the accident, and now that he had been publicly exonerated, they felt compelled to make atonement and pay their respects to a man whose character, trust, and friendship had once meant a great deal to them.

Most striking to Allie were the faces she didn't recognize. A few wore ill-fitting suits that they were obviously not accustomed to wearing, but most of them had neither jacket nor tie. Many were haggard and unkempt, and had the look of lost souls, alone and struggling to cope with challenges presented by life that must have seemed daunting and overwhelming. Almost all looked uncomfortable and embarrassed at being forced into a large social gathering, yet they were willing to face that discomfort because of their love and respect for the man lying in the casket. Many of them had difficulty looking Allie in the eye. Some offered handshakes or stiff embraces. Others kept their hands at their sides or in their pockets. But they all came determined to pay their respects, and Allie could see that it took a special kind of courage for them to do so.

Some were not able to offer much more than their presence. "Hi, my name's Jim. I'm a friend of your dad's. I'm really sorry."

Others stated the obvious. "I'm Fred. I know your dad from the program. I'm sorry for your loss."

Many offered something more, and it was a story Allie heard all evening. "Your father saved me." "Your dad was my hero. I'd never have made it without him." "He was my best friend. He cared about me when no one else did." "I'd be dead if it weren't for your father."

One of those visitors was a large, overweight young man in his early twenties. His brown hair was long and straight, and he pushed it back from his forehead as he approached.

"Hi, Allie," he said shyly. He offered his hand awkwardly, and Allie wrapped him in a warm embrace.

"Thanks for coming, T. J. And thanks for being there during Daddy's final days. It meant an awful lot to him."

"Your dad was a great friend," T. J. said. He looked around the room. "He was a great friend to a lot of people."

"I can't believe how many people are here," Allie said with a tone of grateful astonishment.

"Well, it's the least we can do. A lot of people want to be here for your dad, since he was always there for us."

Allie could see that T. J. wanted to say something more but was clearly struggling with his emotions. He looked toward the ceiling, blinking rapidly as he cleared his throat. "It's okay, T. J.," Allie said, compassion and patience in her voice, as she gave him an encouraging look.

T. J. took a deep breath and looked directly at Allie. Tears rolled freely down his cheeks, but he managed to smile. "Your dad was a very special person," he said, his voice steady now. "He could have been a big wheel again if he wanted to. He could have been wealthy and powerful and famous, but he didn't care about any of that. He used to tell me that what matters more than any of that is living your life with real integrity, and that means always doing the right thing—even when no one is watching. And that's what he did. He devoted his life to helping people who really needed it—people like me. The rest of the world may not have noticed, but he made a real difference, Allie, he really did."

The funeral mass was held at St. Martin's Church the following morning, and again, a massive crowd attended. After the funeral, a line of cars stretching nearly half a mile followed the gleaming black hearse as it wound its way through Beverly, passed Danny's house, then moved back in the other direction toward Mount Olivet Cemetery, just beyond the southwestern outskirts of the neighborhood. Heavy clouds hung low in the gray November sky, and a gentle mist began falling as the mourners parked their cars along the blacktop road that wound through the cemetery and approached the open grave. Father Fitzsimmons said the final prayers and invited the mourners to file past the casket to say their last good-byes. One by one, the somber group filed past the mahogany casket, some touching it, others making the sign of the cross, still others leaving a flower behind. No one spoke. The group dispersed in silence and moved toward their vehicles, picking up their pace as the gentle mist became a steady drizzle.

Allie was the last to leave. The young funeral director handed her an umbrella, and then he and Jason moved toward the car, keeping a respectful distance as they allowed her to say her final farewell privately. She stood alone before the casket, shivering as she watched the raindrops splash on the polished hardwood surface. "Good-bye, Daddy," she said aloud, tears mixing with the rain on her face. "I've been so lucky to have you in my life. You've been the most selfless person I've ever known, and such a great example for all of us. You lived a great life, and I'm so proud I could share it with you. I'm going to miss you terribly, but I know that somehow you'll always be with me. I love you."

She leaned over and kissed the casket, then straightened up and wiped her eyes. She took a deep breath and turned away from the casket. Chuck and Jason stood stoically in front of the dark limousine, side by side, hands folded in front of them, oblivious to the rain. "Hey, sillies, get out of the rain," Allie called out to them, smiling through her tears. "You'll catch pneumonia."

Allie was shivering as she and Jason climbed into the backseat of the limousine. Jason put an arm around his wife, then glanced over his shoulder in the direction of the grave as

Chuck slowly pulled away. The cemetery was deserted, except for a lone figure several hundred feet away, standing next to a bicycle and looking toward the grave. "Who do you suppose that is?" he asked.

Allie turned and looked. "Wait, Chuck!" she called out from the backseat, just as Chuck was about to pull into traffic on 111th Street. She squeezed her husband's hand. "I need to go back for a minute. Wait here."

"I can drive you back, Ms. Moran. It's no trouble," Chuck volunteered, but it was too late. Allie had already grabbed her purse and jumped out of the car, and was walking briskly back toward the grave.

The bicycle was lying on its side a few feet from the grave, and its rider was standing in front of the casket, his back toward Allie as she approached. One hand covered his eyes as he wept.

"Hello, Pat," Allie said softly as she approached from behind.

Pat Jordan started at the sound of her voice. There was a look of surprise and embarrassment on his tear-soaked face as he turned and faced her.

"I'm sorry, Allie," he said, his voice breaking. "I wanted to come to the wake last night, but I was in bad shape. I couldn't face all the guys like that … I'm so sorry."

Allie reached out and held him in a long embrace, gently patting his back as his body was racked with deep sobs.

"I don't know what I'll do without him, Allie," Pat stammered as she held him close. "He was my rock. No matter how badly I slipped or how many times, I knew he'd always be there for me when I needed him. I still need him, Allie."

"You were very special to him, Pat. He talked about you all the time."

"I kept letting him down! He'd get me straightened out and then I'd blow it and fall off the wagon and go on a bender. After all these years and everything he did for me, I still haven't gotten it together. I've failed him."

Allie stood back and looked steadily at Pat. He looked terrible. The face that had once been so handsome looked worn and haggard—tortured, even. He was unshaven, his clothes were dirty, and there were dark circles under his bloodshot eyes.

"Look, Pat," Allie said calmly, but firmly. "Daddy never gave up on you, so you can't give up on yourself, okay? Promise me you won't!"

"I'll try, Allie, but I couldn't do it when your dad was around, so I don't know how I'll manage now."

Allie reached into her purse and pulled out a worn leather booklet. It was her father's devotional, which she had placed in his casket. She had intended to bury it with him, but impulsively grabbed it just before the casket was closed.

"This is Daddy's devotional, Pat. I want you to have it. He read it every night and it brought him real comfort."

Pat looked down, obviously touched by the gesture. "Allie, I couldn't. I know how much that meant to him. You should keep it. It belongs in the family."

"I want you to have it, Pat. Daddy would want you to have it. Take it—please! That way, some part of him will still be with you."

She thrust the little black book toward him, and Pat took it, slowly, with both hands, looking at it with reverence. "Thanks, Allie. You don't know how much this means to me."

"I think maybe I do, Pat," she said with a gentle smile. "You take care of yourself, okay?"

Pat nodded, unable to speak. Allie kissed him on the cheek and walked back toward the car, leaving Pat staring at the small black book.

***

Thirty minutes later, the rain had stopped, and another solitary figure, a tall, well-dressed man, approached the grave. He paused momentarily when he realized he was not alone. A lone figure was sitting on a granite bench facing the grave, apparently reading from a small, rumpled book. The tall man approached the grave slowly, a look of profound sadness on his strained face. The man sitting on the bench looked up, nodded silently at the new visitor, then continued with his reading.

Blair Van Howe was surprised by the man's reaction, or rather his lack of a reaction. He was accustomed to seeing strong reactions from people he encountered wherever he went. For most of the past ten years, the reaction had been one of awe and excitement, the reaction that the powerful and famous evoke from mere mortals. Now, the reaction was different, but equally strong. It was a reaction of contempt, disdain, and ridicule.

"Are you a friend of Danny's?" Blair asked the wet, disheveled-looking man.

"Yeah," the man said without looking up. "He was my best friend."

"Mine, too," Blair said softly. "A long time ago. At least, he was a good friend to me. I can't say I treated him very well."

The man on the bench nodded slowly, without looking up. "I didn't, either. But he was always there for me. No matter how screwed up or lost I was, he'd find a way to help."

"I wish he were here right now," Blair said sadly, his eyes becoming watery and his voice cracking. "I've never needed him more ... My life is a royal mess ... I'm not sure I can ever hold my head high again. I guess Danny was right. In the end, we mostly get the life we deserve."

Pat Jordan looked up and stared calmly at the distraught figure before him. "One thing Danny taught me is that no matter how bleak things get, no matter how badly we've screwed up, or how low we've sunk, life can be good again. We can do something meaningful with our lives." Pat rose from the bench and picked up his bicycle. He put a hand on Blair's shoulder as he walked past him. "You don't need to be president to be a hero, Governor." He rode off, head held high.

DISCUSSION QUESTIONS

1. Through his political accomplishments, Blair Van Howe was able to make life better for thousands of people, perhaps even millions. Had he accepted responsibility for the accident at the outset, he probably would not have been able to do so, because he would not have been elected to public office. With that in mind, consider the following:

   A. Do Blair's accomplishments in elected office, which truly served the greater good, justify his actions relating to the accident? Why or why not?
   B. Did Blair make the right decision in perpetrating the lie and the cover-up?
   C. Should the voting public have been willing to forgive the indiscretion in Blair's personal life, given his track record of stellar public service since that time?
   D. If the voters honestly believed that Blair could do a better job than anyone else leading the nation as president, should he have been allowed to serve in that capacity?
   E. Does personal integrity really matter, or should we judge people solely on their accomplishments and

contributions? Should our political leaders be held to a higher standard of personal integrity? Why or why not?

2. Is Blair a good man who made one very bad decision, or is he a fundamentally flawed person? Does the fact that he feels remorse throughout the story reveal anything about his heart or character? Does his confession to Danny absolve him of his guilt in any way?

3. How would Danny's life have been different had it not been for the accident? Would he have been more of a "success?" How do you define a "successful" life?

4. Compare the impact Danny had on the world around him to the impact that Blair had. Who made a more significant difference?

5. What is a real-world hero? Do you see elements of heroism in Danny? Blair? Slazak? Allie? Judge Andy? Do you know any real-world heroes? What makes them special?

6. What people and/or events were most important in changing Danny's life? What sorts of experiences are most commonly "life-changing?"

7. Do you believe that serious misfortune often serves as a catalyst for positive change in a person's life? How or why does that happen? Luck? Fate? Divine Intervention? Determined effort brought on by recognition that change is imperative? Other reasons?

8. How would the lives of the McGraths, Morans, Van Howes and others have been different if Terry and Ashley McGrath had left home to pick up their puppy five minutes earlier than they did? Consider the fact that if Ashley had never been given her stuffed animal, they wouldn't have spent time looking for it and would have left the house sooner. All these lives, perhaps even the presidency of the United States, were affected by the fact that someone gave Ashley that stuffed animal. Can you think of other instances where seemingly trivial events had profound impacts on the course of events? Give examples, from your personal life and the public arena. Why does this happen? Is it nothing more than pure chance?

9. Did Victor Slazak live a meaningful and successful life? Consider the following:

   A. Did he knowingly sacrifice his life? Did he do so to rescue Ashley McGrath? To get revenge against the evil cop?

   B. Slazak was the best at what he did, and yet he was not well liked, mostly because of his tendency to show disdain, intolerance, and impatience toward others, and because he simply didn't care whether he was liked or not. Should this kind of attitude be tolerated in the workplace? Outside of the workplace? Can it be justified by exceptional results?

   C. Can you be a success in life if virtually no one likes you? If you have no close relationships whatsoever?

   D. Was Slazak a hero?

10. Consider this proposition: Most people are either inherently self-centered or inherently selfless at their very core. Do you agree? Are Danny and Blair examples of a truly selfless and a truly self-centered person, respectively? Why or why not? Was Danny always that way? Can a person change his/her nature from self-centered to selfless? Does that often happen in the real world?

11. While visiting Danny on his deathbed, Blair says to Danny, "I should come clean with this, shouldn't I? That's what you would do." Do you think Blair would have come clean before the election if his conversation had not been overheard? Why or why not?

12. One of the lessons Danny taught T.J. was that having real integrity means doing the right thing at all times, even when no one is watching. What did Blair do when no one was watching? How about Danny? How do you think most politicians fare when measured by this yardstick? Provide examples of public figures who have demonstrated this type of integrity and examples of some who have not. Provide examples from your own experiences where someone did the right thing when no one was watching.

13. In this story, a single bad decision by Blair Van Howe had far-reaching and lifelong consequences. Can you think of examples of public figures who made the wrong choice when confronted with an ethical dilemma and then saw their lives profoundly impacted in a negative way? What about others who made the wrong choice and yet emerged from the situation unscathed? Why the difference?